SKANDIA SEVEN

ACE EVANS BOOK 4

TOBY NEIGHBORS

MYTHIC
adventure
PUBLISHING

Skandia Seven – Ace Evans book 4

© 2020, Toby Neighbors

Published by Mythic Adventure Publishing, LLC

Idaho, USA

ISBN: 978-1-952260-98-8

Copy Editing by Aisha Matthews

ALSO BY TOBY NEIGHBORS

The Abyss Of Savagery

The Vault Of Mysteries

Lords Of Ascension

The Elusive Executioner

Regulators Revealed

Avondale

Draggah

Balestone

Arcanius

Avondale V

Third Prince

Royal Destiny

The Other Side

The New World

Zompocalypse

Spartan Company

Spartan Valor

Spartan Guile

Dragon Team Seven

Uncommon Loyalty

Total Allegiance

Kestrel Class

Jump Point

Gravity Flux

Modulus Echo

Zero Friction

Planet Fall

Charter

Jack & Roxie

My Lady Sorceress

The Man With No Hands

ARC Angel

Battle ARC

Broken Crucible

Hidden Kingdom

War INC

Carthage Prime

Cronus Team

Skandia Seven

CHAPTER ONE

THE OPERATORS WEREN'T HANDCUFFED. None of them had weapons, so the law enforcement personnel just herded them toward the large, armored prisoner transport.

"We just supposed to go along with this?" Sly asked.

"For now," Alex replied.

"Don't they know we aren't the problem?" Corporal Hanes asked.

"I guess not," Alex said. "But we aren't helpless here. It's best to bide our time for now."

"Hey, stop talking," one of the policemen barked.

Alex was shocked. The Ahzco factory on Skandia Seven had been destroyed by militant protesters. The plant had lost several workers, and all of the MBS technicians from the *Currency* had been killed. It was a crushing defeat for Oscar Company, and for Alex's own Cronus Team. Ash was hurt and in the hospital. He didn't even know what her status was. There was no doubt in his mind that he and Sly should be with her, and yet they were being arrested as terrorists. It made no sense, but the law enforcement personnel had weapons, and if Alex used the mechanized battle suits against them, it would only confirm the spreading slander against private militaries.

"Can you take control of their ship?" Sly whispered.

"Probably," Alex said.

"Any chance it's space worthy?"

"I doubt that. Besides, we aren't leaving without Ash or Master Sergeant Monty," Alex said.

"Yeah, I'm with you," Sly said.

"What did the EMTs say when they took her to the hospital?" Alex asked.

"Not a lot," Sly said, his face twisted with pain. "The back of the battle suit was twisted and dented in. She was bleeding."

Alex felt a stab of guilt. No one could have guessed that someone would attack from the public transit station. When Ash was hit with a missile from the underground platform, it had come as a surprise to them all. Worse, it was just one part of a well-organized attack against the Ahzco factory, and from what Nyx was saying through Alex's Titan's com-link, there had been multiple, coordinated attacks on mega corporation properties across the planet.

"We'll get to her as soon as we can," Alex said. "But for now, we'll go along and see what's being planned for us."

"Can they really hold us like criminals?" Corporal Sansabar asked. She was a little smaller than most of the other Operators but had a fierce determination that showed in her almond-shaped eyes.

"I suppose they can do whatever they want," Alex said. "Once the term 'terrorist' gets thrown around, basic human rights go out the window."

"And we're just letting them take us?" Hanes asked.

"We're not without resources," Sly said with a little nod toward Alex.

He had special abilities. Every Operator in Ahzco's CDF had Implanted Neural Controller chips surgically placed at the back of their skulls during basic training. Learning to distinguish between the various EM waves emitted by every electronic device took time, and the ability to sync their INC chips with the special computer controls of a mechanized battle suit took even more. But once they mastered this synchronization, they could operate both the large battle armor and the smaller, more agile vehicles with very little help. Alex had demonstrated the remarkable ability to do even more. No one knew why or how, but he could sync his INC chip with any electronic device. He was a mental hacker, who, by the very nature of the INC, could not only gain access to other ships and various devices, but could also slip behind their security measures to take control.

Alex knew that he could sync with the prisoner transport and fly them all out of danger, but that would only prove that they were criminals. So far, Alex and the other Operators hadn't done anything wrong. They had fought and even killed people, but only those who were already trying to kill them.

Unfortunately, even though his INC was still connected to his Titan battle suit, he couldn't communicate with Nyx, his Controller in geo-synchronous orbit. Thankfully Nyx could still speak to him, but he couldn't reply.

What is going on, Alex? Are they arresting you?

Alex held his arm up, made a fist, and stuck his thumb out. He wasn't sure just how good the surveillance cameras on the *Currency* were, but her ability to see him was his only hope of communication.

We're watching, Nyx said, just before Alex was led into the prisoner transport.

It was good to know that they weren't alone, and that Captain Poe would know that they were being detained. Alex didn't know if the Ahzco officer could do anything about it, but he was certain that the captain would try.

There was something strange about the prisoner transport. Alex felt boxed in, and not simply because the prisoner compartment had no windows. It was because the ship was built like a Faraday cage. He guessed it was to keep prisoners from using their tech once in custody. Most people carried some type of Personal Information Link. His was still in a locker on the *Currency*, but it was usually in his pocket or snapped onto his forearm. When the rear hatch closed, he lost all contact with his Titan battle suit. The world went strangely silent.

"Man, that's trippy," Sly said.

"What? Are they blocking the EM waves?" Corporal Hanes asked.

"Looks that way," Alex responded.

"How do they know we can read them?" Corporal Sansabar asked.

"I don't think they do," Alex said. "It's probably a feature of the cargo section of this vehicle. To keep people from using electronics while it's in the air."

"Can you get past it?" Sly asked.

Alex shook his head. "It's some type of Faraday cage. All we can do is wait."

The members of Oscar Company were clearly angry, and Alex knew they had plenty to be angry about. Despite all of his efforts, they weren't able to keep themselves safe from attack. They had failed in their mission to protect the Ahzco factory. They had worked tirelessly for hours trying to save the people trapped in the rubble, only to be arrested when the grisly task was finally completed.

"This is ludicrous," Hanes said. "We're not the enemy, I don't care what the media says."

"Yeah, well, if they want a fight," Sansabar said, "I'm game."

"We should rest," Alex said. "We'll find out what they plan to do with us soon enough."

"And you're really okay with just letting them have complete control?" Hanes asked incredulously. "What if the plan is to line us up and shoot us like animals?"

"I'm sure that's not their plan," Alex said. "And don't worry, if they mean to do us harm, we'll know about it ahead of time."

"Like we knew about the attack?" Sansabar asked sarcastically.

Her words were like a knife in his guts, but Alex knew she was right. He had known there was an attack coming. He had been watching for it all day, but he hadn't expected the bomb to come from a child, or for the enemy to reach them without being seen. It was a failure—his failure—but as long as he was alive, it wasn't the end.

"I'm sorry," Alex said.

"It wasn't your fault," Sly insisted.

"We all knew it was coming," Hanes said, giving his teammate a hard glare.

Sansabar relented a little. "I'm not saying you could have known or done anything about the child. But just knowing something bad is coming isn't enough."

"Granted," Alex said. "But we'll know more this time."

"How?" Hanes inquired.

"If the holding cells they put us in aren't Faraday cages like this transport, I'll be able to search their computer networks," Alex explained.

They didn't ask him how, and he decided that they probably assumed he had a PIL or some other device that would allow him to access the law enforcement tech. In the end, they would all just have to wait and see, but Alex felt confident that he could get them out of trouble if he needed to.

"The *Currency* will have seen us getting picked up," Sly said. "Even from orbit, the flashing lights would have shown up on their surveillance cameras."

Hanes chuckled. "You think Poe will do anything to save us?"

"Won't he?" Alex asked.

"He hasn't been known to care for anyone who isn't a senior officer," Sansabar said.

"And while he's competent at running the ship," Hanes

added, "I wouldn't trust him in a high-pressure situation. He's too cautious."

"We'll find a way," Alex said. "Administrator Brown will help. So will my family."

"I just don't like the idea of getting locked up with no idea why or what the process looks like," Hanes said.

"Every world is different," Sly said. "But we're on a level one planet. They all have some kind of due process."

"Unless Sergeant Evans is right," Sansabar noted, "and we're considered terrorists without rights. It could be pretty bad."

"Not if I have anything to do with it," Alex said, hoping there was something he could actually do.

CHAPTER TWO

Nyx was the last Controller to lose the connection with her Operator. Most of the others seemed uncertain about what they should do next. Some were acting as if they were in a training exercise. She heard talk of going to bed as she moved quickly past them.

There was a helplessness that came along with being disconnected from the Operator. In the field, if a person got hurt, or just left their battle suit, their Controller was completely cut off. No visual feed, no audio, no way to communicate with the person they were next to, or even to ascertain if they were still alive. Ash's Controller had clearly been distraught after the attack. Nyx didn't think the pair was all that close, but it was always painful for a Controller to lose an Operator. And with the entire group of Operators having been arrested, there was no way to know what was happening to any of them.

Nyx went straight to the bridge, only she didn't wait at the entrance like before. Captain Poe was at his usual station, watching the plot on the round display in the center of the command area. He didn't look up as she approached.

"Have you heard what's happening down there?" Nyx demanded.

"Sergeant West, this is an officer's station. You will follow protocol while you're on my ship."

"I didn't mean any disrespect, Captain, but all of the Operators have been arrested."

Poe looked up at her for a moment, as if he were judging whether or not she was telling the truth. Then, he looked back down at the plot as if he expected to come under enemy fire at any second. From Nyx's point of view, nothing on the plot had changed. There were still several ships in orbit, just holding their positions. She couldn't understand why he was so focused on the display.

"Arrested?" Poe asked. "You're certain?"

"Well, I couldn't achieve full communication with my Operator, but from the surveillance video, I could see the law enforcement vehicles approach the factory. It was a little difficult to make out what was happening on the ground in the dark, but they loaded our people into a transport and cut off all communications."

"That could be anything, Sergeant," Captain Poe said. "There were multiple attacks across the planet. I'm sure that the authorities are just trying to keep everyone safe."

"That doesn't make sense," Nyx said. "Why take our people into custody to keep them safe? Why not just order them off world?"

"I'm sure things will clear up soon," Poe replied dismissively. "In the meantime, if you aren't needed on the control deck, you should return to your quarters and get some rest."

Nyx couldn't believe what she was hearing. Was the Captain really ordering her to her room, like a disobedient child? Even worse, was he really going to ignore the fact that an entire company of Operators had been arrested? She felt rage building inside of her, but she couldn't let it out. Although she felt that an outburst would have been justified, Alex still needed her, and she wouldn't be any good to him locked up in the brig.

"Very well," Nyx said. "As long as you are monitoring the situation."

"We're monitoring everything, Sergeant. Now please, let us do our jobs."

He didn't even bother looking up from the display table as he admonished her. Nyx left the bridge, ignoring the looks she received from the other officers. They all felt superior, despite the fact that they were part of the same service, and in truth, their duties were no more important than her own. Flying an interstellar ship wasn't easy, but the autopilot did most of the work. The officers were there to observe and report on the various systems in the ship. Nyx understood the need for that. She also understood that while they were higher in rank than she was, none of that made them superior in any way. Part of her wanted to turn around and tell them to wipe the smug looks off of their faces, but it wasn't the time or the place.

Throughout her entire career, Nyx had never been on a vessel or base where the members of different divisions were so divided. The *Currency* was a small ship, the kind usually assigned to planetary systems to oversee company business when the threat was low. Those types of planets rarely had more than a few ships in the system at any one time, and most were freighters hauling goods in or out of the system. She realized that Captain Poe was, in many respects, out of his depth. He had probably never kept his ship in orbit around a level one planet where several dozen ships occupied the system at all times. The presence of other military vessels in orbit was making him obsessive.

What was truly worrying, was the fact that he seemed not to care about operations on the ground at all. He didn't seem to care if they lost the entire company of Operators, as long as the ship survived. It was hard to believe, but she had seen it with her own eyes. If any help was coming from the *Currency*, it wouldn't be from Captain Poe.

Instead of going to her berth as she had been instructed, Nyx returned to her Controller console. The room was nearly empty. The cubicles were abandoned and only three other Controllers were in the room. They were clustered together in one corner, talking quietly.

Nyx had lost the connection with Alex, but the Titan battle suit that he had been linked to was still powered on. In theory, she could operate it, even fly it to wherever Alex had been taken, but it was against protocol. Operating MBS was not as simple as piloting a ship. They were meant to be manned, and while they could function via remote control, like drones, there were systems that she couldn't control from a distance. Weapons, for instance, could only be fired by the Operator. The suit's external communication systems could only be utilized by the person inside.

Not that flying a war machine to a police station was a good idea, but even if she dared to do it, she couldn't really accomplish anything. The Titan was built for war, not negotiations. She would serve as a mute threat, and nothing more, which wouldn't work in Alex's favor. Instead, she needed to get information. And her computer was already linked to Skandia's planetary network.

Every level one planet ran its own information network, which in turn was connected to the galactic net. Nyx did a quick search for the official response to the attacks across Skandia. There were dozens of stories, some with pictures or even video, of the attacks. Commentary about the attacks, most of which was in favor of simply writing them off, seemed endless. Most of the loudest voices blamed the corporations and labeled the attacks as mere civil unrest.

There were several easily accessible stories about the Ahzco factory that had been attacked, and Nyx skimmed over them. It was obvious at a glance that all of the stories shared one thing in common—they were determined to downplay the role of the attackers. Although there was no denying that the plant had been destroyed, most of the writers and almost all of the commenters blamed Ahzco for the destruction. They postulated that despite the rigorous permits that Ahzco was forced to file, and the numerous inspections conducted by the local authorities to ensure that no munitions were being manufactured in the Ahzco factory, the explosion and subsequent destruction of the building were surely caused by explosives being produced and stored onsite. Nyx's blood boiled as she read the stories. She'd never read such outright lies being reported as truth, even by the major news agencies.

Finally, after nearly half an hour of research, she discovered a short little article that quoted the Oslo security administrator, saying, *"Our job now is to bring those responsible to justice, regardless of their residency on this planet or affiliation with so-called private military."* Nyx sat back in shock. The administrator hadn't come right out and blamed the Ahzco Operators, but it seemed clear that they were looking at people from off-world. Theirs wasn't the only property that had been attacked in Oslo—one of the chief manufacturing cities on Skandia Seven—but given that Alex and the other Operators had been rounded up by law enforcement, it seemed clear that they were in trouble.

Nyx didn't know what would happen if they were actually charged with crimes. It wasn't unusual for someone wanted by law enforcement to flee to another planet, but that wasn't an option for Alex and the other Operators. And yet, with Captain Poe seemingly disinterested in helping his own people, there was a very good chance that Alex would be locked up on Skandia Seven for a long time. Nyx had to do something, but she had no idea what.

As she clicked through more stories, Nyx came across an article highlighting a charity that claimed to post bond for protesters picked up by law enforcement. The lack of account-ability with donated funds seemed shady to Nyx, but it wasn't their goals or values that had caught her attention. It was the fact that people picked up by law enforcement for crimes on Skandia Seven could be represented in court. Every planet's government operated differently, including the rights they granted to people accused of crimes. Fortunately, it seemed that the legal system on Skandia Seven at least made an effort at fairness.

Nyx did a quick search and found that there were hundreds of law firms in Oslo alone. She didn't want a big firm, or even a competent attorney. She was more interested in finding someone desperate enough to jump through a few hoops to earn their fee. There was no way of knowing how any of the lawyers she found listed online felt about private military, or the attacks on their planet, so she needed someone who only cared about making money.

Eventually, she settled on a lawyer named Jakob Berrgance. He operated what he called a "boutique firm" specializing in criminal law. Nyx typed out a quick message asking for his help. The response was almost immediate. It outlined his fees— namely a retainer that covered several hours of work. Nyx sent the credits from her own account and typed out her instructions to the lawyer. She wanted him to visit the detainment center and find out as much information as possible before reporting back to her. Nyx didn't actually believe that the lawyer would be allowed to see Alex, but he could probably find out why the Operators were being held and what was expected to happen next.

Nyx didn't even believe that an arrest report would move Captain Poe, but she wouldn't stop fighting just because the ship's captain was too blind to see that he had an obligation to the men and women serving under him. There had to be a way to help Alex, and Nyx was determined to find it.

CHAPTER THREE

THE TRANSPORT LANDED and the rear hatch opened. Alex finally felt like he could breathe again as the sounds of thousands of electronic devices created a gentle roar in the back of his mind. Being locked inside of the transport's Faraday Cage had been like losing the ability to see or hear.

"Everyone out!" one of the law enforcement officers shouted.

Alex, Sly, and the remaining members of Oscar Company all complied. Even if they had wanted to fight, they were too exhausted. None of them had any weapons, or, for that matter, the slightest idea where they were. They were Operators on a world that few of them knew anything about. Without the connection to their Controllers via the mechanized battle suits they fought in, the Operators were effectively lost. Worse still, Alex knew that the odds were high that no one on the *Currency* knew where they were either. They had been swept away in the dark of night with no tracking or communication abilities. Perhaps Chief Administrator Cathy Brown would be able to help, but he couldn't count on that. He needed to learn as much as he could before he was locked inside of another Faraday Cage.

"Where are we?" Sly asked.

It was dark and the compound around them had high walls. Alex couldn't see any part of the city over the walls, which wasn't a good sign. They could have been taken anywhere. Their only reason to believe that they weren't too far away from the Ahzco property where their MBS awaited them, was the length of the journey and the fact that Alex could sense a lot of EM waves.

"No idea," Alex replied. "But I'm working on it."

"Good to know someone is," Sly replied.

"What's he talking about?" Corporal Hanes asked.

Those in Oscar Company were companions in the effort to protect the MBS factory on Skandia Seven, but they didn't have high enough clearance to know about Alex's advanced INC abilities.

"Yeah," Corporal Sansabar said. "What are you two not telling us?"

Sly looked at Alex, who shook his head. They trusted the members of Oscar Company, but if word leaked, even by accident, they might lock Alex in a Faraday Cage, or worse still, separate him from the others.

"Nothing," Sly said.

The others looked suspicious as they were herded toward a building that looked like a bunker. Alex could see in the light from a metal door overhead that the structure was built from thick stone blocks. There were windows, but they were very narrow, and he could see wire mesh inside the glass.

"Looks like a prison," Alex said.

"Wonderful," Sly replied.

"Once we're inside, there won't be any getting out," Hanes whispered. "We outnumber the guards."

"They have weapons," Alex said. "We don't. Just stay calm. We'll get out the right way."

"I hope you're right," Sansabar whispered, her voice barely audible.

They were taken into what looked like a garage. The floor was bare concrete, the walls built from unpainted blocks of stone. There was a metal door on the far wall, and a window through which Alex saw several more law enforcement personnel watching them.

"Spread out," one of the officers barked. "Hands against the walls."

Four of the law enforcement officers stood in the center of the room, blaster rifles held at the ready. Two more began patting down each Operator. Alex was one of the first. A man ran his hands over Alex's arms and down his torso. It seemed like a waste of time to Alex, who was wearing compression fatigues just like the rest of the Operators. If any of them had a weapon, or even a PIL, it would stand out. The man searching Alex ran his hands all around Alex's waist, and then down each leg.

Once he was finished, he was turned around and made to sit on the floor with his back to the wall. Another officer was taking the Operators inside the building, through the thick metal door, one by one. Alex let his mind skim over the EM waves. Every electrical device emitted waves. Most were minor, like the hum of insects in the forest.

It didn't take long for Alex to discover the private servers that powered the law enforcement computer system. There were thick, overlapping layers of protection to keep an outside force from hacking into their files, but Alex's abilities allowed him to bypass the system's security measures. When he synced his INC to a computer, in many ways, he became a part of the system, or more accurately, it became a part of him. He could operate the system by a sheer act of will and explore all of the secrets that it held. Alex let his mind connect to the private server, which it did with a satisfying snap.

There were reams of useless information stored on the system, from personnel records to reports generated for every arrest the officers made, and every call for help that they received. Alex wasn't interested in most of it. But somewhere in the building, someone was filling out an intake report on one of the Operators. It was mostly identifying information. The info was being filled in at a steady pace, which told Alex that the subject was cooperating. He was glad that no one seemed to be resisting the locals. It wouldn't help them to be seen as hostile. The last thing that Alex and his team needed was for additional security measures to be taken against them.

He read through the report and noticed that in the "crimes committed" field, the only charge was terrorism. He had known, or at least suspected that much, already. Alex searched through the various systems until he found the head of law enforcement's personal computer, and immediately opened the "messages" application. There was the usual spam and special interest messages, mainly from retailers. But the one that attracted his full attention was from Latisha Monroe, City Administrator. Alex opened the message. It was like he was seeing it in his mind's eye, almost like he had a computer display inside his head.

Chief Hanley,

It has been decided that all private military personnel involved in the attacks that took place earlier today will be prosecuted for terrorist acts. You are hereby ordered to bring all private military personnel within the city limits of Oslo into custody, and to hold them without access or visitation.

We are activating planetary security protocols. We will forward more instructions soon. All private military personnel are to be considered hostile, and lethal force is approved should any resist your authority.

From the Office of
Latisha Munroe
Head Administrator
Oslo City, Skandia Seven

It was the worst-case scenario. Alex felt a sense of dread rising inside of him. If they tried to escape, they would almost certainly be shot and killed. If they went along meekly, they would almost certainly be shipped off to a detainment facility and handled without any human rights what-so-ever. Neither option was appealing to Alex, but he wasn't sure what else to do. He had the ability to send a message mimicking the Head Administrator and calling for their release, but a sudden and unexplained change of the original orders would surely result in a call to the city administration office. The law enforcement officers were trained to investigate mysteries. They wouldn't carry out the orders and might even discover what he was capable of doing. What Alex needed was a solid plan, and that would take time. Yet he wasn't sure how much time any of them had.

Alex ran a quick search to find out more about planetary security protocols on Skandia Seven and discovered a large file with more information on the protocols than he needed. As he sat on the concrete floor, watching the guards with guns, he used his INC to move the computer file to a section labeled *APPREHENSION AND CONTAINMENT OF ENEMY COMBAT-ANTS*. He had just started scanning the document when a woman with wide hips that were accentuated by a thick gun belt stopped in front of him and waved for him to stand up.

"What's your name?" she asked.

The name patch on her uniform said Reed.

"Alex Evans," he replied.

"Alright, Evans, come with me."

She sounded bored and didn't seem concerned that he might attack her. Not that any of the CDF Operators had shown any signs of resistance, but they were in a criminal detention center and he expected a level of security that seemed to be lacking.

He followed her to the heavy metal door. The electric locking system buzzed, and she pulled the door open. Alex realized that he had missed the security system, which operated on a separate, isolated, offline server. It was quiet, almost a whisper among the other EM waves, yet there it was controlling every door, the closed-circuit video surveillance system, and emergency alert sirens. He could sync with it as easily as he could take his next breath, and yet he wasn't sure what good it would do. He could open every door and free all of the prisoners, but that wouldn't stop the officers from firing on them as they tried to flee. Nor would it reveal where they were or how they could get to other parts of the city. As frustrating as it seemed, Alex was forced to bide his time once again.

"Step inside and raise your hands straight up in the air, please," Officer Reed said.

The room she was indicating was small. He didn't want to go inside the small room, but he did as he was told. Reed closed the door behind him, and a whirring sound followed. Alex recognized the scan. It was a deep-penetrating scanner that would reveal any hidden weapons, even things inside the body. He stood with his hands up for nearly a minute, and then the sound ended, and the door opened.

"Let's get you processed," Reed said.

Alex wasn't sure what happened to the people hiding weapons and he didn't really want to know. He followed Officer Reed from the room to a small cubicle where an officer sat at a computer terminal. If it was possible, the man at the computer looked even more disinterested than Reed. His name patch read *WALKER*.

"Name?" Walker asked.

"Alex Evans."

"No middle name?"

"Oh, it's Chester."

"Any aliases?"

"My call sign is Ace," Alex replied.

"Home planet?"

"My family is here, on Skandia Seven."

Walker almost looked surprised, but the emotion faded just as quickly as it had appeared. He was using an old-fashioned analog keyboard. His fingers rattled over the keys almost faster than Alex thought possible.

"What city?"

"Oslo," Alex replied.

"Look man, if you don't tell me the truth, it's only going to hurt you in the long run."

"I *am* telling the truth. My father is Bruce Evans. My mother is Penelope. They own a home here, although I'm not sure what the address is. I grew up on NP8261. But my father was transferred here a few months ago."

"Fine," Walker said. "Who do you work for?"

"Ahzco, Corporate Defense Force."

"What's your position?"

"I'm a Sergeant in the Operator's division."

The questioning continued for nearly fifteen minutes, after which Alex was turned over to another officer who scanned his prints, mapped his retinas, photographed his face, and took a

DNA sample. They even forced him to read from a plaque on the wall to record his voice.

Alex did everything he was told, forcing himself to stay present in the moment. He wanted to continue searching the detention center's systems and find a way out for his friends, but cooperation was his first priority. He wanted to project the image that he was not a threat or even a complication. When possible, he took in his surroundings, but all that he was certain of was that the building was large, and he was only seeing a small fraction of it. Alex didn't even bother asking the questions that were on his mind. Instead, he listened. The people moving him through the system didn't talk to him, but the others nearby had no qualms about speaking to each other. The attacks were all that anyone could talk about. It was clear that not everyone agreed with the idea of holding the men and women of the private military forces on Skandia Seven responsible for the attacks. It was the first time he'd heard dissent from the media narrative outside of the CDF. The law enforcement officers were doing as they were ordered, just as Alex would. But it didn't mean that they agreed with the order, or that they were convinced that what the media was telling everyone was the truth.

"You'll go in here."

He was back with officer Reed. She pointed him into a large holding cell. Three walls were made from bare concrete blocks, the floor a slab of concrete with a drain in the center. There were metal benches along the concrete walls, and the fourth wall was made from some sort of transparent material. It was dirty, covered in smudges on the inside. Alex walked into the room, expecting to feel his connection with the detention center's computer system cut off at any second. Instead, he was hit with a foul stench, a wicked combination of body odor, urine, and vomit.

The door to the holding cell slid shut behind him. Alex turned and watched Officer Reed walk away, her thumbs hooked inside the belt that hung on her wide hips.

"What now, Sergeant?" asked one of the corporals from Oscar Company who had been taken in ahead of Alex.

He did a quick count and saw that they were all being held together in one cell. It wouldn't take long before the entire group of Operators was in the nasty room with its vile stench.

"We wait," Alex said. "I'm sure that Captain Poe will have this sorted out in no time."

He didn't really believe that, but it seemed like the right thing to say. The other Operator didn't believe it either. He chuckled.

"You don't know Captain Poe," the man said.

Alex moved to the bench opposite the transparent wall and let his mind search through the detention center's files. There was plenty of information to share with the others, but he decided to wait until everyone was present. There were two security cameras outside of the cell, near the transparent wall. Alex synced with the security system's computer. It was a simple set up, created to control the building. It ran everything from the lights to the temperature controls. He began searching through the security camera feeds until he found the two looking in on the holding cell. He kept them up in his mind, the images revealed to him in the same way that the video feed from his MBS showed him what was happening around him. Alex had to close his eyes to block out the sensory data from his eyes, but once he did that, he could see the camera footage easily.

It took a while, but Alex went through all of the cameras. There were twelve inside the detention center, which had six small cells for long-term occupants and those who were a threat to others or themselves. Each cell had a camera, and there were two on the large holding cell where Alex and the others were kept. The remaining cameras covered the various areas that prisoners were led through. There were two more cameras in the garage area where they had been searched, and almost twenty cameras on the exterior of the building and the surrounding grounds.

There was only one building that wasn't under video surveillance, and it was impossible to know what was inside. But Alex got a proper idea of the building's exterior, and even what was beyond the walls. He knew that he could log into the main computer system, order a transport to the nearest space port, charter a shuttle that could take the Operators up to the *Currency*, and unlock all the doors between the holding cell and the main or rear entrance to the building. But there was no way to do that without alerting the officers, who might shoot first and ask questions later.

Calls were coming in over the station's communication system. More prisoner transports were inbound. Alex had no idea how many people were going to be brought to the detention center, or how long they might be there. Getting out was his priority, but he couldn't do that without making things worse. He was just a Sergeant, and the politics of their arrest on Skandia Seven were way above his pay grade.

"Oh, this is wonderful," Sly said as he walked into the holding cell. The look on his face made Alex grin.

"Join the CDF," Alex teased. "It'll be fun!"

"Yeah, I think I would toss my cookies, but it's been so long since I ate anything, there's nothing to toss."

"Lucky for us," Hanes said.

Almost the entire group had been processed. As soon as the last member of Oscar Company was shown to the holding cell, Alex gestured for everyone to sit down.

"Just be still for a few minutes," Alex whispered. "Then I'll explain things."

The other Operators clearly had no idea what Alex was up to, but they were all accustomed to following orders. Everyone sat down on the benches and looked around. No one spoke, no one made any big movements. In the meantime, Alex began recording the camera feeds. He let the recording run a full two minutes, then replayed the recording on a loop so that the video feed to their holding cell would be overwritten.

"Alright," Alex said, standing up. "Gather in. I don't think they've got audio, but I don't want to risk it."

The others approached him. He could see the wariness on their faces. They didn't know what he was capable of doing, or even what he was doing at the present moment. All they knew was that their worlds had been turned upside down through no fault of their own.

"What's going on, Sergeant?" Corporal Sansabar asked.

"Okay, what I'm going to tell you has to be kept a secret at all costs," Alex said. "I've got an INC, just like the rest of you, but something happened to me on Carthage. I don't know what, or how it happened, but I can sync to any computer system."

"You're full of it," Hanes snapped.

"Nope," Sly said. "I've seen him do it."

"On Carthage?" Sansabar asked.

"Yeah, my INC taps into computer systems that aren't built for it," Alex said. "Like the ones here in this building."

"You really expect us to believe this?" Hanes asked incredulously.

"No," Alex said.

He sent an order with his mind, the way a person might wink at someone, or flex their nostrils, only Alex wasn't controlling his body. He opened the door to the holding cell. There was a heavy *chunk* sound as the locking mechanism disengaged, and the holding cell door popped open.

"Believe me now," Alex asked?

CHAPTER FOUR

"You did that?" Hanes asked.

"Yes," Alex said. "I've got the security feed on a recorded loop so that they don't know we're talking, but we need to hurry."

"What for?" Sansabar asked. "If you can unlock the doors, we should leave. We haven't done anything wrong."

"She's right," Hanes said. "What are we standing around here for?"

"Wait," Alex said. "We can't just leave. The guards have standing orders to shoot us if we try to escape."

"What?" Sly said.

"We've been listed as terrorists by the city administrator, which is why we were arrested," Alex said. "I saw the memo she sent to the head of law enforcement. They're serious about holding us."

"Why?" Hanes asked. "What are they planning?"

"I don't know yet," Alex said. "I need more time. We will get out, but we have to be ready. If we just leave now, the odds are good most of us will get killed."

"Screw that," said another member of Oscar Company.

"Things may calm down on their own," Alex said. "Cooler heads may prevail. But if not, I'm working on a plan to get us out. The most important thing is that no one can know what I can do. They find that out and they'll never let any of us go."

"You want us to sit around and do nothing?" Hanes said.

"No," Alex responded. "There are more military personnel on their way from other corporations. From what I've seen of their security footage, there are no other holding cells in this building."

"So?" Sansabar said.

"So, we need to pick a corner, and make sure people don't start trouble," Alex said. "We should rest in shifts. Sly, you're the designated news gatherer. Make a few friends and find out what happened at the other sites where the protesters attacked."

"Intel," Sly said. "I've got it, Team Leader."

"Hanes, you and Sansabar keep Oscar Company in check," Alex continued. "Once it's time to go, we don't need injuries slowing us down."

"That may not be possible," Hanes said. "I can't stop a fight if we don't start it."

"So, make sure it doesn't start," Sly said.

"For now, they aren't our enemies," Alex said. "And neither are the law enforcement officers working here. I get the feeling that they don't like locking us up any more than we do."

"Yeah, I picked up on that," Sansabar said.

"The media can't have everyone hoodwinked," Hanes said.

"We'll get our side of the story out," Alex said. "But our first priority is getting a plan together to ensure that we're all safely released."

They heard the buzz and clank of doors opening close by. Alex stepped toward the door to their cell and pulled it closed. The lock popped back into place, just as the door from the processing area opened and a stranger in brown fatigues was ushered in. He looked angry and frightened. Alex moved away from the door as Officer Reed waited for the space to clear. She was clearly a pro, with lots of experience working with prisoners.

After Alex backed up, the door unlocked. The newcomer in brown fatigues was hesitant to go inside. Reed gave the man a shove. She was clearly stronger than she appeared, and he nearly fell as he stumbled inside. The door closed with a metallic bang.

The Operators from Oscar Company had divided in half. Some were sleeping on the metal benches in one corner of the holding cell. The others stood guard over them. Alex was so tired that he actually felt a pang of jealousy. Despite the harsh, unsanitary conditions, the thought of laying down and closing his eyes sounded wonderful. Instead, he leaned against the transparent wall and focused on the security system. There were twelve more people in brown fatigues being processed, and another transport was landing in the courtyard outside of the garage area.

Alex knew that he needed to get a message to Nyx. Captain Poe might not be the type of officer to take action, but Alex knew that one way or another, Nyx would be trying to help him. He had no doubt that he could get his people out of the detention center, but it was all for naught if they didn't have a plan for getting out of the city, or better yet, off world.

Sly was already making friends with the newcomer. And Reed soon brought another prisoner in brown fatigues through the corridor to the holding cell. Alex guessed that there was just enough space for the three different groups of prisoners to squeeze into the holding cell, as long as each group followed the example set by the CDF Operators. But Alex had no idea how many groups might be picked up. Things were insane after the attack on the Ahzco factory. He couldn't remember exactly how many different plumes of smoke he had seen across the city. It seemed like five, but that was really just a guess.

Alex turned his attention back to the law enforcement main servers. From there, he could access the planetary networks. It would be simple enough to log into a messaging service and send an email, but unfortunately, Alex had never set up an account. On NP8261, he hadn't needed a mail account, and once the CDF recruited him, he had gone all in on their services, including a company-only mail service. He couldn't gain access to the Ahzco network outside of the ship.

Instead, he did a quick search for his mother on the city's social media pages. It didn't take long to find an organic growers' co-op that had Penelope Evans listed as a member. He found her contact info and using an unoccupied computer terminal, sent her a quick message.

Hi Mom, it's Alex. I need some help.

Waiting for a reply was difficult. The newcomers in brown

fatigues were in no mood to socialize. Sly came wandering back over after the first three had been short with him. Fortunately, they were staying on the far side of the holding cell. Ahzco's greater number of Operators kept them helpfully intimidated.

"Find out anything?" Alex asked.

"They're with Hazzle Corp," Sly said. "That's all I could get from them. They're pretty angry."

"They might have been caught off-guard by the attacks," Alex said. "If they lost people, they may not be in the mood to socialize."

"Yeah, I'll keep trying," Sly said.

Alex checked on the message to his mother, but there was no reply. It was nearly dawn and odds were good that she was either still at the hospital or asleep at home after a long night. Alex kept an eye on the security camera with a view of the terminal he had used. If someone showed up to that station, he couldn't risk them finding out that one of the prisoners had used it.

More and more people were brought into the building. Once all the Hazzle Corp detainees were processed, the next group was brought in. They wore gray, one-piece flight suits, and like the others, they obviously weren't happy about being picked up. Unlike the Ahzco and Hazzle personnel, however, the men and women in gray had their hands restrained behind their backs. Several struggled as the police officers unloaded them from the transport.

"The next group could be trouble," Alex said.

"Beautiful," Sly replied.

"Nothing we can't handle," Hanes added.

"We're not the enemy," Alex said. "Remember that."

Hanes lifted his hands in a sign of surrender, but Alex knew exactly how the man felt. They needed a target that they could reach, someone to take their frustration out on. The holding cell would descend into violence sooner rather than later. It was only a matter of time with so many warriors taken captive and locked up in close confines.

The sun was rising, and soon there would be shift change at the detention center. With it would come a greater risk that Alex and his abilities would be discovered. He checked the unused computer terminal again and felt a jolt of relief when he saw that his mother had responded.

Alex! Where are you? Your father's okay. I got him home, but there are news reports that the police are arresting private military. Are you okay?

It had been a long time since Alex had seen his mother. In the interim, he had been injured in the line of duty and came close to dying on a number of occasions. Yet somehow, none of those events had rocked him as much as reading the brief message from his mother had. He felt tears stinging his eyes. It wasn't worry that was getting to him, though; it was the concern and love that he knew his mother felt for him. He loved her too, and suddenly wanted to see her more than anything in the entire galaxy. But the last thing he could afford to do was have her coming to the detention center. He needed her help, but in a way that wouldn't get her into trouble.

I'm okay, he wrote back on the messaging site. *We've been taken into custody. We're still in Oslo, but I'm not sure where. I need you to help me discover where I'm at, so that I can find a way to get us out. And please delete these messages as soon as you get them.*

"I've got a line to my family," Alex whispered.

"How's that help us?" Hanes asked.

"His father works for the Company," Sly said. "He saved people during the attack."

"I still don't see how that helps us now," Hanes said. "We need to contact people with the juice to get us released."

"I'm working on it," Alex said. "But it's no secret that we've been arrested. They're reporting it on the news."

"Your father should be able to access the CDF network," Sly said. "He could get a message to the *Currency*."

"Right, I'll get that going. Perhaps Administrator Brown could help too," Alex said. "In the meantime, we stay cool and don't get caught up in our emotions."

He was trying to warn Hanes without calling him out directly. Alex could pull rank, but that authority would only go so far. Especially in such a high-tension environment. Alex sent a message asking his father to make contact with their ship in orbit, then did a search for the addresses of the police detention centers using a mapping program. It didn't take long for Alex to recognize the building in which they were being held from the program's satellite images of the city.

The pieces of the puzzle required to pull off their escape were coming together, but he still wasn't sure that escaping was the right thing to do. It would certainly allow the media to paint them as criminals with no regard for Skandia's laws. But unless Alex could show the rest of the Operators that help was coming, things were bound to get ugly. People could die, and

Alex didn't want that. He needed a solution that would get them out of the fix they were in without making matters worse. A plan was slowly forming in the back of his mind, he just couldn't see it yet. The stress and fatigue were getting to him. His mind felt foggy, and the burning sensation behind his eyes returned with a vengeance. Unfortunately, there was no time to sleep.

On the security feed, Alex watched as the first gray-clad prisoner was ushered into the building. It was a man with a tattoo that covered his neck and one side of his face. As soon as the door closed behind him, the man threw himself into the law enforcement officer, who went down hard. The detainee had his hands bound behind his back, but got to his feet with a lurch, then kicked the downed officer twice before three more rushed in. One had a stun baton and Alex knew what was coming. The man turned and screamed in rage. Alex couldn't hear the man's shout, but he saw his face contorted in rage, the veins in his neck bulging out like high tension wires.

The officer with the stun baton thrusted it at the detainee, who tried to avoid it but couldn't. His body shook as the voltage shocked him and then he collapsed to the ground. One of the three officers was helping the guard who had been kicked. There was blood on the man's face. The other two officers worked over the fallen detainee. They were both armed with non-lethal weapons—one had a slapjack, the other, a plain wooden baton—but they beat the detainee mercilessly. It only took a few seconds before the man was left on the ground, barely conscious.

They jerked him to his feet, but the detainee couldn't stand on his own. He sagged between the officers, who carried him to a tiny room, much like the one with the scanning equipment, and tossed him inside. They closed and locked the door. Alex couldn't see inside, but he could imagine it. If any of the CDF Operators resisted, they would be treated the same way. And Alex had to make sure that didn't happen.

CHAPTER FIVE

LOMAN WAS on an express transit less than twenty-four hours away from the Skandia system. There were eight other people on the shuttle, which wasn't as posh as most interstellar transports, but was much faster. Unlike other ships, express transit bypassed the spaceports and trade lanes in the connecting systems, taking the passengers straight to their destination without slowing down or stopping.

Loman recognized three of the other passengers as news reporters, and two others were social media influencers who he'd heard of before. It didn't take much work to look them up on his PIL and confirm who they were. Loman didn't recognize the other three, but they acted just as busy and self-absorbed as the rest.

Skandia Seven had become the hottest planet in the galaxy overnight. Loman was pinged with messages from Ian Gentry and several upper-level officers within the Security division of

Ahzco about the attacks. Fortunately, none of the other passengers had noticed that the executive VP of Security for one of the galaxy's biggest corporations was on the same shuttle. They were too focused on their own privacy and on keeping up with the Galactic networks' breaking news reports about the attacks to even notice Loman's presence on board.

As the shuttle passed through the intersecting systems, connectivity went in and out in short bursts. Like everyone else onboard, Loman downloaded as many news stories coming out of Skandia Seven as possible before losing his connection. He put on large, noise-canceling headphones and huddled in a seat several rows back from the others. The bathroom facilities on the shuttle were near the front, just behind the cockpit, so the only time that Loman was at risk of being recognized was when one of the other passengers returned from the bathroom. He kept his head down to avoid giving them a clear view of his face and read about the attacks.

In all, thirty-one facilities had been attacked, and more than a dozen businesses had been set on fire. The protests, which were erupting across all of the planet's major cities, turned violent quickly. The media was pointing fingers at the almost twenty mega-corps that had private security teams on Skandia Seven. Loman knew that they were all there, just as his own people were there, to protect company property and employees. He couldn't speak about anyone else, but he was certain that his people hadn't engaged the protesters. They were armed with the lowest level, non-lethal weapons available, and had been issued strict orders not to engage if at all possible.

What Loman didn't have was any reports from the ground

in the Skandia system. His troops there had not reported in, nor had the officers on board the *Currency*. It was an unacceptable lack of information. All that Loman knew for certain was that he had to get in-system as soon as possible and see what was taking place for himself.

The latest news articles from Skandia Seven were reporting a lot of law enforcement activity. It was no surprise to Loman. He would have thought that the police would be working overtime to bring the protesters to heel. After all, there were widespread reports of destruction of private property and theft. But it didn't take a criminal mastermind to realize that the protests were the perfect cover for crimes of all sorts. The people lurking in the shadows loved civil unrest, when the attention of society's watchmen shifted away from them, and they could carry out their devious plots in the light of day.

"It's happened!" One of the reporters shouted from the front of the shuttle.

Loman looked up toward the front, barely daring to peek over the tops of the seats between where he and the other passengers sat.

"What are you going on about now?" asked one of the passengers who Loman didn't recognize.

"Skandia Seven has declared a state of emergency and enacted their Planetary Security Protocols!"

"It was only a matter of time," one of the social media influencers declared.

Loman got a sinking feeling in gut. Every planet had protocols in place for invasions, or on the off chance that alien life was discovered. It was a wise practice, but almost every one of the security protocols that Loman had ever looked into was essentially a call for martial law. Security protocols provided the excuses necessary to bypass civil liberties and individual rights. Some planets even allowed citizens to brazenly gun down anyone who couldn't prove residency on the planet. Whatever was happening on Skandia Seven, Loman knew that his people were in danger.

He checked his PIL again, saw that it had a weak connection to the galactic network, and began downloading more news stories. The first that popped up confirmed his worst fears. *PRIVATE MILITARY FORCES DECLARED TERRORIST THREATS TO SOCIETY.* The increase in law enforcement wasn't initiated to keep the protesters in check; it was to round up the Operators on the ground. He felt like he was going to be sick, while the other passengers seemed to revel in the news.

Loman typed out a quick message on his PIL, not daring to use the dictate function as he normally did. The message was addressed to Captain Poe of the *Currency* and cc'd to Colonel Chastain, who was busy moving units to the Askerria Sector. The message was short and to the point, demanding a report on the troops sent down to Skandia Seven.

The signal to the galactic network was lost as the shuttle approached the next space tunnel. They would pass through one more system before reaching Skandia. Loman hoped that his message got through, and he hoped that his people were okay. Until he reached Skandia, however, hope was all that he could do.

CHAPTER SIX

"THEY WOULDN'T LET me see him," the lawyer said.

Nyx had piggybacked on the ship's com system to get a private call down to the planet on her PIL. She was at her station but had her Personal Information Link synced to her Controller headset. No one else could hear her conversation—not that there were many people around to hear it anyway. Most of the Controllers were on other parts of the ship. Only a few were in the Control Center, and they, like Nyx, were glued to their computers, reading the news stories or watching videos coming out of the planet below.

"I didn't expect them to," Nyx said quietly. "Did you find out what they're being held for?"

"The news reports say terrorism," he said quietly. "The officials at the detention center wouldn't say anything. They wouldn't even confirm that he was there."

"So, what does the terrorist thing mean?" Nyx asked. She

had an idea, and it certainly wasn't good, but she wanted to know the specifics.

"Essentially, it means a suspension of their due process," the lawyer explained. "They can be held indefinitely without charges ever being filed."

"How is that legal?"

"Strictly speaking, it isn't. But I'm hearing reports that the Prime Minister is issuing a state of emergency and enacting Planetary Security Protocols. That means martial law, elevated military presence, and a complete bypass of parliament."

"So, the Prime Minister has complete control?" Nyx asked.

"Yes," Jakob Berrgance said. "I'm not a political person, but essentially, there are two sides fighting it out right now. There are global-first, free trade advocates, and there are people calling for a united galactic government."

"And the Prime Minister is one of the latter?"

"You guessed it," the lawyer said. "I suspect that they'll ship all of the private military personnel they rounded up overnight to a penal colony on one of the moons."

"So, we have to get them out before that," Nyx said.

"Good luck," the lawyer said. "Unfortunately, they don't have any rights. The police could walk into their cells and shoot them dead for no reason. It's barbaric, but some people are actually calling for it."

"And there's nothing you can do to help?"

"Nothing from a legal perspective. I have friends in law enforcement, although most of them think I'm as bad as the criminals I defend. Everyone has a right to council, you know.

Anyway, I can get a little more information, but that's the best I can do."

"Alright," Nyx said, feeling more helpless than ever. "Do what you can and get back to me as soon as possible."

"I will, Sergeant West."

The connection ended, and Nyx had to fight back tears. Things were going from bad to worse. She sat still for several minutes, wrestling with her emotions and trying to figure out what to do next. She could report what she knew to the Captain, but it wasn't anything he couldn't find out for himself by simply checking any one of a dozen news sites. Worse still, her relationship with Captain Poe was already strained and pushing him to do more wouldn't make things better.

What she needed was a way to get them out of police custody, but they weren't being put on trial. There was no bail hearing, no visitation, or even the right to speak with an attorney. It felt to Nyx like the entire planet was out to get Alex and the other Operators. She hated feeling so helpless.

Her PIL pinged, letting her know that she had received a new message. When she checked it, a spark of hope flared to life within her mind. The message was from Bruce Evans, who she knew was Alex's father.

Sergeant Nyx West, this is Alex Evan's mother. He asked me to send you a message. He says he's synced into the police servers and has control of the security systems, but no way to get off-world. He asks that you pass this information along to Captain Poe, and that you send word back through us.

It was signed, Penelope Evans, and Nyx felt the sudden urge to meet Alex's parents. She wanted them to know that she cared about him as much as they did, but obviously it wasn't the right time. She couldn't meet them without Alex, and as long as he was being held as a terrorist, she had to focus all of her efforts on finding a way to save him and the other Ahzco Operators.

"I received your message and will take it to the Captain personally," she said, speaking into her PIL as it transformed her speech into text. "Please stand-by."

She jumped to her feet and ran out of the Control Center. There were a few other Controllers and crew members who saw her running and stared as if she were crazy, but Nyx didn't care. She had a message from Alex, and she needed to show the captain. When she reached the bridge, however, she was shocked to find it nearly empty. The pit in the center was occupied by the first officer, and Captain Poe was nowhere to be found.

"Sir," Nyx said from just inside the entrance to the ship's bridge. "I need to speak with Captain Poe. It's an emergency."

First Lieutenant Rory Jones looked at her and tried to smile but failed. There were dark, puffy bags under his eyes, which were bloodshot. His uniform was wrinkled, and he was leaning against the display table that the captain always seemed to be obsessed with whenever Nyx had seen him on the bridge.

"He's unavailable," Lieutenant Jones said. "He just went down for a six-hour break and gave strict instructions that unless the ship was under attack, he wasn't to be disturbed."

Nyx wanted to scream that she didn't care if the captain was tired, but it wouldn't help Alex. She could tell by looking at the first officer that he was about to fall over. Everyone was tired. The situation on the planet had gone from bad to worse, and there were so many ships in orbit that the current circumstances required constant attention from the ship's crew.

"I have a message from our Operators on the ground," she said.

"Really? I was told they had all been arrested," Rory Jones said, showing a little more life than he had before.

"They were," she explained. "But my Operator, Alex Evans, got to a computer terminal and was able to send a message via his father's CDF messaging account."

She could tell by the look on the lieutenant's face that he didn't understand.

"His family lives on Skandia Seven, in Oslo," she explained. "His father is Bruce Evans, a mechanic at the factory that was destroyed. He saved several people when the building collapsed. Alex sent them a message and asked that they forward it on to Captain Poe through me."

"What's the message?" Lieutenant Rory Jones asked.

"It confirms they're being held by the authorities, and requests further orders," she replied.

"If they've been arrested, there's nothing we can do," Jones said. "We got a message over an hour ago from the Skandian Prime Minister ordering us out of orbit and out of the system. We have twenty-four hours to comply, or they will consider us a hostile threat."

"What does that mean?" Nyx asked.

"We don't know for certain," Jones replied. "Most planets have weapons that can be fired into orbit. I think Captain Poe plans to wait here as long as possible, but with no way to retrieve the Operators from police custody, I suspect he'll break orbit and set a course out of the system."

"You mean he'll leave them behind?"

Rory nodded. "He can't risk losing the ship."

Nyx felt an icy wave of fear run down her back. She understood the logic, but it wasn't in her nature to give up. The message from Alex would only serve to hasten the Captain's retreat.

"Then we shouldn't tell him," Alex said.

"We can't hold back pertinent mission intel, Sergeant," the lieutenant argued. "I have to tell him."

"Then we have six hours," Nyx argued. "We'll find a way."

He looked at her with more than a little pity but didn't stop her as she left the bridge and hurried back to her station. The circumstances were threatening to extinguish the spark of hope that she was keeping alive, but she would never give up. Nyx wasn't helpless, and nothing could ever make her stop fighting for Alex.

She dropped into the seat at her console and typed back a message to his parents.

Please forward this message to Alex: Captain Poe has been ordered out of the system by Skandian authorities. I suspect he will comply in the next seven to eight hours. If you can get out of police custody, you should do it. How can I help?

She sent the message then closed her eyes and rubbed her face. She couldn't believe that things had gotten so bad so quickly. If Alex was going to break out of police custody, he would need a way off of the planet. She opened her eyes and began searching for shuttles that could get Alex and the other Operators off world and to the *Currency* before she left orbit.

Tears filled her eyes as an official message popped up on the first charter flight website she was checking. *ALL FLIGHTS OFF WORLD HAVE BEEN RESTRICTED BY ORDER OF THE PRIME MINISTER.*

No, Nyx thought, *it's not fair.* Even if Alex could break free, there was no way that he could steal a shuttle and fly it into orbit. The ship would be visible to every radar system on the planet, and if they had weapons that could fire into orbit, they could easily track a shuttle and destroy it long before it escaped atmo. The tears brimmed over and began to fall. The thought of leaving Alex behind felt like someone was tearing the heart from her chest. But she finally realized that there was nothing she could do to help him. He was completely on his own.

CHAPTER SEVEN

THE MESSAGE from his mother made Alex angry. Not at his parents, and certainly not at Nyx, who he knew was working tirelessly to find a way to help. But his anger toward Captain Poe was intense. The coward was running. He didn't care about anyone but himself and his precious ship. Alex didn't understand how a man like Poe could rise to the rank of captain, but then, he'd seen a colonel betray the Vice President. Rank didn't always mean that a person had merit or morals.

"What's wrong?" Sly whispered.

The holding cell was filling up fast. Several of the men and women in gray flight-suits had resisted and each one had been beaten. The rest, realizing that it was useless to fight, ultimately complied with the law enforcement officers as they were processed. Several were already in the holding cell. But Alex could see the anger and resentment on their faces. It was only a matter of time before they lost control. He only hoped that none of his own Operators were involved when the newcomers lost their cool.

"I got word from the *Currency*," Alex said. "Captain Poe has been ordered out of the system."

"And he's going to leave?" Sly asked in disbelief.

"Looks that way," Alex said.

"Nah, it must be a mistake. They can't just leave us down here to rot," Sly argued.

"Captain Poe only cares about himself and his ship," Hanes said. "Everyone knows that. He's never been in combat. We spent the last two years in orbit over Nieuw Aarde in the Dutch system. Ahzco has a huge factory there that makes electrical components for their consumer lines. It was so boring, but Poe strutted around like he was about to be named the new VP of Security."

"How much time do we have?" Sly asked.

"Six hours, maybe," Alex replied.

An emergency message came in on the police server, and Alex scanned it.

"All flights have been grounded until further notice," Alex said.

"Great," Sly complained. "If we run, there's nowhere to go."

"It gets worse," Alex said. "They're shipping us to a penal colony on Nattamara."

"What's that?" Hanes asked.

"One of the moons," Alex said, shaking his head. "There has to be a way."

"There might be," Sly said, with a mischievous grin. "Let me do my thing."

He walked away before Alex could find out what he was up to. One of the sleeping Operators got up off of the metal bench, and Alex sat down. It felt so good just to take the weight off of his legs and feet. He couldn't believe how quickly his revulsion at the holding cell had been swept away by his fatigue.

"What is he doing?" Hanes asked, joining Alex on the bench.

"I have no idea," Alex replied.

They both watched in silence as Sly approached the group of newcomers in gray jumpsuits. At first, they were stoic and looked suspicious, but their attitudes quickly changed. Sly nodded, gave one of the newcomers a fist bump, then walked back toward Alex.

"My new friends say hi," Sly said, squatting down in front of Alex.

"Who are they?"

"Zen Tech Operators," Sly said. "And they are pissed."

"I bet," Alex replied.

"You didn't mention having been in the Carthage system by any chance?" Hanes asked.

"Do I look stupid?" Sly replied. "No way, man. That's on a need to know basis, and don't nobody in this room need to know it."

"So, what's your plan?" Alex asked.

"We need a transport, right?" Sly replied.

"Yes," Alex said. "The sooner the better."

"Well then, we should take the one they're sending us to that moon in," Sly said. "You can sync up with the controls and cut the pilots out."

"Well, yeah, probably," Alex said. "But there's bound to be

armed guards. As soon as the pilots reveal that they've lost control, the guards will kill us all."

"That's where our Zen Tech friends come in. We need to get them weapons."

"You're out of your mind," Hanes said.

"No, it's possible," Sly said. "They can smuggle them onto the transport in those bulky suits they wear."

"How are we going to get weapons?" Hanes argued.

But Alex already knew the answer. The plan had merit, if he could manage to get weapons and if the *Currency* didn't leave the system before they could hijack the prisoner transport.

"Leave that to me," Alex said, going right to work.

His first task was to get a message to the *Currency*. If they knew he had a plan, perhaps Nyx could convince them to stay in the system. He leaned back against the wall and closed his eyes. He could hear Sly and Hanes whispering beside him, and the sound of other voices in the holding cell added to the background noise created by the EM waves of the city, a soft rustling sound, like wind through autumn leaves that have yet to fall.

There was a lot to do if the plan was going to work. Getting the weapons wouldn't be easy, but in his search of the building's security system, he had seen officers step into a room unarmed, and come out with blaster rifles. Alex didn't know if the armory was manned. There might be an officer inside the room. The camera angle didn't allow Alex to see inside the space, but it looked like a storage room, and Alex was banking on the prospect that it wasn't guarded. He was also banking on the possibility that there were smaller weapons in the armory.

Rifles were great, but they couldn't be hidden inside the Zen Tech flight suits. They needed small arms, or at the least, stun batons.

Before Alex planned the heist to get the weapons, he sent a quick message to his family. The less they knew, the better, and while Nyx might need details to convince Captain Poe to stay in the system, there wasn't time. Besides, Alex didn't want to mention his abilities in writing that might be recovered in an investigation, which would surely take place once they attempted escape.

He had just finished sending the message when a calendar alert rang through the servers like a bell. Apparently, the message was automatically sent to every device, and Alex saw it in his mind's eye. *MORNING BRIEFING IN 15 MINUTES.* It was the perfect opportunity to get the weapons.

Alex could move through the computer systems with the power of thought. It was like thinking of a movie he had seen, and remembering the different scenes as he debated just how realistic the holo-film really was. All he had to do was think of the isolated security system. It had no wireless connections, and no link to outside servers, yet Alex's INC could communicate with the device as easily as one might slip on a comfortable robe. His mind shuffled through the door locks and security cameras, until he found the feed from the two cameras located just outside the holding cell. Everything on the system was digital, and it didn't take Alex long to record a five-minute loop and start playing it. Whoever was monitoring the feed would just see the detainees sitting around, looking frustrated.

With less than ten minutes until the briefing started, Alex

outlined the route to the armory. When it was time, he and Sly would lead a person from Zen Tech to the room. They would steal no more than six weapons, then return to the holding cell. If all went well, it would only take them a few minutes.

From the other security feeds, Alex could see the officers leaving their desks. The server clock showed the time as 0714. Alex had no idea how long the briefing would last, but they couldn't waste any time.

"Alright, get one of the Zen Tech people," Alex said.

"Roger," Sly said, standing up and moving back toward the gray-clad Operators.

"I still think it would be better to make a break for it," Hanes said.

"And go where?" Alex demanded. He didn't like shooting down ideas, but Hanes wasn't considering all the factors. "We've got no money, no place to go, no way to survive on this planet as fugitives. The entire world is on lockdown. So, the only way we get off Skandia Seven is to hijack the transport."

"And if we fail?" Hanes said.

"We won't fail," Alex said.

Sly returned with a surly looking Operator with a pink scar down the side of his face.

"This is Cutter," Sly said. "He volunteered, even though he doesn't believe we've got a man on the inside."

Alex nodded, knowing that Sly had lied to cover up Alex's abilities.

"I told him you have people here, but he's not the trusting type," Sly continued.

Alex didn't respond. He just got to his feet and moved to the door. The lock cycled with a reverberating clang, and he pushed the door open.

"See," Sly said. "I told you."

The holding cell fell silent. Alex turned to the others who were completely focused on him.

"We get one shot at this," Alex said. "You're all professionals. We could run, but we'd be hunted down and killed. Not to mention the media frenzy would make matters worse. So, stay here, we'll be back, and if all goes as planned, we'll take control of the transport ship that they're planning to use to move us. It's our only shot of getting out, off of the planet, and back to our respective ships."

There were several nods, but no one spoke. Alex could see the disbelief in some people's eyes, even amongst several of the Operators from Oscar Company. They all wanted out of the holding cell, and it was hard to watch Alex and Sly stroll away. It was even harder for Alex to lock the door again, despite knowing that if someone decided to run for it while they were out, it would ruin everything he had worked for. The surveillance cameras had all been rigged with loops of empty corridors and doorways. Alex had to assume that whoever monitored the security system stayed on station even during the briefing. There might, in fact, be others who weren't in the briefing, and in that case, they would have to deal with them as quickly and quietly as possible.

"Just remember," Alex said. "If we get caught, don't resist. Odds are that they won't kill us, and we'll still have a shot at taking control of the transport."

"Copy that," Sly said.

Cutter just nodded.

"Alright, let's do this," Alex said, using his INC to open the door that led from the holding cells to the processing area.

The door popped open and Alex moved silently through it. His heart was beating in his chest like piston, and he could feel sweat emerging all over his body. He was unarmed, and without any type of protection. If one of the law enforcement officers saw them, they might be shot, and there was no way for Alex to defend himself or his friend.

Fortunately, the processing area seemed deserted. There were several computer stations standing empty, the display screens scrolling through pictures in stand-by mode. Alex ignored the computers and moved to a hallway that led toward the garage where he and the other detainees had first been held. There were several doors on both sides of the hallway, and it was difficult to remember which one he was looking for. The perspective was different, and his nerves were shooting warnings through his mind like flashes of lightning. Alex felt like there was a voice in his head screaming for him to hurry.

"Look at that," Sly whispered, as they came to armory door. "They were nice enough to label it for us."

Alex had guessed correctly and felt a tiny wave of relief. Sly reached out to open the door, but it was locked.

"Great," Cutter whispered. "What now?"

"Everything is on a timer," Alex lied. "Just give it a second."

In reality, his mind was skimming through the security system. Terror squeezed his heart. What if the armory wasn't part of the system? What if it required a physical key? Alex hadn't seen anyone else unlock the door, but it was still possible. His mind screamed that it was more than possible, that it was highly probable. But before his fear could morph into full blown panic, he found the lock in the system and ordered it to open. There was a small click, and Alex tried the handle again. It opened.

Lights came on automatically as the door opened, and Alex was right about the room. It was just another storage room, not any larger than the room where he had been scanned for weapons. But the walls were lined with racks of blaster rifles.

"We have hit the mother lode," Sly said in awe.

"Unbelievable," Cutter muttered.

Alex wasn't sure if the Zen Tech Operator's exclamation was out of excitement or incredulity, but he ignored the surly man and looked at the bins beneath the racks of rifles. They found a variety of items, from sidearms, to plastic hand restraints, and even a range of power supplies.

Sly snatched up a laser pistol, found the right size power supply, and rammed it home. The weapon powered on and Sly cycled it through the various modes.

"It's got stun capabilities," he whispered.

"Screw that, set them to kill," Cutter said in a husky voice.

"No," Alex argued. "We can't fire lasers that could compromise the ship."

Cutter grunted, and Alex took that for agreement. The pistols weren't tiny, but they were small enough to hide in the bulky flight suits. The tactical weapons were built on heavy frames that could be enhanced with a wide variety of accessories like flashlights, laser aiming, and even retractable blades that would spring out if someone tried to snatch the pistol from the officer wielding it. They each took two, after loading the power supplies and checking the charge. Whoever was in charge of the armory made sure that everything was in working order and ready to go at a moment's notice.

"Think they'll notice their guns are missing?" Sly asked.

"I hope not," Alex said.

"If they do, at least we can fight back," Cutter grumbled. He looked as if he wanted to burn the detention center to the ground.

"The police were just following orders," Alex said.

"You didn't see what they did to my friends," Cutter said.

In fact, Alex had seen what they did to the Operators who resisted. Four of the members of the Zen Tech group were in isolated cells with multiple injuries. Alex resisted the urge to say how stupid they had been for trying to fight the law enforcement officials while their hands were bound behind their backs. It might have been the truth, but it would only antagonize Cutter. Alex's plan hinged on keep the Zen Tech Operators on his side.

"Let's move," Alex said. "Their briefing could end at any time."

They hurried back through the building, and were almost to the holding cells, when officer Reed turned a corner and stepped into the hallway right in front of them. They froze for a moment, the three detainees staring at Officer Reed. Alex saw the surprise on her face and instantly knew that they hadn't wandered into a trap. It was just an unfortunate accident.

Her hand dropped to the grip of the pistol on her wide hips, but before she could draw the weapon, Cutter fired. The pistol made a high pitch whine after it discharged. The stun level voltage made officer Reed's body spasm as she toppled over.

"Grab her," Alex said in a commanding whisper. "We've got to hide her somewhere."

"If they find her, we're cooked," Sly said.

Alex knew his friend was right. They needed a place that wasn't on the security video, some place people were unlikely to go. And he knew just the place.

CHAPTER EIGHT

"OH, THIS IS GENIUS," Sly whispered as they pulled Officer Reed into a tiny room labeled *JANITORIAL SUPPLIES.*

There were buckets, mops, brooms, scrub brushes, and large bottles of industrial cleaning solvents; all stacked on metal shelving. Reed was beginning to come around, and while Alex was certain that she wouldn't have the strength to overpower the three of them, he understood that she didn't need to.

"Quick," Alex said, pulling a disposable cleaning rag from a box, "stuff this in her mouth."

Sly wadded the rag into a ball and stuffed it into Officer Reed's mouth. Alex noticed the way that it smudged her lipstick, which she hadn't been wearing before, and it occurred to him that she had taken the time to put on make-up. Perhaps she had gone off shift and wanted to look her best when she got home. He couldn't know for sure without asking her, and there was no time.

Cutter was keeping watch at the door, while Alex used an electric extension cord to tie her arms behind her back. He looped the cord around the metal supports of two shelves that were side by side, hoping that the weight of two shelves would hold better than just one. Reed's eyes were open by the time he was done, but only halfway. It didn't appear that she understood what was happening to her.

"It would be faster and safer to just kill her," Cutter growled.

"She isn't the enemy," Alex said. "Besides, hurting her would just give the others an excuse to kill us."

"Like they need an excuse," the big Operator said.

"He's really a lovely person once you get to know him," Sly said dryly.

Confident that they had Officer Reed secured in the janitorial supply closet, they turned off the light and closed the door. The hallways were still empty. Alex scrolled through the security feeds that his INC projected in his mind. The way back to the holding cell was clear.

"Go!" Alex said. "Before we run out of time."

They hurried through the corridor that led to the holding cells. Once they arrived back in sight of the other detainees, Cutter held up the two pistols he was carrying. A wicked looking grin crossed his face. Alex didn't know much about other corporations, or how they trained their defense forces. There were stories, of course, tell-all books and even movies about the rigors of this company's military force, and that corporation's training. But being around Cutter and seeing how the Zen Tech Operators had acted when they were brought to the detention center gave Alex a feeling of dread. They seemed to be the kind that reveled in violence, who were apt to strike first and think second.

They passed through the heavy door into the holding cell and Alex locked it behind them. The pain behind his eyes was getting worse. A growing heat felt like it was scorching the back of his eyeballs and there was nothing he could do to escape the pain.

"You did it?" Hanes asked.

Corporal Sansabar was sitting up on the metal bench, rubbing her shoulder and looking at the Zen Tech Operators suspiciously.

"We got the weapons," Sly said, holding up one of the pistols.

"Any problems?" Hanes asked.

"One," Alex said. "We ran into Officer Reed, but got her stuffed in a supply closet. Hopeful she won't attract any attention."

"If she does, we'll be ready when they come," Cutter said.

"No," Alex replied. "That's insane. We can't fight the entire police force while we're trapped in this room."

"He's right," Sly said. "We're sitting ducks in here."

"We stick to the plan," Alex insisted. "They're going to ship us off-world and that's what we want."

"How are you getting out of here with those weapons?" Sansabar asked.

"We aren't," Alex admitted. "They are."

Alex handed his pistols over to a couple of the Zen Tech Operators. Sansabar's eyes narrowed. She clearly didn't like the idea of giving weapons to strangers when she, herself, had none. Alex couldn't blame her, but there was a slim chance that since the Zen Tech Operators had all been searched upon entering the detainment center, they wouldn't be searched again before being moved to the transport.

"Remember," Alex continued, turning to face the detainees from other corporations that were in the holding cell, "we get one chance at this. The law enforcement officials have been cleared to use deadly force if we resist. All flights have been canceled, except for the transport that is supposed to take us to the lunar penal colony."

"How the hell do you know all this?" asked one of the detainees.

"We've got an inside man," Sly said.

"One of the intake officers is a friend of a friend," Alex said.

"You're from this place?" another detainee asked.

"My family is here," Alex said.

"His father works for Ahzco," Sansabar spoke up. "We met him at the factory before the attacks."

"Not everyone on Skandia Seven believes the media hype," Alex continued. "And there are a lot of people who don't like what the PM is doing."

"The PM?" asked the first detainee who spoke up.

"The Prime Minister," Sly said.

"He's put the planet on emergency security protocols," Alex explained. "I don't know a lot about that, but I could see the memo on the computer as I was being processed. They have the authority to use deadly force against us if we resist."

"So we wait," Hanes said. "At least until we're on the transport."

"Yes," Alex said. "Once we break orbit, I'll give the signal and the Zen Tech Operators will deal with the guards."

"Stun only," Cutter said, as if the words left a bad taste in his mouth.

"Yeah, we wouldn't want to blast holes in the transport," Sly said.

"Wait a second," said the first detainee. "We're talking about a security transport. We'll be locked in place, and the cockpit will be separated from the passenger cabin. It's impossible."

"No, it isn't," Alex said. "I can make it work, even if we can't get inside the cockpit."

"And we're just supposed to trust you?" asked one of the detainees from the Hazzle Corp group asked.

"Does anyone else have a better idea?" Alex asked.

The room fell silent.

"This is how we play it," Sly said. "There will probably be more detainees than just us on the transport. Hazzle Corp, you're in charge of spreading the word that everything is good once we have control of the ship."

"When we're in orbit," Alex said. "We can return each of you to your respective vessels."

"If we run now," Hanes said. "Most of us won't survive."

"Eventually they'll catch us all," Sansabar added.

"But we could go out fighting," Cutter said.

"You can die fighting," Alex said. "But wouldn't it be better to live to fight another day? If I'm wrong, you'll still have the weapons. You can go out in a blaze of glory on the moon."

To Alex's surprise, that actually brought a smile to Cutter's face. It wasn't a pretty sight.

CHAPTER NINE

Nʏx ᴡᴀs ᴡᴀɪᴛɪɴɢ for a message from Alex. When it came, she was filled with joy. Just knowing that he had a plan to escape made her feel hopeful. Yet her own role in the plan was small, and probably impossible. Her feelings about Captain Poe were not positive. He was a small-minded, risk-averse man with whom she had already had conflict. If there was one thing that Nyx didn't enjoy, it was confronting people with things they didn't want to hear.

Conflict was always hard. But Nyx had to admit that she enjoyed being removed from the danger of armed conflict while still playing a role in the outcome. It was, she supposed, not unlike being a general on the ancient battle fields of long ago. To be able to formulate a plan and guide the action from a safe distance, without actually joining in the fray, was much easier than confronting someone face-to-face. But she would never convince the hesitant Captain Poe with a strongly worded text message. She had to put herself in harm's way, so to speak, if she had any hope of keeping the *Currency* in the system long enough to rescue Alex and the other operators.

So, after momentarily savoring the elation of hearing that Alex had a plan, she spent the next several hours wondering what it could be as she waited for Captain Poe to wake up and return to his post. She kept her Flex PIL activated on her forearm and ensured that any incoming messages would sound a tone loud enough to get her attention. The last thing she wanted was to miss Alex as he was trying to contact her. Fatigue was a constant during any mission. Walking up and down the hall of the command deck helped to keep her awake, her mind turning over the many possibilities of Alex's plan.

He had been smart not to spell it out for her. Involving his parents was a necessary risk, but eventually, the authorities would figure out their connection. If they were willing to declare martial law, they might also be inclined to arrest innocent citizens. Nyx could only hope that Alex's parents would be okay, but she had enough to worry about with Alex incarcerated and facing the possibility of abandonment. She couldn't let that happen.

Eventually Captain Poe appeared. He was a tall, striking man in a well-pressed uniform. Visually, he was everything a person expected in a space captain, but Nyx knew that his physique obscured the quaking fear of an indecisive, risk-averse officer who was anything but captain material. She had to push those feelings aside. He looked well-rested and Nyx couldn't help but compare him to his first officer, Lieutenant Jones, who looked like death warmed over as he stood his watch on the bridge of the *Currency.*

As the captain moved toward the entrance to the bridge, so did Nyx. She waited respectfully as he swept past her and into the command center of the ship. Watching from the corridor, she saw that all of the other senior officers were at their stations. Lieutenant Jones stood at attention.

"Sit rep," Captain Poe said in his deep, strong voice.

"All is well, Captain," Jones replied. "A few more ships have entered the system, only to be informed that all traffic onto Skandia Seven is restricted."

"They're serious about clearing us out," Poe said.

"It appears so, Captain," Jones continued. "No one has left orbit yet. Nothing to report on the *Currency.* We're green across the board, and ready for your orders."

"Very well," Poe said, before clearing his voice and speaking loudly so that the officers at their stations could hear him clearly. "I have word from Vice President Haley requesting an update on our situation. As soon as I have completed that report, we will make our way to the FTA space tunnel and out of the Skandia System. Please make sure—"

"Captain!" Nyx said. She hated to interrupt but she felt that he didn't have all of the information he needed. "May I speak with you?"

"No, Sergeant West, you may not," Poe said, his eye twitching with irritation.

"But sir, I've had word from Sergeant Evans. They're planning an escape and have requested that you don't leave the system."

West hesitated for a second before he replied. Nyx thought that he was considering his options, but she was wrong. None of the officers on the bridge showed her the slightest indication of support either. Even Lieutenant Jones looked down, either out of shame or weariness, Nyx could not tell.

"We are leaving the system, as requested by the Skandian authorities," Poe said. "We cannot risk aggravating what has already become an interstellar incident."

Nyx felt as if the captain had just slapped her across the face. Was he actually saying that the operators had caused the attacks? She couldn't understand his logic. He knew the members of Oscar Company and their orders to protect Ahzco property. He had been informed of every action taken down on the planet at every step along the way. Yet he sounded as if he actually believed the news reports coming out of the planet rather than his own men and women on the ground.

"Sir, we can't just leave them behind," Nyx insisted.

"I will take the time to explain myself just this once, Sergeant. And after that, you will return to your post and stay there. I will seek out any information that I need from you."

Nyx felt an icy stab of fear. His mind was made up, and if the *Currency* left the system before Alex could escape, he would be recaptured, perhaps even killed. She felt her eyes stinging with tears at the unfairness of Captain Poe's orders.

"The men and women who are trained as MBS Operators know the risks that they take," Captain Poe said. "Their lives are not more important than the mission they are tasked with carrying out. It may seem harsh to you, but that is the reality of the CDF, Sergeant West. Your connection with your operator is understandable, but you must set your feelings aside and do what is best for the mission."

"And running is best?" Nyx challenged him.

She hadn't planned to challenge Captain Poe. It went against every instinct that she had, but her temper was up, and she spoke boldly, without regard for her own wellbeing or the status of her career.

"That's what you're suggesting we do, isn't it?" Nyx persisted. "That we run away, save ourselves. I'm not sure what orders you're operating under, Captain, but it sounds to me like you're abandoning the mission."

"How dare you?" Captain Poe growled.

The officers on the bridge were silent, totally captivated by the aggression in Nyx's accusation. Challenging a superior officer was detrimental to one's career. Insinuating that the captain of a CDF was a coward was career suicide.

"How dare *you*, sir?" Nyx snapped back. "Those are our people on the ground. They stood under fire from the protesters. They worked tirelessly to save the people we're all tasked with protecting. And you are turning your back on them."

"They failed!" Poe said in a thunderous voice. "The mission is over. Staying here will only draw the ire of the authorities and pull us into a conflict that serves no purpose."

"It sounds like you'd rather save your own neck than make sure our people get home," Nyx said, her entire body trembling with rage and fear.

"Lieutenant!" Poe shouted. "Take Sergeant West to the brig for insubordination. I do not want to see her face on this command deck ever again. She will face charges for her lack of control and disgraceful conduct. It's clear that she is letting her emotions get the best of her."

Lieutenant Rory Jones looked up as he moved slowly from the command station toward the entrance to the bridge. Nyx wanted to run away, and at the same time, to charge straight toward the towering Captain Poe and rip his throat out. But she didn't move, nor did she look away. She stared at the captain so that he knew she saw through his phony excuses.

"You are a coward and a disgrace to that uniform," she said.

"And you are besotted, insolent, child who just sealed her own fate," Captain Poe replied. "Get her out of my sight!"

Jones was beside her and reached for her arm. Nyx didn't struggle, but she didn't leave immediately either. She realized that she had one last chance to get Alex's message to the captain. He may not have wanted to hear her voice again, but he was going to.

"I have word from Sergeant Alex Evans of Cronus Team. They have a plan of escape and have specifically asked that the *Currency* to stay in orbit as long as possible. The authorities from Skandia Seven gave you twenty-four hours, Captain. To leave a moment sooner is cowardice."

"That's enough," Lieutenant Jones said quietly.

Nyx didn't resist him. He tugged at her elbow and she turned and walked with him down the corridor. She felt shaky and weak, but her last glimpse of the captain confirmed that he was staring at her. He had heard every word, and better still, so had the entire bridge crew. It was a long shot, but her only hope of stopping Captain Poe from leaving the system was to challenge him. The odds were slim, but it was possible that he wouldn't want to lose face in front of his crew.

Jones pressed the button at the lift, and the doors opened immediately. They stepped inside and he pressed the button for the lowest level. Nyx felt her body quaking with fear. She didn't want to be stuck in the brig. She had never been in trouble in her life. The very idea of being locked in what amounted to a jail cell on the ship made her feel like she might be sick.

"That wasn't smart," Jones said in a quiet voice as the lift began to descend.

"I had to try," Nyx said quietly.

"Not smart, but courageous," he admitted. "You said what you needed to say, but unfortunately, it won't do any good."

Nyx felt her heart drop. They were going to leave the system without Alex. The odds of him surviving were so small that it seemed impossible. And she wouldn't even be there to watch over him, to say good-bye.

"No," she said. The spark of hope she had been sheltering winked out with that single word.

"The captain won't listen to you or anyone else on the ship," Jones said as the lift doors opened, and he started leading her down the corridor. "He thinks he's above all of us. That's we're simpletons, incapable of intelligent thought."

"So that's it, then?" Nyx asked incredulously. "He just leaves our people behind?"

They came to a thick metal hatch. Jones punched a series of numbers into a touch-sensitive display beside the door and it popped open. He pulled the hatch wide, revealing a dank room with metal walls, a bench, and toilet. Jones waved her inside.

"I didn't say that," he said. "You can always do something, even when it seems like all hope is lost."

She stepped into the little room. There was a weight to the brig, a constricting quality that made it hard to breathe. Jones pointed to her forearm and she thought he was asking for her Flex PIL, which was still snapped around her wrist. She looked at her arm and began to remove the Personal Information Link, but when she looked back up, the lieutenant was closing the door. It shut with a booming thud. Nyx felt the tears pouring from her eyes. They were a result of the pent-up stress from her confrontation with the captain, but also because she still had the PIL in her hand. She was being locked away, but she wasn't helpless. With the PIL she could send messages, log into Skandia's planetary network, and even tap into her controller console.

Even in the grimmest of circumstances, hope refused to die. It glowed back to life inside of her. She wiped the tears from her eyes with the sleeve of her fatigues and sat down on the metal bench that served as both seating and bedding in the brig. The captain may have wanted her shut down, but his actions didn't reflect the feelings of everyone on the *Currency*. There were people on board who felt the way that she did. In fact, they were looking to her to do what they couldn't. And with the Operators on Skandia counting on Nyx, she knew she couldn't let them down. There was work to do, and Nyx had only just begun.

CHAPTER TEN

SEVERAL HOURS PASSED before it was finally time to move the detainees. Alex had snatched a couple of hours of fitful sleep, but he was awake when the transport came into the yard. He had tapped into the station's communication system and was listening as the ship requested permission to land. He waited until he could see it on the security footage before telling the others.

"It's here," Alex said.

"Yeah, but is the *Currency* still here?" Sly asked.

"I can't say for certain," Alex said. "Nyx hasn't responded to my messages."

He had sent several through his parents, who were clearly worried about him. Alex did his best to assure them that he was okay, but it was hard to do via text messages. When he wasn't dozing, Alex had skimmed the news from Oslo, searching for any updates on Ash or Master Sergeant Monty. There were plenty of stories about the attacks, and all of them mentioned the private military personnel, but only to paint them as the aggressors. No one seemed to care what had happened to his friends, who were injured in the fighting, just as no one wanted to hear the real story about how the attacks had been a coordinated effort by the protesters or someone using them as cover.

Alex didn't know who the enemy was, but someone with power was behind the attacks. Perhaps a business rival, but that wasn't likely. The news stories were anti-big business, and a company big enough to launch attacks against multiple corporate entities on an FTA planet all at once would certainly qualify as the enemy in public opinion. The only upside to the mission was that Alex had gotten to see his father, and he knew that his family was safe. He had already given them full access to his bank accounts and urged them to use his salary to pay their bills until they knew what the future of Ahzco's business on Skandia Seven would be. He hoped that they would stay, but if the company pulled out, his father might lose his job. Worse still, he might be transferred back to a level three planet. Alex didn't want that, and had shared as much with his parents, but his father had a lot of years with Ahzco. It would be a big decision for them once the time came.

"Better go and tell the others," Alex told Sly. "Remind them to be cool."

"Yeah, okay," Sly replied.

As soon as he got up, Corporal Sansabar slid over beside Alex on the metal bench. The holding room was crowded. Everyone was antsy. They had been locked up long enough that people were starting to grumble about being hungry or needing to use the facilities, which no one wanted to do since the three toilets were right out in the open.

"You okay?" Sansabar asked.

"Yeah, sure," Alex lied. In truth, the pain behind his eyes was severe. Staying linked to the detention station's computer systems was taxing.

"You don't look great," she said.

"Well, thanks," Alex replied with a grin.

"I mean it. We're all tired, but you've got the weight of the world on your shoulders."

"We'll be out of here soon," Alex said. "I can rest then."

She nodded. "Just know that I've got your back. Oscar Company is here for you."

"Thanks," Alex said. "I don't even know your call sign."

"Sand," she replied.

"That makes sense," Alex said. "It's because you have sand, right? As in courage, toughness, a refusal to back down—I can see that."

"I guess," she said. "They started calling me that in basic. I really thought we'd be called into battle. Instead, we've been glorified babysitters. The only battle I've ever been in was at the factory."

"I get the distinct impression that you'll be in more soon enough," Alex said grimly. "If that's what you want."

"I'm willing," she said. "But I don't know how useful I would be. Sometimes I think I've lost my edge."

"Doesn't appear that way from where I'm sitting," Alex said. "It feels good knowing that you've got my back."

She didn't smile, not exactly, but he could sense a certain

satisfaction in her. And he wasn't just trying to flatter her. From the moment they'd first met, he could tell that she was the kind of operator who did what needed to be done. He couldn't imagine her freezing up in the line of duty.

Alex stood up and held up a hand. He had seen a group of officers moving through the processing center and it seemed obvious that they were going to move the detainees to the transport vessel.

"Remember," Alex said. "Just do as they tell you, and when we're on board the ship we make our move. Just wait for my signal."

"Just don't wait too long," Cutter said. "We owe these bastards some payback."

Alex couldn't change the other detainees' feelings. And he had seen their comrades beaten for resisting. Several were still locked in isolation cells to keep them from causing trouble.

The outer doors opened with a clang, and six law enforcement officers walked through. They all had stun batons, but two had blaster rifles. Everyone in the holding cell turned to look at the officers. They moved to the heavy, metal door that kept the prisoners confined in the holding cell. The lock clicked and one of the officers swung the door open. He was a big, well-muscled man with a thick mustache.

"You're being moved," he said in a gruff voice. "You will step to the doorway one at a time. Hold your wrists together and follow our instructions. We'll be taking you in groups of five at a time. If you resist, we'll used our stun batons, and if that doesn't work... well, we have a more permanent solution."

Alex understood that he was referring to the rifles. The big man pointed straight at Cutter, and for a split-second, Alex feared the worse. So far, he had been able to keep an eye on the closet where they had tied up Officer Reed. No one had found her, but Alex was afraid that somehow the officers had discovered the missing weapons.

"You, in the gray flight suits. You're first," the big law enforcement officer ordered.

Cutter stepped toward the door and held out his arms. "Anything to get us out of this stinking place."

Another one of the officers stepped toward Cutter with plastic constraints, which he snapped around the Zen Tech operator's wrists. The law enforcement officers took all of the Zen Tech operators out of the holding room together. Alex watched as they were herded back through the detainment area and out through the same garage space where they had been brought into the station. Outside, the group was led up a narrow ramp that unfolded from the side of the transport.

"Any trouble?" Sly asked.

"Not so far," Alex said. "We were lucky they didn't get searched again."

"Yeah," Sansabar said. "Fortunately, the locals seem anxious to be rid of us."

"No one likes a dirty job," Hanes said.

It wasn't long until the officers were back. They took the Hazzle group next, leaving the Ahzco operators for last. With each passing moment, Alex's stress level increased. The pain behind his eyes became sharp—a hot, piercing throb that stabbed into his brain. He decided that it was time to release his link to the station's main servers. He had learned as much as he could, and while he still hadn't heard from Nyx, there wasn't really anything that would change their plan. Either he could take control of the transport or he couldn't. And if they were successful in getting control of the vessel, the *Currency* would either be in the system or it wouldn't.

"They're coming," Alex said, as he saw the law enforcement officers moving back through the processing area.

"Did they ever get the group from the isolation cells?" Sly asked.

"Negative," Alex replied. "They must be saving those for last."

"At least they didn't find the woman we took down," Sly whispered, just as the door opened.

Hanes led the way out of the holding cell. Alex was in the middle of the group, his hands bound together in front of him. A few other officers glanced up, but none seemed suspicious or even really interested in them. Sly was right in front of Alex, with Sansabar behind him. The pressure that had been weighing on Alex seemed to lessen as they left the building. The big, overhead garage doors were up. Clean air wafted in and Alex breathed deeply. The holding cell had been rank, and releasing his link to the security system left him completely untethered. It was a relief after having been synced to the detention center computer systems for so long.

"This looks like a definite improvement in our situation," Sly said as they stepped out of the garage into the sunlight.

"If you think so," chuckled one of the officers escorting them out.

"What's that supposed to mean?" Alex asked. "Where are they taking us?"

The officer didn't answer, and Alex already knew the plan, but it seemed like what a person who didn't know what was happening should say. Alex didn't want to do anything that would cast suspicion on them.

"No talking," barked the big officer with the mustache.

At the ramp that led into the transport, a man in a different uniform stopped them. He looked military. Instead of solid-colored clothing, he wore a mottled blue and black fatigue garment. He was armed with a laser rifle that was also different from those used by the law enforcement officers.

"This the last of them?" the solider asked.

"No, we've got a few hard heads in iso," the mustached law officer replied. "We'll carry them out next."

"They can't walk?" the soldier asked.

"We'll see," the man with the mustache said.

"Alright, come on board and continue filling the seats," the soldiers told the group of detainees. "No spaces. Once you're on board, we'll remove your restraints and make sure you're secured in your seats. Any questions?"

"What if we don't want to be secured in our seats?" Sly asked.

"This is a military operation," the soldiers said. "You are enemy combatants. Failure to comply will result in death. No exceptions."

"Yes sir," Sly said softly.

"Let's move," the solider ordered.

Alex followed the group up the ramp and into the transport.

It was clearly meant for prisoners but it looked brand new. There were rows of upright seats and Alex could see that the people already seated had their wrists bound to restraints built into the arm rests.

A quick scan of the ship revealed four times as many prisoners already locked in as those that had come from the holding cell. Alex had guessed that the transport was picking up several groups of prisoners, but fortunately, the ship was nearly full. He doubted that they would make any more stops before heading for orbit.

In the back of the ship, Alex saw several medical pods secured to the walls, with power lines attached. Master Sergeant Taylor Montgomery was secured in a section of spread out seats in the back. He had a large bandage on his leg, and his skin looked strangely pale. He didn't nod or make any sign that he recognized Alex. There were wounded from other corporations as well, and eight soldiers stood guard over the group.

When Alex reached his seat, he sat down and looked toward the front of the passenger cabin. There was a doorway, but he had no idea if it led to the cockpit or elsewhere. Either way, he knew that he could take control of the ship. The EM waves from the ship's systems were strong. Alex immediately let his INC sync to the transport. He felt as if he had gotten exponentially bigger. The ship had state-of-the-art systems, from the engines to the navigation computers. He let the information feed into his head as one of the soldiers removed his plastic restraints and closed the built-in cuffs over his wrists.

Alex was already exploring the security controls. They were

just one of many systems within the ship that had fallen into Alex's control once he synced to the transport's computers. The ship could practically fly itself and Alex knew that he would have no trouble piloting it, despite the fact that there were three soldiers in the cockpit. He couldn't see them, but he heard them talking over the ship's com system. They were making their final preparations before lifting off as the soldiers carried in the four Zen Tech operators that had been beaten for resisting in the detention center.

"Almost time," Sly said. "We good?"

"Affirmative," Alex whispered. "The ship won't be a problem."

"Did you see the Master Sergeant?" Sansabar asked. "There's something wrong with him."

"He looked drugged," Sly said. "They probably gave him something to keep him calm."

"But they didn't repair his leg," Alex said. "It looks like they just bandaged it up."

"Why would they do that?" Sansabar asked.

"I don't know," Alex said. "Give me a second. I'm looking for something."

His eyes were closed, and he was going through the medical files that had been sent to the ship's archives. There were orders and lists of prisoners in the computer system, but it was the medical information that he was most interested in. He found a file listed as Timmons, Ashton Cpl.

The file was strange, with a lot of administrative pages that didn't interest Alex. Then came the medical details. Ash's injuries had required emergency surgery. Two vertebrae had been fractured, and there was swelling among the disks. Alex didn't understand all of the medical jargon, but he learned that Ash was in a medically-induced coma after having several vertebrae fused together, and more than a dozen lacerations sealed.

"Ash is alive," Alex said.

"You found her?" Sly asked, unable to keep his voice down.

Alex looked at the nearest guard, who either hadn't heard or hadn't cared what the prisoners were talking about. Alex nodded and Sly leaned his head back against the seat, breathing a long sigh.

"Where is she?" he whispered.

"On the transport," Alex said. "She's in a medically-induced coma."

"Oh man, that sounds bad."

"The file outlines the surgery and recommends follow-up care," Alex whispered. "We'll get her on board the *Currency* and they'll be able to fix her up."

"Yeah, okay," Sly said. "At least she isn't being left behind."

"That's right," Alex said. "We're all getting out of here together. It won't be long now."

Right on cue, the ship lifted off. It rose slowly up into the air. Alex looked at Sansabar, who was watching the guards.

"I'm going to be pretty wrapped up in what I'm doing," Alex whispered to her. "If the guards do anything I should know, elbow me."

"Sure," she replied. "You've got it. No worries."

"You do your thing," Sly said. We'll be your eyes and ears out here."

"Good," Alex said.

He closed his eyes again. He didn't know if the ship had view ports, but there were external cameras all around the exterior of the transport. He watched the city shrink below them as the ship soared higher and higher. The engines were at seventy percent power and easily shrugging off Skandia Seven's gravity. All systems were in the green, and the power supply was at ninety-two percent of its capacity. Alex knew that leaving orbit would be the largest drain on the vessel. Once they reached orbit, the power expenditure would be drastically reduced.

They were on course, and everything looked good, at least to Alex's untrained eye. Flying a Titan battle suit wasn't the same as flying a transport vessel, but the computers were doing the bulk of the work. Occasionally the pilots pressed a button or adjusted a dial, but they were the redundant systems, and Alex had already found a way to lock them out of the ship's computer controls.

Alex backed out of the mind consuming link so that he could ask his friends a few questions. He was still synced to the transport, his head throbbing with the effort, but he didn't feel the need to keep up with everything happening second-by-second.

"We've got twenty-six minutes until we reach orbit," Alex said.

"Great," Sly said. "I may just take a little power nap."

"No, you need to keep up with the guards," Alex said.

"There are eight," Sansabar said.

"We're out numbered," Alex said.

"But not by much," Sly argued. "And we have way more bodies."

"Any idea what's through that door?" Alex asked.

"None," Sansabar said. "I've been watching. No one has gone in or out, but there could be more guards in there."

"Any chance you can lock it?" Sly asked.

"No," Alex said. "I already checked. Once we hit orbit, I'll open the restraints. Our friends should know what to do."

"Better keep your head down then," Sly said. We can't afford to lose you to friendly fire."

"He's right," Sansabar said. "You get as low as you can. We'll make sure you're alright."

"Okay," Alex said, trying to relax but finding it was impossible. There were twenty-one minutes left before they rose up to take control of the ship. Until then, his nerves were raw, and the tension felt like electricity shooting through his body. But at least they were moving toward something. He would be able to do his part and hope that the others did theirs. If everything worked out, they would soon be back on board the *Currency* and the nightmare of their incarceration would be nothing more than a memory. And if things didn't work out, well... he didn't want to think about that.

CHAPTER ELEVEN

NYX WAS USING her PIL to monitor the ship's progress. As a remote console, the Personal Information Link was extremely limited. She did manage to hack into her controller station, and from there, pick up the *Currency's* exterior and surveillance footage. Unfortunately, there wasn't much to see, and the cameras didn't help her cause. She couldn't take control of any of the ship's systems. The controllers had access to the ship's systems, but not direct control. The only exception was the communication system. Every controller had direct access to their operator, plus access to their team, tactical, and even ship-wide communications.

She had heard the communications officer send their plans to leave orbit to Skandia Orbital Control. Their course was set, and only a few hours after Nyx had been thrown into the brig, the *Currency* had left its geo-synchronous orbit and begun moving toward the FTA space tunnel. The Skandia System was on the Free Trade Association's trade route, which meant that the *Currency* could be going anywhere. In the meantime, Nyx had been wracking her brain, trying to discover a way to stop the ship from leaving the system.

There was the unlikely possibility that someone was monitoring her controller station, which meant that she couldn't tap into the planet's network to check for messages from Alex. She might only have one chance to make herself heard from the brig, and if that were the case, she couldn't waste it by sending Alex a message that she was helpless. When she made her move, it would have to be significant, since her PIL would almost certainly be taken from her once the captain discovered that she still had it. And it wasn't just her career at stake. Lieutenant Rory Jones had thrown caution to the wind and allowed her to keep the one device that would actually give her a chance to salvage things from the brig. But she couldn't waste that chance, and whether she liked it or not, time was running out.

She had considered transmitting a message over the ship's internal speakers, calling for the crew to rise up and demand that Captain Poe wait for the operators that they were leaving behind. She wanted to give an impassioned speech describing how Alex was going to break free of whatever confines the authorities had locked them up in and return to the ship, but she knew that most of the crew wouldn't care. The *Currency* was the most segregated vessel she'd ever been on. Growing up at a scientific outpost, there had been a natural division between the scientists doing research and the engineers that kept the station in optimal operating conditions. There were even some people who considered the longtime residents of the station to be superior to the short-term researchers who only came aboard the station for short stints. It was silly, and easily recognizable, but the biggest difference between the cultures of space station and the *Currency* was the sheer animosity between the divisions. Her parents hadn't socialized with the rough necks and engineers on the space station, but they hadn't hated them either. There was a common bond that should have been present on the *Currency* but was sadly lacking.

The crew wouldn't risk their careers, or even spend the energy to help the other divisions. It seemed that Lieutenant Rory Jones was the rare exception, and it made her wonder if more people like him weren't just waiting for her to sound the call for mutiny. But deep down inside, she knew it was a hopeless cause. And not just because she doubted that anyone would respond, but because the communications officer would have the ability to cut her connection to the ship's system. She wouldn't get very far into her speech before the feed to the rest of the ship was severed.

She filed the idea as a last-ditch effort. Her PIL allowed her to see where the ship was on its trajectory toward the space tunnel. They had less than two hours before they would slip out of the system and Alex would be on his own. She had hope that her resourceful counterpart could find a way to survive, and even get out of the system, but the odds were against him. The entire planet was looking for a scapegoat and a way to show their strength against an enemy, and the media had conveniently sacrificed the private military forces on Skandia Seven for the slaughter. Public executions weren't outside of the realm of possibility.

She was growing hopeless when a new signal came in over the ship's communication system. Nyx had no access to the bridge or what was being discussed. She didn't know if the communication officer recognized the signal or not. To Nyx, it was just a series of numbers and letters. There was no way to know if the captain was ignoring the hail or telling the com officer to respond. All that she could hear was the messages that were received or sent. Fortunately, the message was accepted, and Nyx was able to listen in.

"Ahzco Controller ship *Currency*, this is Executive VP Loman Haley. Do you copy?"

There was a slight pause. Nyx was stunned and guessed that Captain Poe was surprised as well. But the deep, resonant voice of the captain responded after only a few seconds of silence.

"VP Haley, we read you. This is Captain Poe of the *Currency*."

"Where are you going, captain? I've been sending a request for a report but haven't heard from you."

Nyx felt anger spring up inside her. She knew that Poe hadn't responded because he knew that he would be told to hold his position. Of course, communications could be intercepted or lost, so that gave him plausible deniability. But if Poe had refused to give the VP a report of the situation in the Skandia System, it was a major breech of military protocol.

"The system is in lockdown, sir," Captain Poe replied. "Skandia Seven issued a state of emergency and enacted Planetary Security Protocols. We've been ordered out of the system and are in the process of complying. I had planned to report as soon as we were clear of the system."

"You're leaving our property and our employees undefended?"

"Unfortunately, our operators failed to protect the factory in Oslo and were apprehended by the authorities. We were investigating the situation when we were ordered to leave the system."

"Are you telling me that our operators still on the planet, and you are taking the only Ahzco war ship out of the system?"

"All flights to the planet have been restricted," Poe attempted to explain. "Our drop ship was shot down. We felt that it was best to withdraw rather than attempt an ill-fated rescue that was doomed to fail. As you're surely aware, the media have painted us as the villains, and I feared that refusing to comply with the Skandian authorities might have adverse consequences for the company."

There was a pause in the conversation and Nyx knew that it was the perfect time to act, but she was suddenly so afraid that her entire body was shaking. All she had to do was tap the screen of her PIL and tell VP Haley the truth, but in doing so, she was driving a stake through the heart of her career. In the end, it was the mental image of Alex that prompted her to action.

CHAPTER TWELVE

LOMAN WAS in the back of the transport, huddled low, using a wireless ear transmitter and doing his best not to raise his voice. He was the kind of executive who felt that the people who worked for him were his greatest assets. And Loman took pride in knowing as many of them as he could.

Captain Ladarius Poe wasn't what Loman thought of as a superstar, but he certainly looked the part. Tall, strong, handsome in his CDF uniform, but with as unimpressive a record as Loman could think of. The man had a knack for avoiding trouble in the field. Not that anyone had ever used the word "coward" to describe Poe, but "lucky" had been used on more than one occasion. Loman wasn't superstitious, but he hadn't vetoed the idea of assigning Captain Poe to some of Ahzco's most valuable systems simply because he had a reputation for repelling trouble.

But that reputation appeared to have been a mirage. Loman was furious. The factory on Skandia Seven was one of their newest MBS plants. It produced the Titan and Valkyrie battle suits and cost nearly a hundred billion credits to build. Losing it was a major blow to the CDF, who were now limited in the numbers of their most fearsome battle suits. And Captain Poe was satisfied with leaving the system just because some bureaucrat on Skandia suggested it. That made no sense to Loman whatsoever, who believed in presenting a strong image to those outside of the CDF. Not to mention that they still had operators on the planet. Leaving them behind was a major misstep on Captain Poe's part.

"Adverse consequences?" Loman asked.

He was about to lose his cool when a new voice came through the connection.

"Vice President Loman, this is Nyx West. Alex is leading an escape attempt and he requested—"

The line went silent. Loman waited a second but there was nothing else. He didn't know if the ship's comms were being jammed or if the *Currency* had suddenly been vaporized.

"What? *Currency* are you still there?" Loman asked.

"We're here, sir. I'm sorry about that interruption," Captain Poe said, his voice steady, almost inspiring. "It seems that we picked up a pirate transmission."

"The hell you have," Loman said. "That was Sergeant West. What was she saying about a rescue mission?"

"It's nothing," Captain Poe replied, attempting nonchalance. "Rumors and insinuation. There's no proof that our operators ar—"

"I want to hear from her, Captain," Loman demanded. "I don't know what is happening on your ship, but I'm ordering you to stay in the system. My transport will be docking at the system port, and from there I will take a shuttle to your ship. Now, I want to hear what Sergeant West was talking about, and I want to hear it from her."

"Yes, of course," Captain Poe said. "Stand-by, sir. Let me get her to the bridge."

The line went silent and Loman sat up in his seat as the flight attendant approached.

"Are you okay, sir?"

"Oh, yes, just trying not to disturb the other passengers," Loman said. "I'm on a call."

"Do you need anything? We should be docking in a few hours."

"No, no," he said. "I'm fine. Thank you."

The attendant nodded and turned back toward the other passengers. Loman risked a glance to the forward part of the cabin. The reporters and social media celebrities seemed engrossed in their own worlds. It was the only positive thing about his flight.

Loman was tired, hungry, and needed a shower. He had only been to the bathroom once since boarding the express transport. The risk of being seen and recognized was just too great to have taken care of his own needs as he should have. It was easier to avoid food and drink as much as possible, so that he could endure the long flight without requiring frequent trips up the aisle and within sight of the other passengers. His teeth felt fuzzy, and his eyes burned, but he stayed put and endured for the sake of privacy.

"Vice President Haley," Captain Poe's voice was clear through the tiny earpiece that Loman wore. "We have Sergeant West here."

"What were you saying, sergeant?" Loman asked.

"Sir, Alex is planning an escape," Nyx said. "Cronus Team and Oscar Company were taken into custody by law enforcement, but he was able to get a message out, and requested that we stay in the system."

"When was this?" Loman asked.

"Nine hours ago, sir," Nyx replied. "He's been sending us messages through his father's account, but we haven't heard from him in a while."

"Do you think it's legitimate?" Loman asked.

"Yes sir, I do," Nyx said.

"Mr. Haley, sir," Captain Poe spoke up. "These messages are highly unusual and were delivered through third-party messages. It's my feeling that they are nothing more than wishful thinking at best, and a complete hoax at worst."

"But our people are still down there, Captain," Loman said. "We don't leave people behind."

"Your orders were to protect the Ahzco manufacturing plant in Oslo," Poe stated. "Outside of that, we were to do nothing that might incite further media slander against the company. Well sir, the operators on the ground failed in the mission to protect the factory, and I was keen to salvage what little I could of this op. To that end, I felt it best if we honored the wishes of the people of Skandia Seven by leaving the system."

"Your interpretation of orders is not what I would consider

to be in the best interests of the company or the CDF, captain," Loman said curtly.

"Yes sir, I realize that leaving my operators behind is unorthodox, but we were ill-prepared to mount a rescue, and I thought it best to gather further resources and return to the system prepared to get our people back."

"Did you speak to the authorities and find out why they arrested our operators?" Loman asked.

"They're being held as terrorists, sir," Poe replied.

"Did someone tell you that, or did you just read it off of the planetary network like everyone else?"

There was a pause that told Loman everything he needed to know about Captain Poe. He made a mental note to remove the man from active duty as soon as possible. He might make a fine administrator or even a freight captain, but he was not CDF material, no matter how good he looked in a uniform.

"We made inquiries but received no reply from the authorities on Scandia Seven, sir," Poe finally responded. "The only word we were able to get was the request that we leave the system."

"How much time was given?" Loman asked.

"I'm sorry?" Captain Poe replied.

"How much time did they give you to leave?" Loman asked. "Did they tell you to leave immediately, in two hours, or six hours? How much time did they give in their request that you leave the system?"

"Twenty-four hours," Poe said.

"And when was that message received?"

"2300 hours, sir."

"How long ago was that?" Loman said, knowing that with multiple time zones, 2300 hours could have been any time. It further irritated him that Captain Poe was trying to avoid the question by forcing Loman do the math.

"Fourteen hours ago," Captain Poe said.

"So, you had a request, possibly from our operators, that you stay in the system," Loman said, "on the chance that they found a way to escape from the authorities on the ground, and you didn't stay even although you still had ten hours left to comply with the order to leave?"

"In my opinion, sir, the rumors of an escape attempt were far-fetched and foolish," Poe replied. "And sir, might I add that if Sergeant Evans is trying to escape, such an action might be considered an act of aggression by the CDF and result in the planetary defenses firing on our ship."

Loman couldn't believe his ears. Captain Poe was hopeless as a military commander. As soon as Loman could get on the ship, he would take control, but there were still several hours until the express transport would reach the station.

"Captain," Loman said as calmly as he could, "please hear me and follow my orders to the letter. You are to stay in the Skandia system. Please move as close to the system port as possible, so that I can transfer aboard your vessel ASAP. In the meantime, I want Sergeant West given everything she needs to be able to communicate with our operators on the ground. Is that absolutely clear?"

"Yes sir, I read you," Captain Poe said.

"And keep me updated. I need to know everything you know."

"Roger that, sir," Captain Poe said.

Loman slumped back in his seat wondering what else could possibly go wrong and fearing that he would soon find out.

CHAPTER THIRTEEN

IT WAS ALMOST TIME. The ship was approaching orbit. Alex still didn't know who or what was in the other compartment of the transport, but he couldn't worry about that any longer.

"Sixty seconds," Alex whispered.

"Is there any way to only open the restraints on certain seats?" Sly asked.

"Yeah, why?" Alex asked.

"Because if you release us all at once, bodies will go flying and we won't have clear lines of fire."

It was frustrating to run into yet another issue. Alex realized that releasing everyone at once was a bad idea, and yet only releasing some but not others would make his task even more difficult. He had to reorder the chain of events in his head so that he could get everything done. And time was running out.

"How many rows behind us are the Zen Tech operators?" Alex asked.

"The third and four rows behind us," Sansabar said. "Counting from the front that's row seven and eight."

"Okay, good," Alex said.

"As soon as you're free, I want you both to get weapons," Alex said. "Send the Zen Tech people into that forward compartment."

"You got it, Ace," Sly said.

"Who's going to stay with you?" Sansabar asked.

"Don't worry," Alex said. "I'm not going anywhere."

He closed his eyes and leaned forward. Everything happened all at once. There was a lurching sensation, as if the ship were cresting a tall hill. It was the transition out of the planet's gravity field as the ship made orbit. Alex could hear the pilots through the ship's communication system.

"Skandia Orbital Control, this is *Reaper One*. We've just entered orbit. Switching to zero-g maneuvering."

"Copy that *Reaper One*. We have you on radar. You have a clear route all the way to Nattamara."

"Very good, Control. *Reaper One* is beginning main phase burn. Standby."

"Skandia Orbital Control is standing by."

Alex muted the ship's communication system. It was a simple override of all microphones, from the pilots' helmet mics to the ship's intercom, that allowed the pilots to speak to the guards watching over the prisoners. Fortunately, the command was located deep within the comm system, and it would take the pilots a while to discover it once they started looking. In the meantime, Alex had other work to do.

The restraints on the arm rests were made of thick metal.

There wasn't a person in the entire galaxy strong enough to break them open, but Alex did it with a single thought. He opened all the restraints on rows seven and eight.

There was an outburst of surprise, then the high-pitched whine of laser pistols firing and recharging. One report sounded different, and Alex knew the guards had gotten a shot off. People were shouting, but there was no time to calm the prisoners and explain things. Alex renewed his grip on the arms of the seat he was in and braced his feet under the seat in front of him.

"Get ready!" he said loud enough to be heard over the shouting.

He released the restraints on his own row of seats. The wrist cuffs popped open, but he was ready. So were Sly and Sansabar. They leaped into the air and kicked off the back of their own seats just as Alex opened his eyes and sat up in his seat. Four of the eight guards were floating in zero-gravity, completely unconscious. That was good, but Alex feared they weren't out of danger yet. He turned and saw that the Zen Tech operators, along with several others, were spinning in the air above the other prisoners, trying to get control of themselves.

Alex stood up, but kept his feet braced under the seats and turned to make sure all the guards had been stunned. There were four more in the back, floating near the wounded. Everyone was shouting and struggling to get free.

"Get the weapons from the guards!" Master Sergeant Montgomery shouted from the back of the ship.

"Move them to the front row," Alex instructed. "We'll lock them down there."

People were shouting at Alex and all of the other detainees who had been set free. They didn't know what was happening, but Alex had no time for explanations. There would be an opportunity to calm the prisoners and free everyone once the transport was completely under Alex's control.

"Cutter!" Alex shouted. "Get in that compartment."

He pointed to the front of the ship. The big Zen Tech operator launched himself off of the head of another detainee who was still strapped to his seat. The man in the chair was cursing Cutter, but the big operator was sailing toward the front of the passenger cabin with his pistol held out in front him. He passed Alex and was almost to the doorway when another guard appeared. The soldier had a rifle, which he was holding in one hand. His other hand was holding onto to something, perhaps just the wall, to keep himself steady. He fired at Cutter at the exact same moment that Cutter fired at him.

The flash of the lasers was so bright that Alex was forced to blink. In his mind, an alarm began to flash. The hull of the ship had been weakened and was on the verge of losing integrity.

"Stop shooting!" Alex ordered.

"These rifles don't have a non-lethal setting, Ace!" Sly called back.

One glance at Cutter confirmed Sly's assessment. The big man was clearly dead. His forward momentum hadn't been stopped and he crashed into the bulkhead at the front of the compartment. There was smoke rising from his body. Alex looked up and saw a dark scorch mark on the ceiling.

"We're losing integrity in the hull," Alex said. "See if you can find some kind of sealant or we're all dead."

Alex felt relatively confident that there weren't any more guards in the forward compartment. If there had been, surely, they would have come out, guns blazing, like the guard Cutter had incapacitated. Alex hardly knew the Zen Tech operator, but it made him furious that the soldier had killed him. Alex lifted his feet and pushed off of the seat rest of his chair.

He sailed over the heads of the other prisoners and caught himself on the door frame that led into the forward compartment. He reached out and took the rifle from the stunned guard, who was drifting down toward the deck. Alex slung the rifle over his head, and then took hold of the soldier's arm. He used the door frame for leverage and flung the man back toward the front row of seats where Sly was setting down another unconscious guard.

Sansabar slid into the doorway beside Alex. She was quiet and her face was set with determination. She held the rifle against her shoulder, both hands on the pistol grips of the tactical weapon, and used her feet to brace herself. Alex was surprised by how agile and competent she seemed in the chaos of zero-gravity.

"Let me go in," she said.

"Alright," Alex replied. "But be careful."

She nodded and gave a little kick that sent her drifting into the dark compartment. Lights flickered on a second later and she called out from the interior.

"Clear!"

Alex felt himself relax a little more. He pushed himself over to a chair that folded out of the wall, previously occupied by one of the guards. He braced himself into the chair, holding on with one hand and holding the other up.

"Quiet!" he shouted. "Listen to me!"

The interior of the passenger cabin was filled with nearly a hundred men and women from various private militaries. The one thing that they were all accustomed to was following orders, and despite their fear and their desperate need to be free, they quieted down.

"I'm Sergeant Alex Evans, Ahzco CDF. We're taking control of this transport, but I need you all to remain in your seats and stay calm. We still have to neutralize the pilots."

"Good luck," said one of the soldiers in a groggy voice.

He was held down in the front rows of seats. Sly had discovered that the restraints could be manually engaged by clicking them together. Six of the nine guards were already locked down, and the other three were being guided into seats further back in the passenger compartment.

"The pilots are in an isolated cabin," the solider went on. "You can't get to it from the interior. Even if you cut through the bulkhead, there's space between them. You'll kill everyone on board the moment the cabin loses pressure."

"Keep them quiet," Alex said.

He closed his eyes and gave his full attention to the ship's computer systems. The hull integrity sensors showed that the passenger cabin was down to just eight percent.

"Find some way to reinforce that," Alex said, pointing up at the scorch mark in the ceiling.

"There's one back here, too," Monty called.

"I've got something," Sansabar said from the interior of the forward compartment.

Alex looked over and saw her float out of the other room with a canister in her hands. She floated up toward the ceiling and braced herself with one hand on the roof, and her feet on the back of the second row of chairs. Unlike Cutter, she was careful not to kick anyone. She sprayed what looked like foam from the canister, and it expanded as it came into contact with the ceiling, spreading and turning from white to gray.

It only took a few seconds to cover the entire scorch mark that the soldier's laser blast had made. She quickly moved on and Alex watched as it continued to harden. The alarm stopped without him noticing, and when he checked again, the ship's hull integrity had risen to nearly fifty percent.

"It's working," Alex said.

"What now?" Sly asked.

"I'm going to release everyone, but please don't leave your seats if you can help it," Alex said in a loud voice. "People could be hurt if we're all drifting around."

He closed his eyes and opened all of the restrains except on the rows where the guards had been moved, as well as the restraints holding down the wounded.

"Sly, go check on Monty and make sure Ash is okay. Sand, you're with me," Alex said.

She had already drifted down beside him and secured herself to his seat by hooking a foot around the forward support of the fold-down chair. She held her rifle down but kept both hands on it to make sure it was ready if she needed it.

Alex closed his eyes and focused on the communications system. It was still muted, and the pilots sounded near panic.

"Sergeant Gerber, what the devil is going on back there?" one of the pilots bellowed, while the other tried to contact Skandia Orbital Control.

"I repeat," the pilot said in a calm, but urgent voice. "We are losing hull integrity and request assistance. Mayday, mayday, mayday. Skandia Orbital Control, do you read us? This is *Reaper One*, in transit to Nattamara..."

Fortunately, they had no idea that their comms had been muted. Alex checked the ship's trajectory. They were moving away from the planet, and several ships in orbit had begun maneuvering from where they were into intercept positions.

Alex leaned over to the intercom that was built into the wall next to the seat. There was a microphone built into the system, and Alex unmuted it so that the pilots could hear him.

"Pilots of *Reaper One*, this Sergeant Alex Evans in the passenger compartment. We have taken complete control of the ship, including all flight controls. Please cease and desist from any efforts to pilot the ship."

Alex didn't need to unmute the pilot's mic to hear it through the INC connection in his mind.

"Who is this?" one of the pilots replied. "What the devil are you talking about?"

The other pilot immediately began trying to report that the ship was under attack to Skandian Orbital Control. It was almost humorous.

"This is Sergeant Alex Evans, Ahzco CDF. We have complete

control of your vessel. Please notice the warning light on your instrument panel."

Alex set the depressurization warning to its "on" position. It was a safety protocol to keep the air from being evacuated while there were pilots in the cockpit.

"Do I have your attention now?" Alex asked.

The voices ceased for several seconds. When the pilot spoke again, he sounded nervous.

"If you vent the atmo we'll die," the pilot said. "We aren't wearing our pressure suits."

"Then do exactly as I tell you," Alex said. "We have no desire to kill any of you. That's not what we're about."

"Tell that to the guards you had to take out to get control back there," one of the other pilots said angrily.

"They were stunned," Alex said. "Nothing more. They're waking up as we speak. I have them locked into the seats right in front of me. Nine men."

"So what?" asked the first pilot. "You want us to turn around?"

"Negative. I want all of you to sit back and do nothing."

"You don't want us to fly the ship?"

"No, I don't," Alex said. "This vessel practically flies itself. I'm going to make contact with the ships that my fellow detainees belong to and transfer them back to their own vessels. When we're done, you'll get your ship back."

"You really expect us to believe that?" the angry pilot snarled.

"I don't care what you believe," Alex said. "But if any of you do anything else to the ship, including adjusting your seats, I will vent the atmo."

"Skandia Orbital Control has military satellites. They'll shoot you down once they realize what you're doing."

"I guess you'd better hope not," Alex said. "Now sit back, shut up, and let us do our jobs."

"Wait," the first pilot spoke up again. "You said you're with Ahzco right? The *Currency*?"

"Yes," Alex said, knowing that he was giving the pilots and any of the guards bright enough to pay attention too much information about himself.

"The *Currency* left orbit. She's headed for the space tunnel."

"Good to know," Alex said.

"That true?" Sly asked as he drifted back to where Alex sat.

He had to check the ship's radar. Each vessel was listed on a key. The *Currency* was not in orbit on their side of the planet. Alex had to admit that the chances weren't good that the *Currency* had moved to the far side of Skandia Seven. She had been in a geosynchronous orbit above Oslo. That shouldn't have changed.

"I can't find her on radar," Alex admitted. "Not anywhere."

CHAPTER FOURTEEN

"So, what do we do?" Sly asked.

"I don't know," Alex admitted.

"Can we take this ship out of the system?" Sansabar asked. "Maybe catch up with them?"

"It's possible," Alex said. "But I don't like the idea with the hull damage we've sustained. Passing through the space tunnels might put more strain on her."

"Stupid guards," Sly said, looking at the soldiers who were lined up on the first row of seats.

"We might be able to transfer to a different ship," Alex said. "Maybe even a transport that could take us out."

"Maybe a mega yacht," Sly said. "I wouldn't mind that too much."

"Don't get your hopes up," Alex said. "They took our I.D.'s, so we don't have access to any funds. I don't think anyone is going to be keen on transporting a bunch of operators with no credits and only the promise of repayment."

"We have weapons," Sansabar said.

"Yeah, I like the way she's thinking," Sly said.

"We'll worry about it once we get everyone else offloaded. There are several ships moving to intercept us already."

"You mean they didn't cut and run like Captain Poe?" Sansabar said. "Must be nice."

"How's Ash?"

"I don't know," Sly admitted. "Master Sergeant Monty is staying with her. She's sealed up in a medical pod, but the lights on the controls were all green."

"Green is good," Alex said. "Better let me make contact before the other ships start firing at us."

"Is that a possibility?" Sly asked.

"Maybe," Alex said.

He closed his eyes again and focused on the communications system. He had heard the pings as the prisoner ship was hailed. He decided to send a reply to all the ships but made sure that his transmission wasn't going to Skandia Orbital Control or any of the commercial ships in the area.

"This is the prison ship *Reaper One*," Alex said. "The operators of the Ahzco CDF have taken control and we are preparing to return all detainees to their appropriate vessels."

The response was immediate and as Alex guessed it would be, full of suspicion. Taking control of the ship's auto pilot, he ordered the ship to reverse thrusters until the ship was stationary. The closest corporate vessel was a Hazzle ship called the *Omaha*.

It took her forty minutes to reach *Reaper One*, but when she did, Alex prepared the ship for the transfer of personnel. The *Omaha* extended a transfer tube, which suctioned to the side of the *Reaper One*. Once the tube had been pumped full of air, the brown-clothed Hazzle personnel who had shared the odorous holding cell with Alex and the operators from Ahzco were allowed to pass through. It was a relatively simple maneuver for Alex. He basically held the ship still and let the other vessels do all the work.

In total, nine other ships lined up and took people off of the *Reaper One*. It took four hours from start to finish. Alex had to mute Skandia Orbital Control. They were livid, calling the pilots and guards cowards and traitors. Of course, they had no idea what was happening on board the ship. Which left Alex with the question of what to do with them.

"That leaves the Zen Tech operators, a group from Bazmore Enterprises, and us," Sly said.

"We should move soon," Sansabar said.

She had discovered that the front compartment was a lounge area, with a large video display that could show everything from the ship's external cameras to the radar and all the ship's systems. She stayed in the doorway between the cabins, where she could keep an eye on Alex and also watch the display.

"I agree," Alex said. "But where do we go?"

"Doesn't the radar show you other ships?" Sly asked. "Just find the next one, or better yet, the *Currency,* and get us out of here."

"This ship's radar is small, just a short-range device used for maneuvering in close quarters. She relies on a feed from

Skandia Orbital Control for the bigger picture." "And they're not sharing," Sand said.

"Not for a while now. They're trying to block comms too, but only partially succeeding."

"So why haven't they fired on us?" Sly asked. "What's stopping them?"

"The other vessels nearby," Alex guessed. "It could be bad for them to damage a mega corp ship."

"This is a brand-new vessel," Sansabar pointed out. "Maybe they just don't want to destroy what they recently paid so much to build."

"That makes sense, too, but I'd rather not continue to give them an easy target. The farther we are from the planet, the clearer our comms will be. Hopefully we can finish the job and find a way out of the system."

He didn't mention that the patches to the hull were failing. The hull integrity sensors were showing a fifty percent degradation over the last few hours. Every time they opened the airlock to release another group of detainees, the patches succumbed to the vast pressures of hard vacuum. The current reading showed nineteen percent, but the longer they were in space, the more likely it was that the patches would give way and every person on board the *Reaper One* would die.

"Let's get someone from Zen Tech and Bazmore to start hailing their respective ships," Alex said.

"Roger that," Sly said, pushing off from the bulkhead near the intercom.

The Ahzco operators were split between the forward lounge and gathered around Master Sergeant Monty. Alex had thought he might want to take charge of things, but he seemed content where he was. Sly had whispered that he thought the master sergeant was in a lot of pain, but it was impossible to tell by looking at him. The older operator looked cool, calm, and collected. His eyes had cleared, and while his skin was a bit pale, he didn't seem diminished.

The Zen Tech operators were gathered in a cluster. After sealing Cutter into a body bag, they had settled into a group of seats away from everyone else. The Bazmore group was doing the same. It was clear that they felt intimidated by the other groups both having weapons, but for the most part, there was no animosity between the different parties.

"So," Hanes said as he drifted toward Alex, "the *Currency* abandoned us. Is that true?"

He caught himself on a conduit that ran along the wall. Alex was in no mood to try and boost the flagging emotions of the other operators. His head was filled with stabbing, white-hot shards, and his stomach was roiling after hours of zero-gravity. They were so close to freedom, and yet it appeared to be out of reach.

"What do you think?" Sansabar asked.

"I think Captain Poe wouldn't think twice about leaving us behind. So, what's the plan."

"I don't have one," Alex said, mentally checking the ship's radar again and seeing no change in the space around the ship.

"Well that's encouraging," Hanes said with a smirk on his face.

"Maybe it's time someone else comes up with something," Alex said.

"How about we hold these fine folks hostage," Hanes suggested, waving at the soldiers who were locked into the front row of seats. "Tell the authorities on Skandia Seven that we'll kill one of them every hour until they bring us a ship that can carry us home."

"I saw that in a movie once," Sansabar said. "It didn't work out for them."

"It never does," Alex replied. "And we aren't killing anyone."

"We might not have to," Hanes said. "It's possible that their people think more of them than ours think of us. They might come running with a ship just to save their lives. What do you think?"

"I suggest that we keep thinking," Alex said.

At that moment, a message came through. It was the Bazmore ship responding to the hail that had been sent out by one of their operators on the *Reaper One.*

"We read you, Owens," the person on the communication said. "We've been trying to get to you, but the ship is malfunctioning. We're patched up now and should be able to reach you in half an hour if you can come to heading 243 degrees."

"We can manage that," Alex replied.

"Good. We will meet you ASAP. And good job getting free of those Skandian bastards. This is the *Delta Gain,* out."

Alex made the adjustments almost without thought. The ship was so advanced that all he had to do was input the heading to the navigation computer, which he could do just by thinking about it thanks to his INC, and the ship would fly itself. The auto pilot gave him speed options, and as Alex selected the fastest approach, and the ship began to maneuver all on its own. But scanning the comm system and making sure that the pilots didn't manipulate the ship forced him to stay more connected to the *Reaper One's* computer systems than he wanted to. In fact, all Alex wanted at that moment was to escape every EM wave in the galaxy. If someone had offered him a solitary life on an unoccupied world with no technology, he might have accepted. The only thing keeping him tethered at the moment was his desire to see Nyx again.

When he had been put into the Faraday cage upon first being taken into custody, the absence of any EM waves had seemed like he was losing something. It was as if a huge, essential part of his body had been amputated. But the absence of his awareness of thousands of EM waves was nothing compared to the feeling deep in his chest that had arisen from not being able to speak to Nyx. She was always there when he used his INC. It was like her voice lived inside his head. They might be hundreds of miles apart, and yet they were always connected. And part of him knew that the *Currency* was gone because there was no reality in which she wouldn't contact him if the ship hadn't left the system.

When one of the Zen Tech operators came floating toward Alex, he first noticed Sansabar stiffen beside him. His would-be protector hadn't left his side in the hours since taking control of the ship. She was tireless, and seemingly very protective. Alex looked up to see what had elicited the reaction and saw a female operator approaching. She had tattoos across the bridge of her nose and around her eyes. It made her look strange, and somehow fearsome.

She bounced against the ceiling and then drifted down in

front of Alex. There was a pride to her bearing, and Alex saw one of the stolen laser pistols tucked into the waistband of her flight suit, just inside the open zipper.

"We have a problem," she said.

"What's wrong?"

"The *Empress Sword* isn't answering our hails," she said.

"What's your name?" Alex asked.

"I'm called Jai."

"Is the *Empress Sword* the Zen Tech ship?" Alex asked. Jai nodded as she sized Sansabar up with a contemptuous glance. "Maybe she's being jammed. We're getting a lot of interference from the planet."

"Or maybe she was attacked by another ship," Jai countered.

There was an awkward pause as Alex tried to decide exactly what the woman meant by the statement.

"Are you saying that you think we had something to do with it?"

"You've found the ships for everyone else," Jai said. "We're not expendable. You can't just use us to do your dirty work then leave us behind."

"We wouldn't do that," Alex said. "The truth is, we haven't found our ship either. We'll have to figure out what to do next once we deliver the Bazmore people to their vessel."

"Then you won't mind if I stick around for the discussions," Jai said.

"Not at all," Alex replied.

"I don't think she was asking you a question," Hanes said. He sounded as if he was enjoying the Zen Tech operator's angry insinuations.

Alex looked at the corporal from Oscar Company and did his best to imitate Master Sergeant Gellar's disapproving stare. He threw his hands up as if to say he was sorry and, in the process, lost his hold and began floating away. Alex gave him a shove that sent Hanes spinning away.

"Hey!" he cried out as he flipped backward.

"Here," Alex said, offering Jai a hand. "A spot just opened up."

CHAPTER FIFTEEN

THE SKANDIA SPACE Port was crowded. With planetary flights canceled for the time being, and the majority of the visitors being either media or activists drawn to the system by the attacks, getting from one place to the other was a bit like paddling a boat upstream. That Loman had made it from the express transport to a local charter service without being recognized was a small miracle.

Once he saw his face in the shiny reflection on a wall panel of polished chrome, he realized that he did look different. Since the protests began, he hadn't taken the time to do his usual routine. His hair was longer, and a thick growth of beard covered his face and neck. His clothes were wrinkled, and he was sure he smelled bad. Most people didn't give him a second glance, and fewer still wanted to get close to him.

The kiosk was unoccupied but had self-help terminal. Loman worried that all of the charter services would be booked up with so many people in the space port, but with the flights to the surface canceled, the charter schedule was free. He booked passage out to the *Currency* on a small ship with passenger cabins that included a full bathroom.

He was taken on board immediately and had showered before the ship left the port. By the time it reached the *Currency*, which was only fifty kilometers away from the space station, Loman had shaved, brushed his teeth, and changed into clean clothes. He felt much better than before, although a hot meal and eight hours of sleep would have been nice.

The *Currency* extended a space tube which locked onto the charter ship, tethering the vessels together. Loman had to propel himself through the zero-gravity from the charter ship to the CDF cruiser, but it wasn't the first time and he didn't think it would be the last. He made the transition without difficulty or personal embarrassment. When he cycled through the airlock, he expected to see Captain Poe, but it was an exhausted first officer who greeted him.

"Vice President Haley, welcome aboard sir."

"Lieutenant Jones," Loman said, leaning forward and looking hard at the name badge. "I assume you're keeping up with what's going on."

"Yes sir, in fact, the Captain sends his apologies but felt he couldn't risk being away from the bridge to meet you. We still have no word from our operators on the transport ship *Reaper One.*"

"It has to be them," Loman said. "Take me to the bridge."

"Yes sir," Jones replied. "This way."

He began walking and Loman followed him. They passed

people in the corridors on the way to the lift that would take them up to the command level of the ship. Loman had been on every class of ship in the Ahzco fleet. The smaller control ships, like the *Currency*, were his least favorite. Built for economy and crewed by a fraction of the men and women on most ships, it had that small town feeling where everyone knew everyone else's business.

"Were you in favor of leaving the system?" Loman asked Lieutenant Jones once they were alone in the lift.

"Following Captain Poe's orders, sir," Jones said.

"That's not what I asked."

"I would never question my captain's orders, sir."

"Let me tell you something, Lieutenant. I'm not looking for blind fools who only do what they're told. If you want to rise in the ranks of the CDF, you need to think for yourself and speak up when the opportunity arises. A good commander makes his ideas heard and isn't afraid to speak his mind, even when it might not be perfectly in line with his superiors."

Jones cleared his throat before speaking. "Yes sir."

They had reached the command level, and the lift doors were about to open, but Loman reached over and pressed the button to keep them closed.

"I'll ask again, Lieutenant Jones. Were you in favor of leaving the system without your operators?"

"No sir," Jones said in a steady voice, his eyes meeting Loman's and not shying away. "There was still time to give the operators a chance to make their escape before we departed. If we had stayed, they might already be on board."

Loman nodded. "My thoughts exactly. Take me to Poe."

Jones nodded and stepped to the door, which slid open. A group of controllers were waiting and looked as if they were about to say something about the two men holding up the elevator until they recognized Vice President Haley. They quickly stepped aside, and Jones walked briskly from the elevator.

"I suggest you return to your posts as quickly as possible," Loman told the controllers.

They nodded and mumbled their "yes sir's." He wasn't impressed with what he'd seen on the ship thus far. It was spotless, and yet there was something about it that seemed off. Loman guessed it was poor leadership. He had witnessed just about every style of command, from the iron-fisted to the friendly. What he was seeing on board the *Currency* was a certain attitude from the crew that made him wonder why Poe's first lieutenant refused to contradict his captain when it was obvious that Poe had made the wrong decision in leaving the system. He was even more perturbed by the controllers' irritation at something as small as the elevator being a few seconds late. Perhaps even more disturbing was the fact that the group of controllers felt that it was acceptable to voice their irritation to a senior officer. Where were the lines of command? Every good commander ensures that the chain of command is clear and absolute. It was a system that could be easily abused, but at the same time, in conflict, the discipline of a sound command structure allowed a crew to function as it should.

They walked down the corridor to the bridge. Lieutenant

Jones was the first through the doors and immediately stepped to the side and came to stiff attention.

"Commander on deck!" he said in a loud voice.

The bridge wasn't very large. Six officers swiftly came to attention in front of their stations. Captain Poe was in the pit, leaning over the display that showed a three-dimensional projection of the space around the ship. He stood up, pulled his uniform into place on his muscular frame, and in an almost lackadaisical way, gave a salute.

"Welcome aboard, Vice President," he said.

Loman stepped into the bridge and looked down at Captain Poe. In a fist fight, the captain would have all the advantages. But Loman outranked the ship's commander and would ensure that things on the *Currency* were made right. That would have to come later, though. Their first priority was to reach the transport ship that had been hijacked by the Ahzco operators.

"What's their status?" Loman asked as he moved to the railing that surrounded the pit.

"The *Reaper One* is moving. We still haven't heard from them," Poe said. "It's possible that our people aren't on board."

"I doubt that," Loman said. "Do we have a read out on that ship?"

"It's a new design," the chief engineer said. "I've searched the Skandian network, but there's no record of it in the public files."

"But we know that groups are being transferred from it," Loman said. "You've been keeping tabs on the ship, Captain?"

"We have, sir," Poe said. "It does appear to be a mutiny, but at this point, there are no hard facts. The *Reaper One* made contact with several military vessels. They could have moved passengers off or on. We simply don't know."

"Sir," the communications officer spoke up, "there is a considerable amount of interference coming from the planet. They've increased their broadcasts exponentially over the last three hours. We've been trying to contact the transport, but it's doubtful our signal is getting through."

"So we get closer," Loman said. "Bring us right alongside their ship if you have to. If our people are on board, we have to make contact."

"They're on the move," Poe said. "But we're calculating an intercept course as we speak."

"Good," Loman said. "I want to know who's on the ship. And if it isn't our people, then we will find out where they are. If the Skandian authorities make contact again, I want to be notified immediately. I'll deal with them. Is that understood, Captain Poe?"

"As you wish, sir," he said.

The big man's eyes were filled with hate, but he didn't let his anger bleed into his voice at all. Loman could respect a man who could control his emotions. He didn't have to like or trust Captain Poe to work with him.

"Where is Sergeant West?" Loman asked.

"She was allowed back at her post," Lieutenant Jones said. "I can show you to her, sir."

"Allowed back?" Loman asked, still looking at Captain Poe.

"Sergeant West was sent to the brig for insubordination," Poe said. "But we allowed her to keep her PIL and stay connected to her control console just in case she heard from the operators again, which she did not. In fact, we haven't had word—direct or otherwise—in several hours."

"Yes," Loman said. "I'll speak to her about that."

He didn't elaborate, but if the captain thought that Loman meant he would speak to Nyx about being thrown into the brig, he was correct. Loman turned on his heel and followed Lieutenant Jones back out of the bridge.

"The brig?" Loman asked.

"She's a headstrong young woman," Jones said. "She refused to give up on her operator."

"As well she should," Loman said. "Was the captain being honest about letting her keep her PIL and staying connected to her station."

"It wasn't a direct order," Jones said. "But when he discovered that she had her PIL in the brig, he didn't seem displeased."

"An implied order, so to speak," Loman said.

"Exactly, sir," Jones said, leading the VP into the control center.

There were at least twenty cubicles with full controller consoles in each. Nothing about the room or its set up surprised Loman. What was surprising was how many consoles were empty.

"Attention on deck!" Lieutenant Jones said in a loud voice.

Four people stood up. One looked as if he had been sleeping at his station and rubbed his eyes as he looked for the source of the disturbance. Loman ignored him, and two controllers who stood side-by-side, looking as if they had just been caught with their hands in the cookie jar. The discipline on the ship was embarrassing, but Loman would have to correct that later. His focus came to rest on Nyx, who stood by her station. He walked down the aisle and stood before her.

"As you were," he said over his shoulder. The other three controllers slowly sat back down, their heads disappearing behind the dividers between the consoles. "Any word from Alex or the other operators?"

"None sir," Nyx replied. "I've been trying to get a message through to his parents, but the network connection is down."

"Could be jammed," Lieutenant Jones offered. "There's a lot of information going through the network right now."

"Or it could be that someone on Skandia is blocking access," Loman replied. "In times like these, a little paranoia is called for. They're jamming us, Lieutenant. Which means that they probably have an operation in the works. If we don't get our people out soon, we may never see any of them again."

CHAPTER SIXTEEN

"WE'RE CLOSE," Alex said.

"The Bazmore people are ready to cross over as soon as their ship extends the boarding tube," Sly said.

"Still no word from the *Currency?*" Master Sergeant Montgomery asked. He had finally let a couple of members of Oscar Company help him move from the back of the transport to where Alex was stationed at the front. Alex had given the wounded Master Sergeant the fold out seat.

"None. There's so much noise from the planet that we can't hear much," Alex said. "And this bird is blind without a connection to the radar feed from orbital control."

"So, what do we do?" Hanes asked.

"There are two options," Alex said. "We can return to the planet. I doubt they would let us land wherever we wanted, but there's a small chance that we could put down somewhere and escape. Maybe we find a place to hide out until help comes."

"And maybe they shoot us down in the upper atmosphere," Sly said. "Then make up some story about how the dumb operators made a mistake that destroyed the ship."

"That's a good possibility," Alex said.

"What's the other option?" Monty asked. The older operator couldn't seem to take his eyes off of Jai and her exotic tattoos.

For her part, the Zen Tech warrior ignored him, but hung on Alex's every word.

"We stay out here," Alex said. "We don't have radar, but we do have the coordinates to the space tunnel. We could start moving that way and hope for the best."

"But if our ship isn't out there, we're cooked," Sly said.

Alex couldn't help but check the hull integrity sensors. They were down to seventeen percent. He knew that Sansabar had used most of the canister she had found to patch the two breaches made by the guards' laser fire. The second had gone through the deck and into the landing gear. Patching it had taken a lot more of the foam sealant, and Alex didn't know if there was more in the ship, or if it would even help. What he did know was that their time on the transport was limited.

"Someone out there will take us off," Monty said. "The attacks on Skandia will be big news. I saw some of the coverage while I was in the hospital. This system is the center of the galaxy for the moment."

"Most of the people will be media sympathizers or even activists," Alex said. "We might be jumping from the frying pan into the fire if we get picked up by anyone other than our own ships."

"What about the Zen Tech vessel?" Monty asked.

Jai didn't even acknowledge that she heard the question. She just stared at Alex, who wasn't sure if she liked him or not. It was possible that she simply had him under a constant surveillance to ensure that he didn't betray her people. Her focused attention made him feel as if the pressure was twice as intense. She wasn't the kind of person would take failure well. And despite the fact that Alex was surrounded by his friends, he didn't want to fight Jai. Nor did he want Sansabar or Sly to have to defend him. What he wanted was to find a way out of the mess they were in so that everyone was happy. It wasn't really about pleasing people, but about hope. He wanted to believe that there was a way to survive without being captured.

"No sign of it either," Alex said. "But it could be out there. And for now, we need them to find us, not the other way around. I'm still scanning the coms, but it's mostly static. Every frequency is overloaded."

"I didn't even know that was possible," Sly said.

"Anything is possible in a fight," Monty said. "I don't like the idea of going back to Skandia Seven."

"Me either," Alex said "There's no guarantee that we can land, and if we do, the authorities will come after us. Once they catch us, we'll be split up and rescuing everyone will be impossible."

"So we stay in space," Sly said. "Take our chances as we make for the space tunnel. You think they'll shoot us down?"

"Not with everyone watching," Alex said. "They have to maintain the narrative that we're the aggressors. It's our only advantage in this fight."

"If they shoot at us, they end up looking like the bad guys," Monty agreed.

A proximity alert sounded, and Alex closed his eyes. The Bazmore ship *Delta Gain* was close, but the alarm had sounded due to the other ship's boarding tube. Alex fired the stabilization thrusters. The computer had already matched the Bazmore ship's directional drift. Alex kept a watch on the tube using the ship's external cameras. The tube was a simple accordion shaped device, a series of large hoops covered in a filmy material that was able to hold air inside. The tube connected to the transport and used a sealant that was similar to the foam from the canister that Sansabar had found.

"They've made contact," Alex said. "Let's go and see the Bazmore people off and get the airlock resealed."

"Sure," Hanes said, launching himself toward the group of anxious operators waiting near the airlock.

The Bazmore soldiers wore gray and white fatigues. They were quiet and kept to themselves. Alex wasn't even sure if they were operators or if they used mechanized battle suits. He hadn't bothered to get to know the other people on board. His full attention was required for monitoring their ship. Space was a dangerous place, and anything could happen.

"The tube is pressurized," Alex said, as confirmation of his own readings was sent over via comms from the *Delta Gain*. "You can open the airlock and go through."

The look of relief on the faces of the Bazmore soldiers was so genuine that it made Alex smile, too. He could only imagine how they felt. More and more frequently, he found himself thinking of the transport as a death ship and he wanted off. He was just as desperate to get his friends off, too. And the fact that they were all relying on him only made things worse.

The airlock door opened with a hiss, then slid aside. The first of the Bazmore soldiers pulled himself inside and was suddenly flung back. At first, Alex thought that the tube had lost integrity, but just as quickly, he realized that if that were the case, the trooper would have been sucked into the tube. Then he saw the flash of a laser blast.

"Close the door!" Alex shouted. "Shut it!"

Another blast took out a second Bazmore solider. They were sitting ducks in front of the airlock. Alex used the ship's emergency controls to shut the airlock, but not before six armor-clad commandos came flying into the transport.

It was clear at a glance that the commandos were highly trained. They came through the airlock bunched together and then pushed off of each other to split apart. There were flips and bounces as dozens of laser bolts shot out from their pistols.

Sansabar was one of the first hit as she jumped in front of Alex. She made a grunt as her body stiffened and then went limp. Sly grabbed Alex by one arm. He would have been hit by one of the commandos, but in zero-g, the people who got hit didn't fall; they just kept floating, creating small pockets of cover.

"This way," Sly said, as he tugged Alex toward the seats.

Behind him, Monty was a sitting duck on the fold out chair. His injured leg made it painful for him to move, and Jai was beside him, pushing him forward. At first, Alex thought that the Zen Tech operator was trying to help him, but she ducked down behind his out stretched body, using it for cover. A laser blast hit the master sergeant, but Jai returned fire.

Alex and Sly flew down behind the first row of seats. The Skandian soldiers were shouting and several where hit by the commandos' indiscriminate fire. An alarm suddenly started blaring inside of Alex's head, alerting him to another hull breech. He closed his eyes and saw that someone had broken into the cockpit. He could see two commandos in space suits using some kind of thermal gel to create a hole. It was most unfortunate for the pilots, who were surely killed instantly as the air was vented out of the small space where the ship's controls were held. Alex didn't have time to stop the intruders from flying the ship. He sent a mental command to lock down all systems and then opened his eyes.

Sly was up again, propelling himself toward one of the commandos. He had a rifle but knew better that to fire it. Even if he hit his target, the powerful bolt of super-focused light would burn through the body and continue on to damage the transport's hull. They couldn't afford another breach. Sly used the rifle like a club. He hit one of the commandos in the side of the head, just as the soldier was turning to fire at him. The shot went wide and hit the bulkhead. Alex tracked the shot and saw, to his relief, that the blast didn't scorch the wall. He couldn't be certain, but he felt confident that the commandos were using stun blasts.

Following his friend's lead, he bounded up over the seats and kicked off. It was difficult to control himself in zero-gravity. Various shots continued to fire off, and people were shouting as they tried to escape or attack. Alex didn't make a sound. He used the seat backs to keep his trajectory low and build speed until he crashed his shoulder into one of the commandos. The man was like a wild animal, thrashing wildly as they flipped through the cabin. Alex managed to grab his gun hand, but the commando was punching and kicking, trying to get away.

Alex held on for dear life, one hand on the commando's wrist, the other on the top of the gun. He pushed the barrel down, trying to wrench it free. He suddenly felt a searing pain across his shoulder and saw a dark blade lodged there, blood bubbling out of the fresh wound. Alex had to turn away from the commando to avoid the blade a second time, but managed to kick out at his attacker. The sole of his boot connected with the commando's groin. The man grunted and raised his knees toward his chest, spinning to the side away from Alex, who had bounced off of the ceiling and was angling down toward the seats.

He reached out and felt a shock of pain in his right arm. He pulled it back but used his left hand to adjust his trajectory. The commando had rotated all the way around and brought his laser pistol up toward Alex. For an instant, he thought it was all over. The weapon was pointed straight at him and Alex saw the commando squeeze the trigger; but nothing happened.

Alex felt a surge of relief, followed instantly by intense hatred. The commando had cut him and tried to kill him. With a savage cry of rage, Alex pushed off of a seat back with both legs and went straight at the commando like a human torpedo. The man tried to turn away but was too slow to avoid Alex. Punching with his left hand felt awkward but the punch connected, catching the man on the side of his head. He howled in pain as his body spun around. Alex caught hold of him, wrapping his legs around the man's waist and snaking his bleeding arm around the man's throat. He couldn't squeeze with his right arm—the pain was too intense—but he could hold on. With his other hand, Alex seized the commando's knife hand. They crashed together into the bulkhead, but Alex got lucky and the commando hit first. His laser pistol went spinning through the air.

Across the passenger cabin, Jai was pinned down by a commando huddled in the seats a few rows back. The entire cabin was filled with limp, floating bodies, and neither could get a clean shot. The commando looked up as Hanes's limp body came drifting toward him. The man saw the vacant expression on the Ahzco operator's face, and turned his attention back to Jai, who was huddled behind Master Sergeant Monty's seemingly lifeless body, still trying to get clear. He raised his pistol and was about to fire, when Hanes suddenly came to life. The Ahzco operator reached out, grabbed the commando's ear, and tugged. The warrior rose to his feet, screaming in pain, and tried to point his gun at Hanes, but the operator latched on to the commando's gun hand and used it to flip his lower body around. He kicked out with both feet—straight into the commando's face. The man had no choice but to let go of his pistol and try to avoid the savage kick. He couldn't escape completely, but managed to turn the kick into a grazing blow that did little damage. He drew his knife, a long ceramic blade with a razor edge on one side and jagged saw teeth on the other. He brought the weapon up in front of him as his feet found purchase. His legs bent as he turned his body to line up a dive that would take him and his deadly knife straight toward Hanes, but before he could kick off, a laser blast from Jai's pistol hit him in the side of the head.

In the forward compartment, Sly was searching for another one of the commandos. There were several bodies floating in the lounge, where a table and several chairs were bolted to the deck. There were also several large storage lockers on one side of the room. Sly knew that there was a commando inside; he just couldn't get through the bodies. Sudden movement would draw laser fire, so he drifted, waiting for his chance to attack and hoping that the commando didn't see him first.

The big wall display showed video of the *Delta Gain*. The ship was much larger than the transport, and they were still tethered together with the boarding tube. With a glance at the screen, Sly saw that the bigger ship was slowly reeling them in. The tube was stuck to the hull of the transport with adhesive that would be simple to break away from, but if the big ship pulled the smaller vessel close enough, they might be able to secure the two ships together. Alex needed to take control of the transport, but in all the chaos of the attack, Sly had lost sight of his friend. He didn't know if Alex was alive or dead. Out of the corner of his eye, Sly saw movement. There were bodies and debris drifting everywhere in the lounge, but speed or jerky movement was easy to spot. The commando was close, almost within reach. Sly saw the man's legs drifting up toward the ceiling, where a small metal hook had broken off of the wall. It was rounded on one end, like a coat hook, but the broken end was jagged. Sly reached out and grabbed the hook.

The commando must have seen the movement, and he twisted, trying to bring his weapon to bear, but Sly thrust the jagged bit of metal forward, straight into the man's calf. The commando screamed. A laser blast flew over Sly's head. He pulled the commando closer and drove the jagged metal into the commando's thigh. The pistol lashed out and hit Sly just above his left eye, ripping open a nasty gash. It hurt, but Sly ignored the pain and kept pulling the man closer. He had to take hold of the commando's gun hand as the assailant tried to point the muzzle at Sly. With his other hand, he drove the jagged bit of metal into the commando's stomach. The man swung a clumsy, desperate punch at Sly, who could only bow his head to avoid getting hit in the face. The man's hand connected with the top of Sly's head. For a second, the Titan operator nearly lost his grip. His vision narrowed but then he regained his senses. Silver sparks floated in his vision, but he managed to dig deeper with the metal hook.

The commando's foot hit the wall, and he pushed off, twisting Sly around and slamming him into the row of metal lockers. Sly let go of the metal hook, leaving it embedded in the commando's stomach, and he drove his fingers straight into his attacker's throat. The man sputtered and coughed. Sly held tight to the commando's gun hand and used it to turn his body toward his assailant. He rotated in and swung his elbow hard at the commando's nose. It connected with a devastating crunch. More blood and a gurgled scream later, the commando tried to push away from Sly, who wrenched the laser from the man's hand. A second later, the commando was hit in the chest—at point blank range—with a laser blast, and the man's body went limp.

Back across the passenger cabin, Alex wrestled with the commando whose knife was stained with his blood. His right arm held no strength, and he could see the look of desperation in the commando's eyes. Winning the fight meant killing his opponent, and while Alex didn't want to kill anyone, his will to live was even stronger. He rotated his feet up and wrapped them around the commando's head. The man punched at him with his free hand, hitting Alex in the legs and back, but there wasn't much strength to the blows. Alex could see the knife blade. It was black and glistening with his blood. Whenever a drop came free, it floated through the air in a perfect sphere of crimson. The sight of it made him angry, but without the strength of his right arm, it was hard to get leverage on the commando. The best he was able to do was keep the man from causing more harm.

Then fortune turned the tide of the struggle in Alex's favor. They crashed to the deck and the blade caught on the arm of one of the seats. With a shove, Alex drove the blade into the resin armrest, and at the same time, forced the commando to let it go. Then the two men hit the floor. It wasn't hard enough to hurt them, or even break them apart, but it gave Alex a chance to grab onto the leg of the nearby chair, which was bolted to the deck. With his body anchored, Alex wrapped his legs tighter around the man's head, locking them together by hooking his knee over the ankle of the other foot. Alex remembered his hand-to-hand combat training, and squeezed with all his strength, flexing his entire body. The commando gagged, and tried to wiggle free, but the man was floating up from the floor like a balloon filled with helium. He had no leverage, and Alex wouldn't let go. A few seconds later, and the man went limp.

Alex pulled the man down into one of the seats and quickly clicked the restraints over his hands. Unlike the stun blast from a laser gun, the chokehold only knocked the commando out for a few seconds. As he came to and realized his predicament, he roared in rage. Alex slipped one foot under the edge of another seat and stood up. He pulled the knife free from the armrest and held it toward the commando's face.

"I owe you one," Alex said, looking at his bloody shoulder. "Shut up or I'll gut you like an animal."

The commando stopped yelling, but stared at Alex with hatred in his eyes.

"Alex!" Sly yelled from the doorway to the lounge.

"I'm here," Alex replied.

"I'm glad you're not dead," Sly said.

"Me too."

"We've got trouble."

"Tell me about it."

"The *Delta Gain* is pulling us toward them," Sly said. "They're going to try and haul us back to Skandia Seven."

"Well, we can't let them win that easy," Alex said. "We'll just have to do something about—"

He didn't finish his thought because at that second, the entire ship went dark and his connection to the transport's systems was severed.

"Alex? Am I dead?" Sly asked.

"Not yet," Alex replied in the darkness. "But we're in trouble."

"Turn the lights back on, buddy," Hanes shouted from somewhere near the front of the cabin.

"I can't," Alex said. "The ship is dead. Someone has cut the power."

CHAPTER SEVENTEEN

A BEAM of light cut through the darkness. It was coming from the front of the cabin, but Alex couldn't see who was controlling it.

"Sound off," Alex said. "Who's got that light?"

"Hanes," the Corporal responded. "It's attached to the rifle that the guards were carrying."

"I'm still alive," Sly said.

Two other Oscar Company operators and four Zen Tech operators, including Jai, were still alive.

"Did we take out all the commandos?" Alex asked.

"I got two," Sly said.

"I got one," Hanes said, "with a little help."

The other three were taken out by laser blasts from the Zen Tech operators.

"Converge on my position if possible," Alex said. "I've got one of them and he can talk."

Alex looked down at the captured commando who had begun staring off into space. It was obvious from the set of the man's jaw that he was anticipating what was to come. Alex had questions, and he wanted answers, but the commando clearly wasn't going to give the information away freely. Alex bent down close to the side of the man's head and whispered in his ear.

"I know you don't want to talk, but I've got a Zen Tech warrior who will carve you up, bit by bit," Alex said. "Now, you're a tough guy. I can attest to that personally. But we both know that sooner or later, you'll talk. So why not skip the pain and tell us what we need to know."

"Go screw yourself," the man snarled.

He threw his head toward Alex, trying to smash his skull into Alex's face, but it was an obvious move and the Cronus Team leader was ready for it, easily swaying out of reach. When he stood up straight, Sly, Hanes, Jai, and the others were drifting toward him.

"Well, we don't all need to question this guy," Alex said. "Hanes, why don't you take that light and find the other weapons? And let's get the other commandos in the cabin locked down next to this one."

"They're dead," Sly said.

"Are they?" Alex asked, directing his question toward the commando. "Were your weapons set to kill or stun?"

The man didn't respond. Alex handed Jai the knife he had taken from the commando.

"Would you like the honors?"

She took the knife and pressed against the commando's

groin. "Talk!" she shouted at the man, whose expression had gone from one of stoic professionalism to one of stark fear in an instant. "Talk or I start cutting," she threatened.

"St-st-stun," he managed to say.

"So everyone on the ship is still alive?" Alex asked.

"The-they sh-sh-sh-should be," he said.

Alex realized that the stutter was a consequence of stress, not simply fear. It was probably something that he had struggled with for most of his life. He didn't want to feel compassion for the man, but he couldn't help it.

"Alright," Alex said. "Find more lights. Find all the commandos. Before they wake up."

"Roger that," Sly said.

"There were six of you, am I right?" Alex continued to question the commando.

"Y-y-yes."

"And I'm guessing the plan was to cut the ship's power, then haul us back to Skandia Seven?"

The commando nodded.

"Can they do that?" Jai asked.

"Yeah, I'm thinking they can," Alex said.

But a plan was forming in his mind. In space, the vast distances between things made it much quieter to Alex's INC. He could *hear* the EM waves of every electronic device, but those waves grew weaker with distance. When the commandos cut the transport's power, it silenced the ship completely. But it also allowed Alex to hear the EM waves coming from the *Delta Gain*.

"Keep an eye on him," Alex told Jai. "Once the commandos

are all locked down, let's find a way to secure our own people so that no one gets hurt drifting around in here."

Jai nodded. It was hard to see in the dark, but Hanes and Sly had discovered two more flashlights. Alex turned back to the commando.

"How many people do you have on the *Delta Gain?*"

The man tried to look tough, as if he weren't going to answer, but Jai put the blade of the knife next to his ear.

"Twelve," the commando said.

It was exactly what Alex feared. He could sync to the *Delta Gain* and even take control of the vessel, but the commandos wouldn't understand what was happening. They would assume that the crew of the big ship was refusing to obey their orders and would probably kill them.

He closed his eyes and ignored the pain throbbing in his brain. There was no longer any doubt in his mind that using the ability to sync with systems other than the mechanized battle suits his INC was designed to control was costing him physically. He couldn't say what the pain was for sure, but it felt as if the hot, stabbing pains were taking a toll. He didn't know how much longer he could endure or if the toll was permanent, but he realized that he couldn't keep doing it forever. It wasn't getting easier, and that scared him a little. People were depending on him, and eventually, his abilities weren't going to be up for the challenge.

The feeling of his INC syncing to the *Delta Gain* was powerful. The EM waves changed from low-pitched vibrations, like the sounds of an orchestral bass section, to a harmonizing melody that reminded Alex of the classical recordings his mother liked to play in the hydroponics green house on NP8261. Information immediately began to dump into his brain. The big Bazmore ship was stationary, but slowly retracting the boarding tube. He could access the *Delta Gain's* external cameras and see the dark transport slowly being pulled across empty space toward the larger ship.

Alex checked the big ship's radar and was surprised to see how many ships were nearby. Most were news ships, probably recording the entire special operation to get the prisoners back. Alex could only guess what the Skandian authorities hoped to do to him, and his friends, back on the planet. He could imagine a very public trial that would be broadcast over the galactic network to every world in the FTA. He wouldn't let that happen, but was hesitant to do anything for fear of the commandos harming the crew of the *Delta Gain.*

Fortunately, there was another ship approaching. It was still over a thousand kilometers away, but the radar identified it as an Ahzco battle cruiser. The ship's transponder code listed it as the *Currency.* Alex tapped into the *Delta Gain's* communication system and sent a message.

"*Currency* this is Sergeant Alex Evans on *Reaper One,* transmitting through the *Delta Gain.* Do you read? Over."

It took a bit longer than he expected for a reply, but there was still a lot of noise from the planet. Luckily for Alex, the *Delta Gain* had a powerful antenna array built onto the ship, and plenty of power to produce a strong signal.

"We read you, Cronus Team leader," came a static laced reply. "What's your sit rep?"

"We're alive, although most of Oscar Company has been

stunned by a commando attack from the *Delta Gain*. We're securing the *Reaper One* as best we can, but laser fire has significantly weakened the ship's hull integrity. Commandos have cut her power as well, so we only have so much life support. We request emergency intervention."

The pause was even longer this time. Alex wished he could communicate what he was capable of doing to Captain Poe, but that was against the orders that VP Haley had given him on Arcadia.

"We stand ready to help, Cronus Leader. Please advise," came the reply.

It was a better response that Alex had hoped for. He had a plan in mind, one that might neutralize the commandos, but there was a risk. As the *Currency* approached, the commandos might fire on the smaller Ahzco vessel. Worse still, if they breeched the *Reaper One's* hull, Alex and everyone in the passenger cabin could die.

Alex turned to the commando locked into the passenger seat beside him.

"How were you planning to communicate with the commandos on the *Delta Gain*?"

"W-we-we w-wer-wer-wern't," he stammered. "It w-w-was a b-b-bl-bla-black op. Ra-ra-rad-radio s-si-si-si-silence."

"Okay," Alex said. "Thank you for your help. We're going to get off of this ship, but you should know that without power, we can't unlock your shackles and the hull is in bad shape. Your people will have to rescue you once we're gone."

The commando looked at Alex without any pretext. He could see fear in the commando's eyes. Space was a dangerous place, and there were no guarantees. For all Alex knew, if the mission failed, the Skandian authorities might just leave them to die.

He couldn't worry about the commandos or the guards, though. Alex had one mission, and that was to get the detainees off of the prison transport. Once that was done, someone else could worry about the rest. He activated the *Delta Gain's* comm system and transmitted another message.

"Here's the plan."

CHAPTER EIGHTEEN

NYX FELT SELF-CONSCIOUS. She was on the bridge with the Vice President of Ahzco Security and it was obvious that Captain Poe resented both of them for intruding upon his command. A large wall display showed a live video of both the *Reaper One* and the *Delta Gain*. The large Bazmore craft dwarfed the prisoner transport and Nyx could see at a glance that it was larger than the *Currency*. It was a carrier class ship loaded with weapons systems that were visible even from over five hundred kilometers away.

"If Alex is wrong..." Haley said in a whisper beside her.

"He's not," Nyx replied, although she felt helpless without her usual connection to the operator with whom she was always partnered.

"There's been no change," Captain Poe said. "If we continue, we'll soon be in the range of those laser cannons."

"That's a risk we'll have to take," Haley said.

As she watched the two vessels, Nyx's anxiety grew. Everything was on the line and if Alex was wrong, it would cost them countless lives, perhaps even her own. As she watched, the voice she had come to know so well came over the bridge speakers.

"*Delta Gain*, this is Alex Evans on board the *Reaper One*. We have thwarted the attack by your commandos. Please disengage, remove yourself from the vicinity, and allow the *Currency* to pick up the remaining operators."

There was no reply for several seconds. The bridge was utterly silent. Captain Poe looked at the VP and shook his head. When the response came, it was clear that no one on the *Delta Gain* realized that Alex was broadcasting the exchange.

"Prisoner Evans, this is Lieutenant Trey Urloch, Skandian Special Forces. We have taken control of the *Reaper One*, which the criminals on board tried to pirate. You will be returned to Skandia Seven to answer for your crimes against the people. If you resist, we will vaporize your vessel with everyone aboard, and make it look like an accident. The law and the media are on our side this time, and you *will* be held accountable for your actions."

"Are you saying that if we don't comply, you'll kill us?" Alex asked.

"You're damn right. If it were up to me, you'd already be space dust. But someone down there wants to make an example out of you, and my job is to oblige them."

"Lieutenant," Alex continued. "We have on board nine soldiers and six commandos, not counting the pilots and whoever you have in the cockpit. They are in restraints, but none are seriously injured. No one has been killed except for one Zen Tech operator who your people fired on with high-powered laser weapons. Are you saying that you're willing to let them all die just to stop us?"

"Are you saying they are your hostages?"

"I'm saying that we have not harmed these men in our efforts to return to our own ships. We have committed no crimes and have done nothing other than protect the companies who employ us."

"Spoken like a true peacekeeper. Let me tell you something, Sergeant," the Lieutenant spat the last word like it was an insult. "We don't need or want your kind on Skandia Seven. There's nothing I'd like better than to come over there and show you the level of my resolve."

"No," Alex said. "You aren't allowed to cross the boarding tube. Like I said, we have control of the *Reaper One*."

There was another pause. Haley spoke up.

"Sounds to me like they're buying it."

"They can't possibly be that stupid," Captain Poe said.

"They're anxious to show their superiority over our operators," Nyx said. "That's the temptation, not what Sergeant Evans is saying."

When the commando lieutenant replied, it seemed that he was close to taking the bait.

"Our scans show the hull integrity of the *Reaper One* is down to ten percent," the lieutenant said. "The best thing to do right now is to let us come across and escort you back to the *Delta Gain*."

"Negative, lieutenant. Do not cross to our ship."

"We have a responsibility to get you back alive."

"Forget it," Alex said.

There was a pause.

"Sergeant Evans, do you read me?"

Alex hadn't cut the connection, but he was acting as if he had.

"We're in range of their weapons," the fire control officer announced.

"Range?" Captain Poe asked.

"Three hundred, eighty kilometers," the navigation officer replied.

"We'll begin retro burn in eighteen minutes, Captain," the helmsman said.

"Thank you, helm," Captain Poe said. "Mr. Haley, may I suggest that we slow since the *Delta Gain* has made no move to evacuate the area around the *Reaper One?*"

"No," Haley said. "We're going to see how things play out. And if that report about the transport hull integrity was accurate, we'll need to get our people off of that ship as soon as possible."

"You're putting this ship at risk," Poe said, barely controlling his anger. "It's irresponsible."

"This is a war ship, Captain," Haley said, no longer trying to conceal his disgust. "You are a captain in the CDF. If you wish to remain so, I suggest you do as I tell you."

Captain Poe's eyes flashed with seething hatred.

"I do so in protest," Captain Poe said. "This course of action is irresponsible and there are over fifty souls on board this ship. Who is looking out for them?"

"I can do that," Haley said, "without abandoning the operators who are just as much a part of this crew as you are. I regret that it has come to this, but I must ask you to leave the bridge. You are relieved of your duties, Captain Poe. Please go to your cabin and stay there until further notice."

Captain Poe stepped up out of the pit. He was close to Haley and to Nyx, who felt threatened by the big officer. He towered over Haley, who didn't back down from him in the slightest.

"Not everyone sees the CDF as the war mongering army that you do, sir," Poe said. "And there will come a day when you are no longer the commander-in-chief."

"Perhaps," Haley said. "But for now, everyone in the CDF follows my orders. If you don't like it, you can resign your commission and move on. No hard feelings."

"If I did, I would have a story to tell," Poe said.

Nyx knew the captain was threatening to run to the media. He could smear the CDF and specifically, VP Haley, but the executive was unfazed. Nyx wondered if she could be so cool under that kind of direct threat.

"Yes, I suppose you could. But it would be a sad end to promising career," Haley said nonchalantly. "You must do as you see fit, Commander."

Poe left without another word. The tension on the bridge was thick, but Haley didn't even seem to notice.

"Lieutenant Jones," Haley said in a chipper voice. "You have the con. Let's go get our people back."

"Aye, sir," Rory Jones said, moving down into the pit.

Nyx thought the vice president was the steadiest person she had ever met—that perhaps he had ice water running through his veins. But then she noticed his hand on the railing around the pit. The knuckles on his fingers were white, and she realized that he was fighting to stay calm just like she was.

CHAPTER NINETEEN

"HERE THEY COME," Alex said.

"I wish we could see it," Hanes said.

"You're welcome to go out and have a look," Sly said.

Alex didn't join in the fun. He was too busy counting the commandos entering the boarding tube. They were wearing hard vacuum space suits and carrying assault rifles. Unlike the first group of commandos, they weren't going to use non-lethal tactics.

Alex waited, counting the heavily armed warriors and knowing that there was probably an emergency release on the exterior of the hull that would pop open the door to the passenger cabin. Once that happened, the commandos would come in, guns blazing. And the inevitable result would be a hull breach. The air would be sucked out and anyone not in hard vacuum suits with air tanks and insulation to protect them from the cold would die, including the first group of commandos and the guards. It was reckless and cruel, but Alex had guessed that Lieutenant Urloch might be the kind of man who cared more about winning than the lives of the innocent people who he was supposed to protect. And had the commandos not been heavily armed and wearing space suits, he might have felt guilt over what he was about to do.

For a moment, Alex wished he could show the commandos exactly what their commander planned to do. Alex hadn't lied. Most of the dark-clad warriors were unharmed. Most had bumps and bruises, but only one had more serious wounds. The commando that Sly had subdued in the lounge compartment was bleeding from several punctured wounds, but there was nothing Alex could do about that. Hanes had pressed quick clot gauze into the bloody lacerations once the man was strapped down beside the others.

Ten commandos were in the tube, drifting across toward the *Reaper One*. Alex wished that all twelve had gone into the boarding tube, but he decided that if the crew of the *Delta Gain* couldn't dispatch two Skandian commandos, they deserved what they got.

With his INC synced to the large, Bazmore ship's systems, it only took a thought to shut the door on the far side of the boarding tube. There were no cameras in the extendable tube, and Alex had no idea if the commandos were even aware of what he had done. What he did next, however, was undeniable.

The *Delta Gain* was a massive, interstellar, war ship with powerful engines. Still, it took a huge amount of thrust to move the big vessel. Alex engaged the thrusters on the starboard side that faced the small prison transport and began feeding power to the big main engine. In his mind's eye, he saw the video feed from the *Delta Gain's* external cameras through INC. His brain processed the data into a picture. Alex had no idea how it worked, but he watched as the boarding tube stretched wide, then popped off of *Reaper One's* exterior. The transport was dragged into a slow tumble, tethered as it was to the boarding tube. Alex hoped it wouldn't keep them from being rescued, but he would worry about that later. The *Currency* was still two hundred and fifty kilometers out.

Once the tube detached, Alex increased the main engines' power to full, then cut the lights all over the ship and shut down the vessel's artificial gravity. It wasn't a crippling move, but caused enough problems that might not easily or quickly be rectified and that it merited moving the big ship away from the *Reaper One*. Alex watched the ship begin to move away in his mind's eye, and with it, his ability to stay synced to her systems begin to falter. He accessed the ship's comms one last time and sent a brief message.

"*Currency* crew. Don't tarry. We don't have much time left on this vessel and you're our only hope."

He had to cut his connection with the *Delta Gain* before a reply came through. And when he opened his eyes, he saw his friends, and most of the soldiers from Skandia Seven, watching him.

"That's it," Alex said, feeling relieved to have broken the connection with the big ship.

"Now we wait," Sly said.

"And hope that Captain Poe doesn't take too long," Hanes said.

They spent the next half an hour helping the operators who were coming around from the commandos' stun lasers. There wasn't much in the way of provisions on board, but Sly found some water and everyone waited. Alex expected the commandos in the cockpit to power the vessel back on, but the familiar hum of EM waves never reappeared. The only sign of the approaching Ahzco battle cruiser was the series of growing EM waves emitted by her electrical systems.

"Let's move all the wounded," Alex said. "We can get them across first."

"What about them?" Hanes said, nodding his head toward the guards and commandos still locked in their seats."

"We have to leave them," Sly said. "Without power, we can't unfasten their restraints."

"We'll have to cut them loose," Alex said.

"Exactly," Sly said.

"No, not like that. I mean literally, cut them free," Alex said.

"With what?" Sly argued. "We don't have the tools."

"With these?" Jai asked, holding up her laser pistol.

"Yes," Alex said. "They've got an adjustable power output."

"Yeah, but one wrong move and we've just blasted through the hull," Sly said.

"If we leave them here, they'll die," Alex said.

"Not our circus, not our monkeys," Sly replied.

"He's not wrong," Hanes said.

"That's not how we do things," Master Sergeant Montgomery objected.

"We'll get everyone off of this ship first," Alex explained. "Then we'll cut them free and take them on board the *Currency*."

"That might be a problem," Jai said."

"Oh, it's definitely a problem," Sly added.

"The pistols don't have a lot of power left," she went on, ignoring Sly. "There might not be enough power to cut all of the prisoners free."

"Check the weapons they brought on board," Hanes said. "Their pistols were set to stun. They might have more power."

"If that doesn't work, we'll use the rifles," Alex said.

"That's insanity," Sly said.

"We're not monsters, Sly," Alex insisted. "These people were doing their jobs. They don't deserve to die because of it."

"And we don't deserve to die because they followed some foolish orders to arrest us in the first place. We aren't the enemy."

"That's right," Monty said. "And that's why we won't treat them like enemies."

"Who knows?" Alex said. "Maybe Captain Poe has a plan and we won't have to figure everything out ourselves."

"I wouldn't count on that," Hanes said. "Poe's guiding principle is to look out for himself and let everyone else figure it out on their own."

CHAPTER TWENTY

Nyx helped Loman into the Medic battle suit. The lightweight MBS was designed for warfare in atmo but could be converted to hard vacuum. There were no more technicians on board, but Loman and the ship's chief engineer knew enough to put the suit all together.

"You're certain about this?" Nyx asked as she handed him the transparent helmet.

"We can't board or move anyone while that ship is spinning," Loman said. "And I'm the only person left on the *Currency* with an INC chip. It may have been a few years since I last suited up and went to work as an operator, but I haven't forgotten."

Actually, it was more than a few years. Loman had last donned a mechanized battle suit over twenty years prior, but his INC still worked. And he had experience in zero-gravity.

"I've got this," Loman told the young controller. "You get on up to your station and check in. It's been a while since I've had another person's voice in my head."

She nodded and hurried away. Loman lifted the helmet and settled it over his head. It had latches on each side that held the flexible edge down to create an airtight seal. In truth, he was nervous. If they had made even one tiny mistake, he would die outside the ship. In other circumstances, he might have been justified in claiming that his life was too valuable to risk. But Loman had the security division well-organized. While he was the mastermind behind everything that the CDF was doing to thwart the secret powers pushing for a centralized government and breaking up mega corporations, it was really Alex Evans who was the future. His special abilities gave the CDF an edge over everyone else. If Loman had to risk his life to save his star operator, then so be it.

"Ready?" the chief engineer asked.

"As I can be," Loman said, his own voice sounding strange inside the helmet.

"You don't have to do this," the officer said. "We can find another way."

"There's no time. You heard their last transmission. That ship's hull is compromised. And the Bazmore carrier could return at any time."

"Alright sir," the chief engineer said, lifting up an EVA jet pack and settling it onto Loman's shoulders. "I checked everything myself. The airlock's ready. And we'll be standing by to help."

"Just make sure the boarding tube is ready to deploy. We can't afford to waste any time."

"I will, sir. Good luck."

The engineer walked away, and Loman was left standing by the airlock. He could see the cold darkness waiting for him through a small window-sized port. His skin tingled with fear, but he had learned to master his emotions a long, long time ago. He pushed the dangers to the back of his mind and focused on what he needed to do.

Mr. Haley, do you read me, sir?

"Call me Loman if you're going to be in my head."

Roger that Loman. Please call me Nyx.

"How do we look from your end?"

All systems are green. Your suit is ready for hard vacuum, and the Currency *is two klicks from the* Reaper One. *We're ready if you are.*

"Good," Loman said. "There's nothing worse than waiting around."

He reached out and pressed the large red button that opened the airlock door. It slid aside and he stepped into the small compartment. The door closed behind him and the air was pumped out of the room.

Loman checked his weapons. He had a laser pistol on his hip as a last resort, but his primary weapon was on his right forearm, a standard Medic blaster. The barrel was extendable, and he went ahead and activated the weapon.

You're at full power, sir, with over two hours of O2.

"That's good to know," Loman said. "Hopefully this won't take that long."

No sir. Just be careful getting into that cockpit.

"Roger that," Loman said, as the outer door opened.

The executive vice president of Ahzco Security stepped out

onto the edge of the ship. Comparatively speaking, it felt like he was standing at the threshold of a large building. The ship rose up in front of him several stories tall on either side. And in the distance, illuminated by the light reflecting off of Skandia Seven, the *Reaper One* spun round and round. It was an oblong ship, with a thick central cabin, an aerodynamic cockpit in the front, and a small engine compartment in back. The ship was spinning down its central axis, like a bullet spiraling through the grooves on a sniper rifle.

"Here goes nothing," Loman said.

He bent his knees and leaned forward. It didn't feel like falling. He was halfway out of the *Currency's* artificial gravity when he kicked off. It felt like he was swimming, only he didn't slow down as he flew through space. Outside of the ship's artificial gravity field, there was no physical sensation of movement.

Your trajectory is good but check your thruster just to be certain. You're traveling at ten kilometers per hour, so you've got twelve minutes.

"Thank you," Loman said.

The jet pack was computer controlled, and slaved to his Medic battle suit, which gave Loman the ability to control it with his mind. He checked the jet pack's thrusters, which fired smoothly, and he gave them a slightly prolonged burst that doubled his speed.

"Bring up navigation," he said. "I'm a little out of practice and I don't want to miss the target or break my leg hitting that ship too fast."

Sending trajectory data to you now, Nyx said. *I've already run a calculation that's based on your speed and should bring you into contact with the top of the cockpit.*

Loman could see the hole cut in the roof of the space craft. There was movement inside the cockpit, and he didn't know if the commandos who had cut the power were still inside, or if he was just seeing the bodies of the pilots. It made him angry to think that the soldiers could be so callous that they felt no qualms about sacrificing the lives of the pilots. The fact that the Skandian authorities were bowing to the media pressure and blaming his operators for an attack planned and carried out by protesters seemed absurd. But Loman knew enough about bureaucracies to understand that they rarely did things well or rationally. Behind every decision was a personal agenda, and behind every action, there was someone who stood to gain. Unfortunately, that often meant that most of the things governments did resulted in someone's suffering. They were necessary evils, and Loman was well acquainted with the reality that when someone had to be blamed, it was easier to blame the outsider. On Skandia Seven, his people were the outsiders, but they deserved better treatment and he was determined to ensure that they didn't die on the transport ship.

Four minutes to contact. You should begin firing your retro thrusters.

"Copy, firing retro thrusters now," Loman said.

He wondered how things were carried out when people didn't have computers to guide them. It was said that long ago, before mankind spread through the galaxy, explorers navigated by using the stars. But Loman was happy for the help. He followed the navigation program's trajectory and speed recommendations until he was just meters away from the cockpit.

It rotated into an upright position and Loman got a good look through the forward view ports. He saw the pilots still strapped into their seats, but no sign of the commandos who had cut into the hull to gain access. It was possible that they had returned to the *Delta Gain*, but it was also possible that they might be hiding in the cockpit.

"Double check my weapons," Loman said. "I don't want to blow holes through the ship."

Laser is set to the lowest power and full auto fire. It won't penetrate the hull but should stun anyone not wearing armor.

"Yeah, how many shots would it take to penetrate battle armor?"

Three or four. If you run into trouble, I wouldn't hold back.

"You don't have to worry about that," Loman said.

He drifted to within arm's length of the ship just as it rotated back into the upright position. It was a simple matter of grabbing the roof and pulling himself onto the vessel, but a wrong move could propel him away from it. He grabbed on and pulled himself right up to the hole that was cut in the roof.

"I'm on," he said.

Good work, sir. You're doing great. There's no rush. Take your time.

Loman drew his knees up under him and looked down into the cockpit. A yellow laser blast missed his helmet by centimeters.

"Enemy fire!" Loman shouted, throwing himself back out of harm's way.

He realized too late that he had dislodged himself from the ship. By pulling back, he had set his body in motion and the ship slid out of arm's reach. He would drift off and have to re-do his approach. Fortunately for him, Nyx was ready for just such an accident and activated the electromagnets in his hard-vacuum boots. His body flew backward, but his feet stayed connected to the roof of the cockpit.

Easy sir, I've activated your magno-boots.

"And saved my bacon. Thanks, Nyx. That's good thinking."

Did you get a good look inside the cockpit?

"Negative. They fired at me too quickly."

I'm running playback now, frame by frame. I should have a decent picture. Hang on.

Loman wanted to draw his laser pistol, but it wouldn't do him any good. He would need to keep one hand free to help him maneuver in zero-gravity. With a little effort, he pulled himself back down to the roof of the cockpit on his knees, staying clear of the hole. An image appeared in his mind. He could see two commandos huddled behind the seats of the cockpit's main chairs. There wasn't a lot of room to spare in the small space. A hatch had been opened, the cover removed, and emergency power cut-offs were visible.

"I guess that's how they kept Alex from controlling the ship," Loman said.

Yes sir. How are you going to get in there?

"I'll have to take out those two commandos first."

Is that even possible?

"Let's find out."

Loman inched forward, well aware that the commandos

could have changed position. It didn't really matter. In fact, they had done him a favor. With the power off, shooting his laser in the cockpit wouldn't do too much damage. He reached out with his right arm and immediately felt a sting that made the arm feel numb, but at the same time, he began to fire. He waved his arm back and forth, letting the forearm weapon shoot rapid bursts all across the cockpit.

Two more laser blasts shot up through the hole in the roof of the cockpit, but they were nowhere near Loman. If the commandos had been smart, they could have adjusted the power of their weapons and fired through the roof, but they had no way of knowing that he was still there until he opened fire on them.

Are they neutralized?

"Only one way to find out," Loman said.

He eased back over the hole, looking down. Both commandos looked unconscious. He didn't hesitate, throwing himself into the cockpit and firing at point blank range, hitting both of the commandos just to be sure they were really stunned.

There were scorch marks across some of the controls, which he guessed was from his random blasting. But it didn't matter. He wasn't planning to fly the ship. All he had to do was get the power back online.

"Alright, Nyx, patch me through to Lieutenant Jones."

Go ahead, sir.

"Jones, I'm in the *Reaper One's* cockpit. Activating the power now."

"We read you, sir. The *Currency* is standing by for emergency rescue operations on your command."

Loman reached down into the compartment, took hold of the emergency cut-off lever, and turned it back in line with the thick cables that connected the ship's power banks to her systems.

Nothing happened. Loman felt a stab of disappointment. Then, to his relief, he saw a light blinking on the cockpit control board. He pulled himself past the floating commandos and in between the pilot seats. The label on the blinking light said *INITIALIZE*. Loman grinned with success as he reached forward and pushed the button.

CHAPTER TWENTY-ONE

WAITING WAS THE WORST, but at least Alex could feel the EM waves from the *Currency* growing closer and closer. It was an encouraging reminder that they weren't alone.

As they waited for rescue, all of the wounded, including Master Sergeant Mongomery, and Ash in her medical pod, were moved close to the exit. Alex's own wound, a gash in his shoulder, wasn't as serious as he feared. Sly had packed it with quick clot gauze to stop the bleeding, and then covered it with a bandage. The one thing that the ship seemed to have in abundance was medical supplies. It was almost if they were preparing for a fight on board the ship.

"How much longer you think?" Sly asked.

"Hard to say," Alex replied.

After they had gathered all the weapons and moved the injured and wounded, there was nothing else left to do but wait and hope.

"I could use something to eat," Sly said.

"I'm sure they'll have plenty of food for you on the *Currency*," Alex said with a grin.

"I wouldn't call that food," Sly said. "There's nothing culinary about the reconstituted items that pass for meals on board a military ship."

"Food is fuel, nothing more," Jai said.

She was growing more talkative since the commando attack, much to Sansabar's consternation.

"I think that's the worst idea I've ever heard," Sly replied.

Suddenly, a new sound caught Alex's attention. It wasn't audible to most of the passengers waiting to be rescued, but Alex heard it like the steady pounding of a giant drum.

"Is that what I think it is?" Sly asked.

Alex couldn't stop grinning. "It is. They got the power going."

It only took a moment before the lights in the passenger cabin flickered on and the air scrubbers began to blow pure oxygen through the air vents. Alex hadn't noticed how cold the ship had gotten until the life support system began to raise the temperature.

"Starting to feel halfway decent around here again," Hanes said.

"The good news is that I should be able to unlock the restraints," Alex said. "We'll bring the prisoners through last."

Alex synced to the *Reaper One's* systems, many of which were still booting up, but he got an immediate read on the situation. Comms were still loading, but the thrusters were active, and Alex began to fire short bursts that slowed the ship's rotation. He knew it needed to be steady for the *Currency* to extend a boarding tube.

"*Reaper One*, this is the *Currency*. Do you read? Over."

Alex heard the communication signal in his head, and at first, he thought it was Nyx, but he quickly realized that it was just the comms officer on the *Currency*.

"We read you, *Currency*. This is Sergeant Evans. How can we assist in the rescue efforts?"

"Stand-by, Cronus Team leader. We're extending the boarding tube now. We'll alert you when we have pressurization."

"Roger that, *Currency*. Cronus Team is standing by."

It took almost ten minutes to get the boarding tube extended and pump enough air into the collapsible device for safe passage between ships. Once the *Currency* gave the okay, Alex had the door opened and the wounded were ushered through.

"You sure you want to waste time and resources on prisoners?" Sly asked. "You know Captain Poe will just put us in charge of them."

"What choice do we have?" Alex asked. "If we leave them—"

He was cut off by an alarm that sounded in his head. He closed his eyes and let the data reveal itself. A squad of small ships had just broken out of the planet's atmosphere and were racing toward the ruined transport ship.

"What is it?" Sly asked.

Alex held up a hand. The transport didn't have the radar capabilities to pick up the ships. Even from the external hull cameras, they were nothing more than glowing specks. It took him a moment to realize why the alarm was blaring, and when he did, it hit him like a physical blow.

"They've locked onto us," Alex said. "*Currency*, are you reading this?"

"Who locked onto us?" Sly asked frantically. "Someone is shooting at us?"

"Time to move!" Sansabar said, grabbing Alex's arm and pulling him toward the exit.

"Wait," Alex had to concentrate for a second to open all the restraints. They snapped open and Alex looked back at the prisoners.

"Someone is firing on this ship," Alex said. "We have to get across to the *Currency*."

The commandos looked skeptical and the soldier guards looked frightened, but Alex didn't care. He flung himself through the doorway and into the tunnel. There was no walkway, since the boarding tube only worked in zero gravity. Instead, there were evenly spaced canvas straps that Alex used to keep moving toward the ship.

"Weapons inbound, Cronus Team," the comms officer said. "Get your people across and seal that hatch. We have to move."

"Roger that," Alex said, just before he flew across the threshold and into the *Currency's* artificial gravity.

Alex landed hard, sending a fiery flash of pain surging through his shoulder and up his neck. Sly and Jai crashed on top of him. They all scrambled up together, Sansabar tugging on Alex's good arm. The last of the operators flew through the tunnel and Alex looked back. The guards were clustered at the door on the other end.

"Come on!" he shouted.

No one moved. Alex felt a sinking sense of fear inside of him as he realized that the guards and commandos were about to die. He wondered—if he were in their position, would he believe his captors or not?

The guards came racing through the tube. Alex looked over his shoulder and saw with satisfaction that there were operators from Ahzco, Zen Tech, and Bazmore with weapons ready. Not that Alex was worried that the soldiers would somehow manage to best them unarmed, but he didn't want more bloodshed. A show of force would keep the guards in check. They came diving on board almost as one. There were nine, all told, but when Alex looked back, he didn't see the commandos.

"Where are the others?" Alex shouted at the guards.

"It's too late," Sly said. He hit the button that closed the emergency hatch.

"*Currency,* we're all on board," Alex said, shaking his head at the stubborn commandos. They would die because they were unwilling to take help from the people who had overcome their surprise attack. But there was nothing he could for them if they weren't willing to accept his help. "Retracting the boarding tube now."

He cut his link to the *Reaper One*, took a deep breath, then synced to the *Currency's* systems. He realized immediately that the ship was already moving. He cycled through her external cameras, looking for signs of the weapons that had been fired at the prison transport, but instead, he caught sight of a medic in a jet pack racing away from both ships.

"Who in the world?" Alex wondered aloud.

CHAPTER TWENTY-TWO

LOMAN KNEW AS SOON as he had been notified of the danger that there was no way to get back onto the *Currency*. The boarding tube covered the only single person airlock, and the larger hangar utilized a crane to pull the drop ship into position on the belly of the ship. He could have flown across to the *Currency* and held fast to her hull, but there was a high probably that wreckage from the transport might hit the larger ship. The last thing Loman wanted was to get crushed. Instead, he crawled out of the cockpit and propelled himself away from both ships.

Mr. Haley, sir, what are you doing?

"Surviving," Loman said. "And I told you to call me Loman."

I'm trying, but it doesn't seem appropriate.

"Just keep an eye on those fighters."

Yes, sir.

"If they come after me, I won't be able to escape."

Loman knew the odds were long. If the fighters were willing to take on the *Currency*, it would be a protracted fight. The battle cruiser had weapons, but they were built to take aim at large, slow-moving targets, not small one-man fighters. And his weapons were meant to be used against mechanized battle armor, not the thick plates of starships.

There was even a high risk of death if the fighters didn't pursue him. All they had to do was keep the *Currency* busy long enough, or disable her, and Loman would suffocate before he could be picked up.

"How much air to I have?"

Just over an hour remaining.

"See if you can adjust the mixture to make it last longer. I don't need pure oxygen all the time."

I hadn't thought of that. Just a minute.

Loman would give her all the time she needed. He was speeding away from the two ships and had already put several kilometers between himself and the *Reaper One.* He gave his thrusters a tiny burst, one that wouldn't slow him down or change his direction, but that set him slowly turning while he continued on the trajectory away from the two ships. When he could finally see them, it was immediately obvious that there was a problem.

"Why are they still attached?"

I don't understand.

"The *Currency's* boarding tube is still attacked to the *Reaper One.*"

But even as he pointed out the issue, the tube detached from the passenger transport and began to retract. The *Currency* immediately began to move away from the Skandian ship, using thrusters only.

They've parted now. Commander Jones is waiting to fire the ship's main drive.

Loman didn't have to be told that missiles were inbound. It was the only reasonable explanation for waiting to use the ship's main drive engine. There was a possibility that the missiles would sense the *Currency's* heat exhaust and target the Ahzco ship. Although Loman's intuition told him they were shooting at their own vessel.

"That's a desperate move," Loman said.

What do you mean?

"I mean that they're sacrificing their own ship and killing any survivors just so they can spin the story," Loman explained. "I guarantee you that the media ships are recording everything, but from the distance they're keeping, they won't be able to say who fired the missiles. Skandian authorities will say it was us, and that they sent their fighters to run us out of the system."

But they have people still on board the Reaper One. *Surely, they know that.*

"They had innocent pilots in the cockpit, but they cut into the ship anyway."

They might have thought the pilots were helping our operators.

"Maybe, but it's horrific that they killed them," Loman said. "From what I've seen, they didn't want word getting out about what really happened down there. Odds are good that they're getting a lot of sympathy because of the attacks."

Which the protesters started.

"With help," Loman pointed out. "From what you and Lieutenant Jones have told me, they had advanced, military planning to coordinate those attacks to take place at the same time all around the globe."

You think maybe the Skandian authorities were behind it?

"It's possible. And then they blame us, which plays right into the media's fabrication that we're all warmongering barbarians trampling on the rights of innocent civilians every chance we get."

So they arrest the survivors so that they can't tell their side of the story.

"Not that anyone would believe—"

He was cut off when the *Reaper One* exploded in a sudden flash of light. Loman had to close his eyes. When he opened them again, he noticed that the small fighters were getting closer. But so was the *Currency.*

Lieutenant Jones's voice came over Loman's helmet speakers, sounding small and far away.

"Mr. Haley. We have eight small fighters on an intercept course," he said. "Should we fire at them?"

"No," Loman said. "Prepare the point defense system. If they fire at us, we need to be ready. But I don't think they actually want a fight."

They just want to look strong.

"Exactly. They're putting on a show for the cameras."

"Stay on your current heading," Lieutenant Jones said. "We should be able to slow to your speed and give you time to get back on board."

"That's good," Loman said. "We've got to get out of this system before they do something really stupid."

Getting back onboard the *Currency* was nerve wracking, but Loman managed it. Once he was back inside with the feeling of artificial gravity pulling down on him, he finally realized just how tired he was. Space walking was a young man's game. He shrugged off the jetpack and unfastened the latches on his helmet. He was covered in sweat, and desperate for cool shower and a warm bed, but it would have to wait. The fighters were still on their tail, and if they fired at the *Currency*, things could get ugly very quickly.

"Sir, can I help you with that armor?" an engineer asked as he made his way out of the MBS hangar and toward the corridor that led to the lift.

"No, I've got to get to the bridge," Loman declared.

He was stripping off the hard-vacuum components in the elevator, and only had the job halfway finished when the doors opened to the command level. He came walking out, dropping parts and pieces of his suit behind him.

The bridge was crowded. Nyx was there, along with several operators, including Alex. Loman moved past them all and went directly to the railing around the pit where he could see the three-dimensional hologram that showed the space all around the ship. There were eight triangular ships following in the *Currency's* wake, swiveling and swarming around each other. It was clear at a glance that the ships themselves were capable of going much faster than they were flying. They could have raced past the Ahzco ship, but they were holding back.

"Report!" Loman demanded.

"We're on course for the space tunnel," Lieutenant Jones said. "And for the moment, the fighters are holding back."

"As they should. They just want us gone," Loman said. "Loose lips sink ships, as they say. Skandia doesn't want us around to contradict their spin on the situation."

"Mr. Haley," a familiar voice said from behind him. Loman turned and saw Alex Evans. "We have nine of their soldiers on board. They were guards on the transport."

"You mean the witnesses the Skandian's hoped to kill by blowing up the *Reaper One*," Loman said. "Outstanding. You never cease to amaze me, Sergeant. Good work."

Alex looked surprised at the compliment.

"Lieutenant," Loman said with a grin of his own. "Change course. Make for the space station."

CHAPTER TWENTY-THREE

"I WANT those captives taken care of," Loman Haley demanded. "Make sure they're fed and have everything they need."

Alex had seen leaders take charge before, and at times, he had even done so himself, but he'd never seen a single man captivate a room like the executive vice president of security. He was a force of nature, with the kind of charisma that made you want to do whatever he asked.

"Were there other company personnel on the transport?" Haley asked Alex.

"Yes, sir. Zen Tech and Bazmore operators."

"Excellent. They're on board with us?"

"Yes, sir," Alex said.

"Let's make sure they know where we're going. Get the controllers to help them make contact with their people. Those that so choose to do so can get off at the space station. I'm sure there will be plenty of people there willing to hear their side of the story."

Nyx hurried away to get the controllers to their stations. Sansabar and Hanes were sent to gather the group of detainees who had come aboard the *Currency*.

"Lieutenant Jones, I want everyone at battle stations," Loman ordered.

"Yes, sir, Mr. Haley."

"I don't think they'll fight us, but if they try, I want us to be ready." The VP turned to Alex again. "You're wounded?" Loman asked as the bridge began to clear of spectators.

"It's nothing," Alex said, which wasn't entirely true. Moving his right arm at all sent shooting pains across his shoulder, down his arm, and up his neck. But he was caught up in the excitement and didn't want to be left out.

"Your team is down to just two members," Loman said, thinking out loud.

"For the moment, sir," Alex said. "But Sly and I can handle whatever you need."

"Alright then. Get down to the hangar. I want you both suited up."

"There aren't any technicians, sir. They died in the attack on the factory," Sly said.

"You'll have to prep the Titans yourself," Loman said. "Get them ready and geared up."

"Sir?" Lieutenant Jones spoke up. "You're sending Titans out against the fighters?"

"If I have to," Loman said. "Right now, those fighters are waiting on orders from Skandia Seven. The Prime Minster will have figured out what we're up to by now. They're trying to decide if it's worth attacking us with every news agency in the galaxy watching. But they don't know that we saved their guards."

He was nodding, and his excitement was contagious. "They'll be thinking we're just dropping off the other operators, or there's no way they hold back. Alex, I don't want you to fight them. Just disable their ships temporarily. Understand? And do it in a way that can't be traced back to you."

"Yes sir," Alex said.

"Sly, you're his backup. If things get out of hand, you have permission to engage. If it comes to that, do not hold back."

"Yes, sir," Sly said.

"Alright, get moving. This pot could boil over at any moment," Loman said.

Alex and Sly went straight to the lift, and when it opened, Nyx came out with a worried-looking group of controllers.

"What are you doing?" Nyx asked.

"We're getting suited up," Alex said.

"What? Why? You're wounded."

"It's nothing."

"I'm looking at bloody bandages, Alex. You just got rescued after being taken hostage and held against your will."

"I'm fine. We aren't going to fight. You know what I can do if we get close to the fighters."

"I also know what they can do to you."

"Sly won't let that happen," Alex said.

"Yeah, don't worry about him," Sly said. "I've got his back."

"Just don't push it," Nyx said. "Know your limitations."

"I will, I promise," Alex said.

They left her on the command level and went straight down to the MBS hangar. The Zen Tech and Bazmore operators were in the ready room, but Jai and few others came out as Alex and Sly hurried by.

"Are we allowed to help?" Jai asked. "I wouldn't want to cross any lines."

"I think you love to cross lines," Sly said with a smirk.

Jai returned the look, and they both laughed. Alex was taken off-guard by the stoic Zen Tech warrior's laugh. The lines on her face curled around her eyes and danced across her nose in an appealing way.

"We could use a bit of help," Alex said. "We're suiting up."

"Is there trouble?" Jai asked, her mirth suddenly gone.

"The fighters are still out there," Alex said. "The commander just wants us ready on the off chance that they get aggressive."

"I wish we could join you," Jai said. "None of our battle suits are rated for hard vacuum."

"We'll be fine," Alex said. "The ship is armored and has weapons. We're just a show of force."

They went into the hangar and found the backup Titan suits. It occurred to Alex that he was prepping the third Titan MBS he'd been in since the mission began. It wasn't a good trend, but at least he was alive.

The battle suits were on huge racks. Fortunately, there was a hydraulic pulley system to move the Titans into position. The munitions were clearly marked and easy to load into the battle suits. They made sure the power supplies were fully charged and loaded the secondary weapons with mini rockets. They weren't long range weapons and didn't have the explosive yield to match the fighters, but they packed more punch than the laser cannons, especially if the small attack craft had deflector shields.

Once the Titans were moved into the launch bay, which was basically a contained room where the Titans could drop straight down through a retractable floor into open space, Alex and Sly climbed up into the battle suits.

"We're in," Alex said over the com-link.

I have you. Good job prepping the MBS.

"Yeah, I learned a thing or two helping the mechanics build one out down on Skandia," Alex said. "Any word from the bridge?"

Not yet. We're fifteen hundred kilometers from the port, and we'll soon be close to some of the news agency ships.

There was no need for Alex to stay synced to the *Currency*. His Titan gave him access to most of the ship's systems and he didn't need to circumvent the crew. All he wanted to do was keep an eye on where they were in relation to the space station and the fighters following them.

"We're lucky Skandia doesn't have more ships," Sly said over the team channel of their com-link. "We could be in trouble if they had a fleet in the system."

"You made sure Ash was taken straight to the med bay, right?" Alex asked.

"Of course," Sly said. "She's in good hands now, but I wish we were on a bigger ship."

"Because of those fighters?"

"No, because the med bay here is small," Sly said. "And there were a lot of wounded from the attacks. The medical staff is probably overwhelmed."

"We won't be here much longer," Alex said. "Once we drop the guards on the space station, we'll leave the system."

"And go where?"

"Anywhere's better than here."

"What do you think of Jai?" Sly asked.

Alex couldn't help but grin, although he was also struck by pang of guilt. Would Ash be okay with them talking about another woman? He didn't know. He couldn't even say for certain if she had feelings for Sly, but she had certainly seemed very concerned for him when he was caught in the blast on Arcadia.

"I think she's different from any person I've ever met," Alex said honestly. "I wouldn't want to go into battle knowing she was on the other side."

"Me either," Sly said. "I'm afraid of what she'll think of us when she finds out we were at Carthage."

It was true; they had been instrumental in crippling the Zen Tech fleet in the Carthage system. Alex had not only fought their operators, but had also taken out entire drop ships, and disabled the Zen Tech freighter that had who knew how many souls aboard. There were times when the thought of that mission haunted him. He couldn't fathom the number of lives that were lost directly because of his actions and the plan that he had played a part in developing and implementing.

"We were doing our jobs," Alex said. "She would have done the same in our shoes. Maybe she has."

"True," Sly admitted. "But there are times when I think this is all so stupid. We're no different from the Zen Tech operators or any other. We just took a job working for Ahzco and they took a job for a different company. Is that really a reason to fight and kill each other?"

"Maybe not," Alex said. "In some ways, we're just pawns in the hands of the executives trying to improve the company bottom line or win a little more market share."

"And you're okay with that?"

"I don't know," Alex admitted. "All I know is that it's better than the options I had on NP8261. I've traveled the galaxy. I've been to places where I never dreamed I'd go. And I'm entrusted with state-of-the-art gear. I don't know about you, but I don't think I could give up flying. Not now."

"No, me either," Sly said.

"I can't say that I have a grasp on everything philosophically, but I know I want to do this for as long as I can."

"That's a good way to look at it," Sly said. "I suppose that's why you're the team leader."

"Or maybe I was just in the right place at the right time," Alex said.

"No way. There's never been anyone who can do what you can, bro. We're the best of the best and you're a big part of that."

Alex didn't know what to say. He wasn't trying to be humble, but he felt uncomfortable at the center of attention. Alex hadn't done anything to earn the special abilities he was using; they had just appeared. And what Sly didn't know, or anyone else for that matter, was that his special abilities were costing him something. He couldn't say what was happening, but it wasn't good. The stabbing heat behind his eyes was so common that he was beginning to take it for granted—when it didn't overwhelm him.

"If that's true, it's because I have the best partners."

"Awwh shucks," Sly teased.

Well, that much is obvious.

"And I wouldn't have it any other way," Alex said.

CHAPTER TWENTY-FOUR

"Ahzco warship, this is Skandia Orbital Control. You are ordered to leave the system immediately."

The message played over the bridge loudspeaker. It reminded Loman of a parent trying to rein in an unruly child by counting to three. The first two numbers were really just to make the parents feel like they were putting in the effort and to justify the punishment that they're preparing to dish out.

"Have our Titan's stand-by for launch," Loman said.

"Opening Titan MBS bay doors," said the fire control officer.

"Patch me through to Cronus Team Leader," Loman said. The communications officer pressed an icon on her screen and pointed at the VP. "Ace, remember the drill. Follow us but get close to those ships. Don't fire unless they get aggressive with you or you get an order from me."

"Roger. Titans are ready, Commander."

"Launch!" Loman ordered.

The fire control officer carried out the order and Loman turned back to the comms station.

"Put me through to Skandia Orbital Control," he said. "But send the broadcast wide. I want every media ship in the system picking this up."

It took a few seconds to get the broadcast ready. The communications officer's hands flew over her controls. When she had everything set, she turned back to Loman.

"It's ready, Commander."

Commander was the code name for the VP, since mentioning his name or his actual rank would tempt other private military ships to take a shot. It's not every day that the executive vice president of Ahzco security ventures out into harm's way. Loman was known as a competent commander-in-chief. Capturing him would be a major coup for any mega-corp military. Killing him would be profitable for the opposing military, but it would set Ahzco back and make their assets vulnerable. Loman was tasked with protecting nearly two dozen worlds and hundreds of thousands of employees. With the top man out of the picture, other companies would grow bold.

The *Currency* was still officially Captain Poe's ship. He had been removed from duty, but Loman had no intention of firing him. Once they were out of the system, an agreement could be reached with Poe, but until then, Loman was in command. He cleared his throat and spoke clearly so that the bridge communications system would pick it up.

"Skandia Orbital Control, we have passengers to deliver to your space station."

"Negative, negative," came the immediate reply. "Your business license has been revoked, and you are ordered to leave the system forthwith. Failure to comply could result in direct action against your vessel."

"Orbital Control, we are an independent ship transmitting in the clear. According to FTA guidelines, you have no grounds to keep us from docking and allowing passengers off this ship."

"You're in the Skandian system, *Currency*. This is a free world and we don't want your passengers. You are ordered to adjust your heading to three zero niner degrees and proceed to the space tunnel."

"Orbital Control, we have passengers requesting that we deliver them to the space port in this system."

"You are a foreign ship, with foreign passengers. According to the Free Trade Association bylaws, if a ship is deemed a threat, we have the authority to order it out of the system. Ahzco ship *Currency*, you are hereby ordered to leave Skandian space immediately."

Loman smiled. They had walked straight into his trap. He hoped that every ship in the system was watching. It was inevitable that someone had to be live streaming this stand-off, and not just to the Skandian planetary network, but also on the galactic web.

"Orbital Control, do not fire on us. We are attempting to deliver nine Skandian citizens to your space station. I repeat," Loman almost chuckled, "we have nine survivors on board from the *Reaper One*, which your vessels fired upon. They have requested that we return them to the Skandian space port, which we intend to do."

There was no immediate reply. Not only did the *Currency* have the legal standing to dock at the space port and deliver the guards from the *Reaper One*, but by telling Orbital Control about the survivors and announcing that it was their own fighters who blew up the transport, Loman had shown his hand. He intended to deliver a group of people who could back up his story.

Truth didn't matter nearly as much as perception, which was why Loman had announced his version of events. Witnesses could be bribed to say anything; results could be doctored to read a certain way. But by telling his side first, Loman had set the course for the narrative coming out of Skandia. It would be twisted by those with an agenda, he knew, but it was always better to strike the first blow, which is what he'd just done. When the Orbital Control response played over the *Currency's* bridge speakers, Loman knew things were about to get serious.

"Ahzco ship *Currency*, there were no survivors from the *Reaper One* transport, which your personnel took over by force. It is clear that you have committed crimes against the people of Skandia and will not be allowed into port. Change course now or prepare to be fired upon."

Loman held up his hand and the communication officer pressed a button to mute the bridge mics that were transmitting Loman's side of the conversation.

"Get me the names and service numbers of those guards," Loman ordered Lieutenant Jones. "Send word to Cronus Team to begin disrupting the fighters. And have our point defense system ready."

He nodded at the communications officer, who unmuted the com-link.

"Orbital Control, this is the commander on board the Ahzco vessel *Currency*. Do not fire at us. We have nine Skandian natives, all members of your military on board," Loman said, as the names and service numbers popped up on the display screen. "Sergeant Witmore, Phillip, service number 28137-0883."

He read through every name, knowing that somewhere, people were looking up the names and records of the guards. Their pictures would be added to the news stories, their families found and put on video that would be uploaded to the galactic web. The standoff on Skandia Seven was becoming a major story with every name that Loman read. He knew it wouldn't be enough to keep the fighters from firing at them, but he was counting on the ship's armor and their point defense weapons systems to keep them alive. The *Currency* was less than a thousand kilometers from the space port. There were hundreds of other ships in the vicinity of the space station. If he could just get close enough, the Skandians wouldn't be able to justify the risk of firing at him. And of course, Loman had a secret weapon—Ace Evans in a Titan battle suit.

CHAPTER TWENTY-FIVE

CAPTAIN POE WAS in his quarters on the *Currency*, which were opulent, comparatively speaking. His bedroom was twice the size of the berths that Cronus Team occupied, with a private desk and trio of cedar-lined lockers for his uniforms. In addition, he had a private sitting room, with a sofa and two tufted, faux leather chairs.

He sat in one of the chairs, nursing a cocktail that he had mixed with cranberry juice. Another perk of being a senior officer was the means to procure victuals and space on board to store them. The liquor was in a tall bottle that he kept in a small, refrigerated unit that looked like part of his entertainment cabinet. Poe rarely drank, reserving his libations for times when he was certain not to be called into action. A small speaker was transmitting everything from the bridge to his sitting area. He didn't need a visual feed, although he could have pulled that up. The bridge on Ahzco warships had cameras to record the senior officers in the midst of their decision making.

But Captain Poe was only half listening. His attention was on the message he had just gotten on his private account. Upon being relieved of duty, he had messaged his secret benefactor, letting her know that he had stumbled upon an operator with unique abilities in whom she might be interested. He hadn't expected such a swift response. His benefactor was a busy woman with wide-ranging responsibilities. Normally, their interactions took several days between responses. But she seemed acutely interested in the operator that Poe had discovered.

After getting her response, he looked up Sergeant Evans' service record. It was clear that he was VP Haley's poster boy, but other than saving the executive's life, and taking part in the military operations in the Carthage system, there was nothing special to note. Certainly, no mention of the operator's unique abilities. Poe was angered that no one had bothered to mention those abilities to him before the mission. He was the captain, the senior officer in charge. He should have been fully briefed about Sergeant Evans and exactly what the young operator was capable of doing. All Poe knew for certain was that he could hack into other vehicle operating systems. Poe didn't know how, but he assumed that Ace had a special device or had modified his Titan battle suit. It was no secret that the suit he wore on Skandia had been highly customized.

But it wasn't Alex's abilities that confounded Poe; it was his benefactor's interest. She seemed to know more than Poe did. He didn't know how that was possible, but he had no doubt that she was well connected. One of her specialties was cultivating relationships with powerful people. The fact that he was one of those people was not lost on him. Poe had ambitions. He liked being in charge and planned to stay that way.

It made him nervous to think that Haley had sent the prize operator out on a dangerous mission. That the VP insisted on putting the *Currency* in needless danger astounded Poe. He had heard the warnings from Skandian Orbital Control. There was a good chance they would all die if the reckless fool didn't show a little caution. They needed to leave the system. There was a perfectly good space port in the next system where no one wanted to kill them. They could drop off the passengers and be done with the whole, disastrous mission, but Loman Haley was a madman.

Poe looked at his PIL. His instructions were clear. Regain control of his ship and deliver Sergeant Alex Evans to Lynn Faulk at the Crossmenian Station. He sat back and bided his time, taking another sip of the cocktail. It was ice cold, yet it left a trail of heat in its wake as it flowed over his tongue and down his throat. Soon Haley would come calling, wanting to make peace. All Poe had to do was wait, and he was a patient man. In time, there would be new leadership in Ahzco, perhaps even over the galaxy as a whole. He had been assured that there would be a place for him in the new regime. Poe's importance could not be overlooked, and that filled him with a sense of satisfaction.

He reviewed his list of tasks:

Survive the deteriorating situation in the Skandia system.

Get reinstated.

Deliver the boy.

CHAPTER TWENTY-SIX

ALEX WAS EXHAUSTED AND HURTING, but he felt better being in the Titan battle suit. Flying was the most exhilarating thing he'd ever done, and he knew he could never give it up. Piloting a ship surely had its perks, but it wasn't like being connected to his Titan through the INC, which made him feel as if he *were* the battle suit. It wasn't a cage; it was pure, unadulterated freedom.

After dropping out of the *Currency*, Alex and Sly had flown in what was essentially a giant loop. They hadn't come in behind the fighters. Alex feared that might be seen as too aggressive. Instead, they had taken a position above the Skandian ships. A few were ahead of him, and more were behind. They had spread out in a long line just a few hundred kilometers behind the *Currency*. Alex knew that they couldn't keep up with the fighters. Their ships were made for blinding speed and agility. But Alex had a weapon they couldn't see or avoid, no matter how strong their armor or how talented their pilots.

Alex, we've got the green light.

"Okay, preparing to sync now," Alex said.

He could feel the computer systems on the fighters. They were like a hum in the air. Not that there was air in space, or any actual sound at all. His INC registered the EM waves and his brain translated them as sounds.

"Stand-by, Sly," Alex ordered. "I've been given the order to disrupt the fighters."

"Roger, team leader," Sly said.

He was a jovial person who enjoyed good humor. He could make light of almost any situation, but in combat he was a professional. Their friendship was put away, and he treated Alex like a superior. It was just one of the many small things that Alex admired about his friend.

Tell me when you've got a good connection. I'm monitoring all systems.

"Thanks, Nyx. Here goes nothing."

He let his mind snap onto the nearest of the fighters. The EM waves began to feed information straight into Alex's mind. He saw that the small ships were armed with ship-to-ship missiles and deep space torpedoes. The *Currency* had weapons made to shoot down incoming missiles and torpedoes, but if all of the fighters fired their weapons at the same time, some would get through the *Currency's* defenses. It only took a small issue to disable the biggest of ships: a hull breech, damage to an engine, a short in the vessel's electrical system. The *Currency* was a war ship, with thick armor and numerous redundancy systems, but anything could happen in battle. Better to make sure the fighters didn't have the chance to fire on the *Currency*.

He focused on the fighter's controls and activated a directional thruster. The small ship suddenly started angling up and back. Alex could hear the pilot's panic over the ship's communications system.

"Blue four, Blue leader, what's your status? Over," a stern voice said.

"Blue leader, Blue four, my directional thrusters are malfunctioning! I can't stop it."

Alex almost laughed. The ship was angling away from the *Currency*, out into deep space. His connection to the ship was slipping, and the last thing he did was cut the ship's power. The sync was lost, but as Alex watched as the glow of the fighter's engines faded away. Its momentum kept it moving farther off course.

Any idea how long it will take them to restart their systems?

"None," Alex admitted. "But it's keeping him busy for now."

Keep going.

Alex let his mind sync to the next fighter. He got connected just as the team leader was finishing up orders.

"... tighten up that formation. We're weapons hot people."

Alex was split between his Titan and the fighter labeled Blue five, but all of his focus was on the Skandian ship. He perceived the ship's weapons systems coming online and used the opportunity to trigger a power overload.

"Mayday, mayday," the pilot shouted. "I've got an unstable power surge."

"Bailout!" came the stern order from Blue leader. "Get out before it blows."

Alex dropped Blue five and picked up the nearest ship. He waited for a moment, letting Blue five eject. A second later, the fighter exploded in mid-flight and Alex immediately cut off Blue six's engines.

There were eight fighters in total pursuing the *Currency* and Alex had taken out three without firing a shot.

Good work.

"Thanks, I'm going after the leader now."

Roger that. I'll pass that on to the Commander.

"Sly, hold your position," Alex said.

"Roger, team leader," Sly said. "Nice work, by the way."

"We're having fun now," Alex said.

He accelerated. The need to get closer to the lead ship put a burden on the Titan. In space, his speed increased the longer he kept the suit's main thruster engaged, but it wasn't as simple as just pressing on an accelerator pedal and getting an immediate boost in speed. It took Alex a full minute to get within the thirty kilometers or so that he needed to sync to a foreign computer system. He let his mind snap to the lead fighter's ship, just as word came in from Skandian Orbital Control.

"... authority is given. Fire on the Ahzco ship at will."

Alex immediately shut down the team leader's weapons system and communications.

"What the hell?" the pilot snarled.

Alex took control of the thrusters and started a full retro burn. Blue two and three had to swerve to avoid him. Alex forced the ship off course, then cut its power. He dropped the ship from his INC and picked up Blue three. A sudden burst from the directional thruster sent it sliding sideways through space.

"What are you doing?" Blue two shouted. "Look out!"

The two ships would have collided, but Blue two was fast enough to avoid a deadly crash. Instead, he swerved and only got a small bump, but it was enough to send both ships spinning off course.

Alex, you've got company.

The blare of the Titan's missile detection system went off. The klaxon reverberated inside Alex's skull, adding to the fiery throbbing he felt as he pushed his abilities to control the fighters.

"Missiles are in the air," someone on the *Currency* announced.

Two missiles shot past Alex. They were locked on him, but they didn't endanger him at all. He raised his arm and fired a burst of short, but powerful lasers at the passing warheads. One exploded in a burst of light.

"Look out, Ace, we've got incoming missiles."

"Evasive maneuvers," Alex said.

He pulled up and away from the remaining fighter. It had fired at the *Currency*, and then at Alex and Sly.

"How many missiles?"

Just one, Nyx said. *I'm releasing countermeasures.*

Ten rotating flares ejected from the back of the Titan battle armor. They ignited and began to spin behind Alex. He altered course and rotated around so that he was flying backward. The missile flew into the flares and detonated.

"Where's Sly?"

He just took out the missile tracking him.

"Good, I'm going after that fighter," Alex said.

The fighter was still chasing the *Currency* but had activated the small ship's thrusters and was racing past Alex's position. He only had a few seconds of connectivity, but it was enough. His INC synced to the fighter and Alex surged the power supply. Alex's connection to the fighter broke off, and he felt an intense pain in his head. He groaned in agony. The small ship exploded a few seconds later, but Alex didn't see it. The pain in his head was so intense, he passed out.

CHAPTER TWENTY-SEVEN

"ALEX!" Nyx said. "Talk to me. Are you okay?"

Unlike some battle suits, the Titan MBS didn't have pilot vital readings. It was, in Nyx's opinion, a major fault in the suit's design. As his controller, Nyx needed a constant awareness of Alex's health and abilities. She could only guess what had happened. He was wounded and pushed to the point of exhaustion. Perhaps connecting his INC with other vessels was causing him some kind of harm, but she could only speculate, since the Titan didn't give her any measure of his physical well-being.

"Commander," Nyx said, activating her link to the ship's communication system. "I've lost Cronus Leader."

"He was hit?"

"Negative, but I've lost him somehow," Nyx said. "No contact. All systems green."

"Can you get him home?" Nyx could hear the concern in Loman's voice.

"Yes, sir," she said. "I have complete control of his MBS."

"Alright, well, our tail is clear, thanks to Cronus Team. Let's see this through."

Nyx began to maneuver Alex back onto course. The *Currency* was already beginning to slow down, and Nyx knew that Alex would catch up to the ship in time. It might even be easier to come back on board once they were docked at the space station.

"Sly?" Nyx said through the team channel of the com-link. "I've lost Alex."

"He's okay," Sly said. "He's ahead of me now."

"I'm piloting his suit. He's unresponsive. Stay close and help me keep an eye out for trouble."

"Roger that, Nyx. You think he's okay?"

Her gut told her no. Alex wasn't okay. There was something seriously wrong with him. Probably something to do with the new abilities that he hadn't told anyone about. She remembered seeing how drained he looked after using his INC to connect to computing systems that were never meant for outside control. How he had managed to do it baffled her, but the very idea that he could sync to an interstellar war ship and manipulate, much less control, its systems had to put a strain on him. Those same ships required several people to monitor and control those systems. It was no wonder he was in trouble.

"I hope so," she said honestly. "You've both been through a lot over the last forty-eight hours."

"He's carried the load," Sly said. "He may have just passed out."

"I'll get him back on the ship," Nyx said. "Good work out there."

"Thanks, Nyx. Take care of our boy. I've got your six."

The flight into the space port took half an hour. Until she fired the retro thrusters, there was very little for Nyx to do but worry about Alex. He didn't come to until she was maneuvering him back inside the *Currency's* hangar.

"Whass-goin-on?" he asked, his words slurring together.

"Alex? Are you okay?"

"Dunno," he replied. "My head hurts."

"I've almost got you back to the ship. Just relax."

Unlike when she spoke to him, his words came to her over the com-link. But he was firmly in her heart and she knew that if there was anything seriously wrong with him, she would never forgive herself. She had worried about his abilities. It was amazing, but she had a feeling that it was also dangerous. She didn't like thinking about it, so she hadn't. As if just ignoring a problem would make it go away. She felt foolish and scared that she might lose him.

The big hangar doors opened. She could have flown him into the narrow chute that opened directly to the Titan bay, but VP Haley had thought it safer to get him in the main hangar where the medical techs were waiting to help him. She landed the Titan and walked it through the partition to the medics standing by. It was infuriating that other people had to help him, and that she was stuck seeing to the mechanized battle armor.

Once they got Alex out, he was awake, but struggled to comprehend what was happening. Nyx, with the help of some of the Oscar Company operators, got the Titan suit onto a charging rack. Only after she powered down the suit's systems and notified her superior did she have the freedom to rush down to the medical bay. When she got there, a short, but muscular female corporal with caramel-colored skin was standing in the doorway to the med bay, along with Sly and few others.

"What are they saying?" Nyx asked.

"Who's she?" Sansabar asked.

"Sand, this is Nyx, Ace's controller," Sly said. "Nyx, Corporal Ayla Sansabar, from Oscar Company. They haven't said anything yet. They're running a full scan."

"He didn't seem to be hurt too badly," Sansabar said. "The patch on his shoulder had only just barely soaked through."

"Probably just exhaustion," Sly said. "I know I feel like I could sleep for a week."

Nyx worried that it was more than just fatigue, but she wasn't a medical expert, and Alex hadn't really complained about anything. It was just her intuition, but she trusted it.

"Any idea how long we're staying in port?" Nyx asked. "It might be better if he was taken to a larger medical facility."

"Not in this system," Sly said.

"The VP is down talking to the Zen Tech and Bazmore operators," Sansabar said. "He was encouraging them to tell their story."

"I hate that this is all so political," Nyx said.

"No doubt," Sly said. "Give me an enemy to fight over this posturing for the cameras any day."

They stayed by the entrance to the med bay, although they soon slumped down with their backs against the walls. It wasn't long until Vice President Haley appeared. He looked tired too, but there was satisfied twinkle in his eyes.

"How's our boy?" he asked Nyx, who quickly climbed to her feet.

"They're running tests. No word yet," she confessed.

"Well, we're on our way out of the system. I'll be leaving the ship once we reach the Crossmenian Station, but the *Currency* is on its way to the Helena system. I want Alex to get a full checkup."

"Me too," Nyx said. "Thank you."

"Walk with me for a moment, Sergeant," Haley said.

The others watched them go. Nyx could feel their eyes on her, especially Corporal Sansabar's.

"I need you to keep a close eye on Alex," Loman Haley said to her in a quiet voice. "There is no doubt that we've asked a lot of him."

"Yes, sir," Nyx agreed.

"We're going to need him in the days to come, but I don't want to push it," Haley continued. "He needs some rest and recuperation. Once you're on New Helena, you'll have some leave. Make sure he spends it as quietly as possible."

"I can do that."

"I know you can. Look, everything is changing. I honestly don't know what we may face tomorrow, or what we might need from the CDF, but if he isn't up to it, say the word. I'm going to put operational oversight into your file. It doesn't give you the right to say what Cronus Team will do, but if things get scary, you can pull the plug."

"I'm not sure what to say," Nyx replied.

"Say you'll keep the company's best interests in mind, Sergeant," Loman said. "We're at a crossroads, and the things we do now could very well determine the future for millions of people."

"I understand," Nyx lied. She couldn't imagine her actions affecting so many people.

"I believe Alex is at the heart of it all," Loman said. "But he can only do so much. I'll be watching, even from a distance. If I don't see you again, good luck, Sergeant."

"Thank you, sir. It was an honor seeing you in command. I've never witnessed anything like it."

Loman laughed, but he seemed to take the compliment to heart. When Nyx got back to the medical bay, the doctor was waiting.

"We're all here now?" he asked in a condescending tone that made Nyx angry. She couldn't wait to get off the *Currency* and away from the petty rivalries that defined her crew.

"Yeah, doc, go ahead," Sly said.

"Your friend is okay. There aren't any major deficits to be concerned with. He's dehydrated, the wound on his shoulder has a minor infection, and he's suffering from sleep deprivation. It oftentimes looks much worse than it is. But all he needs is rest and fluids, and he'll be fine. We'll keep him here overnight on an IV drip and observation, but I have complete confidence that he'll be fully recovered in twenty-four to thirty-six hours."

"That's a relief," Sly said.

"Can we see him?" Nyx asked.

"He's sleeping. And from the looks of things, you all could use some yourselves," the doctor said. "Hydrate, sleep, and check back tomorrow. I assure you, he's perfectly safe."

"What about Ash?" Sly asked. "Any improvement?"

"Corporal Timmons's brain activity is increasing. She could wake up at any time, or not. Only time will tell. You can check on her tomorrow as well. Now shoo, you're blocking the medical bay."

Nyx didn't like being shooed away. The fussy, old doctor had no idea what they had been through while he sat, oblivious to the dangers, in his med bay. But that was his job and it was the best care that Alex was going to get for a while. The truth was, she could already feel her stress melting away. Alex was alright, and the ship was on its way out of the Skandian system. The danger was behind them, and the doctor was right. She needed food and rest. She would rather have seen Alex. It didn't sit well with her to not see him and she had been too busy when he was carried up from the hangar bay. Waiting wasn't her strong suit, but she would endure with the knowledge that Alex was safe and her work was done.

CHAPTER TWENTY-EIGHT

LOMAN CHECKED in on the bridge. They had dropped off the passengers despite the Skandian authorities' insistence that they refrain from docking. Loman had dealt with enough obstinate bureaucracies to know that each branch loved to piss off the other. Skandian Orbital Control was based on the planet, but didn't actually have oversight of the space port, which was run by another branch of the planet's government. While Orbital Control railed on about how the *Currency* had no rights in the Skandian system, the space port welcomed them with open arms. Loman and the crew of the *Currency* didn't step foot outside of the ship, but he made sure that the multitude of reporters and internet personalities knew exactly where they would be docking. He watched from a distance as the guards and former detainees were greeted by crowds of eager reporters, anxious to hear their stories.

There was no way to guarantee that the guards told the

truth. They could lie, and he wouldn't even blame them. To tell the truth about what had happened would put them at odds with the vocal majority who wanted to hear nothing else but how bloodthirsty and inhumane private militaries were. But the truth was out there. The entire mission, from the moment the prison transport had broken out of atmo, had been caught on multiple cameras. Some would spin the story, but a few would tell the truth. And to the people who cared about the truth, it would be available.

Loman stepped onto the bridge of the ship. He didn't approach the pit, where Lieutenant Rory Jones was standing easily. Everyone at their stations seemed relaxed. There were no more threats coming from Orbital Control, no more fighter crafts coming to hurry them out of the system.

"What's our status?" Loman asked.

"Four hours to the space tunnel," Lieutenant Jones reported.

"Any traffic?"

"Mostly incoming vessels. Everything looks clear."

"Don't get complacent," Loman said. "There are people on Skandia who would give their right arm to see us dead after the stunts we just pulled. I don't want us to leave heightened readiness until we're out of the system."

"Roger that, Commander," Jones said.

"I'm going to give the ship back to Poe," Loman said. The smiles on the faces of the officers wavered. "He'll have orders to take her straight back to the Helena system for refit, including a new crew. You've all done well, and I'll make note of your performance today in each of your records. Ultimately, reassignment will come from Colonel Chastain. But I will make my recommendations."

"Thank you, sir," Lieutenant Jones said.

"Just make sure you finish well," Loman said. "I'll be leaving the ship at the Crossmenian Station."

He turned and left the bridge. He had one more bit of unpleasant business to attend to before he got some much-needed rest. The stress of the battle had taxed his body more than anything he'd done since the ambush that Alex Evans had saved him from in the Helena system. Somehow, it seemed that every time he spent time with Ace Evans, his life got more exciting than he'd bargained for.

The crew had their quarters on the level below the command deck, and above the engineering level. The only exception was Captain Poe, who had a berth on the command level so that he could be close to the bridge. Loman stopped at the Captain's door and pressed the guest announcement button.

After a second, during which Loman was certain that Captain Poe saw a video picture of Loman at his doors, they opened with a swish. The tall, black Captain did not rise. He was sitting in a comfortable chair with a drink on a side table. He tucked his PIL into a pocket of his uniform as Loman walked in.

"May I?" Loman asked, before sitting down.

"Be my guest," Captain Poe said. "Can I get you something?"

"No thanks, I just here to finish up my business. I'm sure you know we're on our way out of the Skandian system."

"I am aware," Poe said.

"You have a fine ship, but your crew is divided, smug, and I hate to say it, poorly disciplined."

"Your opinion," Poe replied.

"It's my opinion that counts," Loman said, trying not to sound condescending.

"For now."

"Yes, for now. That may change, but until it does, I'm the VP of security. When I give orders, I expect them to be carried out. That said, you're a valuable officer and I don't want to lose you. I want you to resume your duties and see the *Currency* back to the Helena system for refit. Once there, you'll receive new orders."

"A new command?"

"If that's what Colonel Chastain believes is best for you," Loman said. "I trust her to make personnel assignments, and frankly, there are other fires that need my attention. I don't have time for politics and games. Buck up, do your job, Captain, and we'll have no problems."

Captain Poe chuckled. "You have a lot of nerve coming on my ship and telling me how to do my job."

"I'm the head of the division," Loman said, trying to keep his anger in check. "You're a captain. You report to Colonel Chastain, and she reports to me. If I want to tell you to wear a pink hat and speak pig-latin on board the ship, I'll do that. If you can't follow those orders, I'll accept your resignation now."

"You've let your position go to your head," Poe said, his voice dripping with malice.

"Captain, I've been in my position longer than you've been in the CDF," Loman said. "Nothing has gone to my head."

"Perhaps you've been in command too long," Poe said. "You are wasteful, reckless, and on the verge of out of control."

"Your opinion doesn't mean shit to me, Captain. Now do you want your damn job back or not?"

"I do," Poe said. He looked like he was about to say more, but Loman quickly rose to his feet and started for the door.

"Fine, do better," Loman called over his shoulder. "I'll be disembarking at the Crossmenian Station. From there, take the *Currency* back to the Helena station."

He didn't bother to inform the arrogant captain that he would be riding a desk for the rest of his career and given the tasks that no one else wanted. Loman didn't like to lose his cool with subordinates, but at times it was inevitable. He left the captain's quarters and headed straight for the elevator. He needed to file several reports before snatching a few hours of sleep, and he wasn't even sure where the guest quarters were located on the little ship.

CHAPTER TWENTY-NINE

ALEX WOKE AND LOOKED AROUND. He felt better, but it was clear that he was in the medical bay. There was a large contraption hanging over his wounded shoulder, using light therapy to speed the healing process. He looked to his left, away from the glare, and saw Ash lying in the bed next to him, her eyes open.

"Hey," Alex said in a raspy voice. He wasn't thirsty but his mouth was dry.

She managed a weak smile but didn't speak.

"How are you feeling?"

She gave a little head shake.

"It's good to see you. We were worried. That missile came out of nowhere. We're back on the *Currency*. Have you seen the doctor?"

Another tiny nod.

"You should rest, Ash. Things will get better."

Alex believed that, but he couldn't help but feel a pang of

worry for Ash. He could see the pain etched on her face. Would she be the same? One second she had been doing her job, working with Alex and Sly, placing herself between a child and an avenue of escape. The next second she was on death's door. She never even saw the missile that hit her. She had been knocked unconscious by the blast, and all she knew when she came to was pain.

He felt tears stinging his eyes, but none fell. He closed his eyes and felt sleep coming to claim him again. There was no reason to fight it. After all, he had done his part. He could hear the medical equipment as his ears hummed and beeped. He could also hear every component with his INC. The EM waves hummed, but his head didn't hurt. There was only the slightest heat behind his eyes, and the absence of pain felt luxurious. He was safe, his labors over for the moment, and he let himself sleep.

When he woke again, a medical technician was changing the empty fluid bag that fed into his IV. The man helped Alex get out of bed and use the bathroom. He didn't feel sick or injured, just tired and a little unsteady. His breakfast was waiting for him when he got back to his bed, and Alex discovered that he was ravenous. He ate the entire tray of food—eggs, pancakes with syrup, round sausage patties, toast, fruit, and a small bowl of oatmeal. By the time he finished, the doctor had arrived.

"You're looking better," he said. "As I expected. How do you feel?"

"Better," Alex said.

The doctor inspected the wound on his shoulder, which had been sealed with bio-adhesive and treated with light therapy.

"This is better, but I want to keep it under light through the morning," the doctor said. "You can have visitors, but don't get worked up. Rest is the best medicine for you right now. I'll be back to check it again. You'll be cleared to leave this afternoon."

"Thank you," Alex said.

The doctor smiled, but it wasn't a happy smile. It was acceptance. The man was clearly unhappy and was barely putting in the effort to hide it. But Alex felt better than he had in a long time. There was no mission hanging over his head, no need to train, or wonder how things would go on a new ship. He didn't feel out of place, or even in the way. He was tucked away, perfectly content, well looked after, and out of danger. For the time being, it was all he wanted.

"You look better," a weak voice said from the next bed over.

Alex turned as the medical tech began arranging the light therapy machine over his shoulder. He wasn't looking at the technician, but at Ash. She was on her side, and there were several tubes visible under the gown she wore.

"Hey, Ash, how are you?"

"Broken and not yet put back together again," she said. "I can't even move on my own."

"That's only temporary," the technician who was working on Alex's therapy machine said. "She's got a nerve block just above the wound so that she can't feel it."

"And can't do anything but lay here," Ash complained.

There was a trace of her defiance, at least. The old Ash was still there, but she looked small and weak.

"What happened?" she asked once the tech had the therapy light set up and moved along.

"On Skandia Seven?"

"No, on your head?" she said sarcastically. "What happened to me?"

"You were shot with a rocket," Alex said. "There were protesters down in that public transport station. They fired some kind of missile or rocket-propelled grenade."

"Not surprising," Ash replied. "It feels like I got blown up."

"It was chaos," Alex went on. "A coordinated attack. We were trying to help you when more protesters showed up on the rooftops of the buildings. The kid's backpack exploded and took out the factory. We spent hours trying to dig out the survivors."

"Your dad?"

"He made it," Alex said. "Saved a few people in the process, but we had losses, too."

"God, what a disaster. What happened to the kid?"

"What kid?"

"The one who dropped the backpack?"

"I don't know," Alex said. "He disappeared. All I can say for certain is that he didn't get killed. He knew enough to get out of there."

Alex went through the all of the events that came after the attack, and before he was finished, visitors started to arrive. Nyx was the first. She looked beautiful to Alex, a sight for sore eyes. When she saw him, her smile was dazzling.

"I'm so glad you're okay," she said.

"I just pushed things a bit too far," he admitted. "I should have listened to you."

"Sure, *now* you can admit it," Nyx said playfully.

"He's the type who thinks he has to do it all himself," Ash said.

"Isn't that the truth?" Nyx agreed. "How are you feeling, Ashton?"

"I'm not."

"They have her on a nerve block," Alex said. "She can't really move."

"What do you need?"

"See, wonder boy over there didn't even ask."

Nyx was sent to fetch Ash's PIL. Sly and Sansabar arrived together. The dark-skinned operator stood by Alex's bed and hardly spoke a word, but Sly wouldn't shut up. He checked in on Alex, but spent his time talking and cracking jokes with Ash. Alex didn't mind. They both knew she would need all the encouragement she could get. The daredevil of their Titan team wouldn't fare well being grounded.

Nyx returned with Ash's PIL and gave them an update. The ship had already passed through the tunnel from the Skandian system to the Crossmenian sector. It wasn't a star system, just a rogue star that powered a space port near an intersection of space tunnels. The *Currency* was preparing to dock.

At lunch time, the doctor sent their visitors away, checked Alex's shoulder, and cleared him to leave.

"It may be tight for a while," the doctor said. "There was some damage to the muscles and that can change the fiber structure. Be careful exercising it for a week or so."

"Roger that," Alex said. "Light duty for me, no problem."

"Yes, well, good for you, Sergeant. You are free to go, but

Captain Poe has sent for you. You're to report to him immediately."

"Straight to the principal's office," Ash said. "No surprise
there."

"Cool it," Alex said. "It's nothing."

He stood up and pulled on his fatigue shirt. It wasn't a
compression shirt, just a loose-fitting button up similar to what
the other specialists wore on the ship. He never saw the technician with a sedative patch step up behind him and slap it onto
his neck.

"What the?"

"Hey!" Ash shouted. "What are you doing?"

Alex wanted to fight back, but there were no attackers, just
the same friendly medical technician. And no matter what Alex
wanted to do, the sedation patch went to work immediately. He
suddenly felt as if he weighed three times as much as normal;
he could barely stand up. His eyelids began to droop.

"Help!" Ash shouted. "Alex, stay with me."

He wanted to comply, to struggle, but it was no use. The
tech set him down on something; Alex wasn't sure what it was.
His thoughts were sluggish; his eyes wouldn't stay open. The
tech gently pushed him back and Alex didn't have the strength
to fight him off.

"What are you doing?" Ash snarled. "You can't do that."

"Just relax, sweetheart. We all have orders."

"The captain sent for him!" Ash said.

Alex couldn't understand why she was upset. He felt so
relaxed.

"True, but he ordered me to get him off the ship," the tech said. "We're just two deserters. See you around."

"No! Don't you dare. Come back."

Alex saw the technician adjust something on Ash's IV. That didn't seem right. She was upset, but Alex couldn't process what was going on. He just wanted to close his eyes. Ash stopped shouting. Her words slurred, or maybe Alex just thought they did. But he wasn't worried. He felt too good to worry, too warm and relaxed. It didn't even bother him when the tech closed the lid to the medical pod. He just let himself drift off to sleep.

CHAPTER THIRTY

WHEN NYX RETURNED to the med bay, she was promptly informed that Alex had been discharged. She was surprised that she hadn't seen him. The only person she had passed after running back to the cabin was the technician who was moving the emergency medical pod that Ash had been moved in down to the storage area on the bottom level of the ship. The lift had stopped on its way down, but she was going up and waited while it finished the downward journey and started upward again.

She had a strange feeling like something was wrong but consoled herself with the thought that Alex had probably gone looking for her on the upper deck where the recreation space was located. The chow hall was on the upper deck too, and he might have run into Sly or Sansabar there. She went up to the chow hall and saw the doctor, but not Alex.

"What's wrong?" the doctor asked.

"I can't find Sergeant Evans," Nyx admitted.

"He was discharged with orders to see Captain Poe."

"He was?"

"I'm sure of it. I gave him the order myself."

Nyx hurried back down to the command level, hoping to see Alex in the corridor, but it was empty. She went past the bridge, peeking in and hoping not to be seen. She was persona non grata with Captain Poe since breaking into the communication exchange he was having with VP Haley. It had been the right thing, she knew, but he hated her for it. The VP coming on board the ship was her only saving grace. The captain couldn't have the one person VP Haley had asked for still locked up in the ship's brig. He had sent her to get cleaned up and to wait for the vice president in her quarters. He made it very clear that he never wanted to see her again, and for her part, Nyx felt the same way. But she desperately wanted to find Alex. She was almost willing to buzz the captain's personal quarters in the hopes of finding her operator, but she decided to wait. The captain couldn't keep him there for long, even if he was lecturing Alex on everything the captain thought was wrong about the mission.

It wasn't long before she saw a familiar face, but it wasn't who she was expecting. Sly arrived on the deck and was headed for the med bay.

"Have you seen Alex?"

"Isn't he in the med bay?"

"No, they released him," Nyx said. "The doctor said he was ordered to report to the captain."

"Well, I guess I could have missed him, but I didn't see him downstairs. I just came up from my cabin."

"That it so strange," Nyx said.

"I was going to check on Ash, but I can help you look for him," Sly offered.

"No, it's okay," she said. "I'll find him."

Sly left and Nyx turned back toward the captain's quarters. She was pacing a few moments later when Sly returned.

"They won't let me in," he said. "Apparently Ash is sleeping, and they have orders not to let visitors in right now."

"Okay," Nyx said, frowning. "If that was the case, you would think they would have told us earlier."

"The medical staff is a bit high on their own importance if you ask me," Sly said.

"Agreed," Nyx said. "So what do we do now?"

"I'll go check his cabin," Sly said. "You stay here in case he's still in with the captain."

Nyx agreed, although she couldn't think of any reason why the captain would keep Alex for so long. A few minutes later, Lieutenant Jones left the bridge. He was walking past her, obviously headed for the lift, and Nyx couldn't help but ask him the question that was on her mind.

"Lieutenant, do you have a second?" she asked, falling into step beside him.

"Sure," Lieutenant Jones said. "What's up?"

"My operator was ordered to report to the captain, but I can't find him."

"Sergeant Evans, right? I saw that order. The captain is in his quarters now."

"So Alex could be in there with him, right?"

"I suppose," Jones said, frowning. "Although the captain doesn't normally permit anyone in his personal cabin. Have you checked all the places he might be?"

"Yes," Nyx said. It wasn't exactly true, but she was feeling desperate. "Is there any chance he got sent onto Crossmenian Station for something?"

"No," Jones said. "We just left. We're in transit for the Helena system now."

Nyx couldn't say how or why, but she knew that something was wrong. Part of her, something deep down, something she couldn't identify, was telling her that Alex wasn't on the ship.

"Is there a way to access who came and went from the ship while we were docked?"

Lieutenant Jones hit the button for the lift and nodded. "Sure, check the security logs. Anyone who left the ship had to swipe their ID."

She thanked the lieutenant and hurried to the control center. Dread was filling her and threatened to come pouring out. Her hands shook as she entered the command to bring up the security logs. There were only a few entries. One of the engineers had gotten off but returned. Vice President Haley had disembarked. And one other name was listed, but it practically jumped from the screen. At first, she couldn't place where she'd seen it before, but then it came back to her like a crack of lightning streaking across the night sky.

The medical technician. She hadn't asked his name but had seen it on the breast of his fatigue shirt. And she had run into him on his way down to the lower deck. It felt as if ice had formed in her veins. She had heard the expression that a person's blood ran cold, but she thought it was just a saying to express fear. When she thought of the emergency medical pod that the missing tech was pushing, however, she felt her blood run cold. She shivered and tears filled her eyes. There was no sign that the tech had left with anything, but she didn't know if the logs would show that. She ran back out of the control center and straight into Sly, who caught her.

"Hey!" he said, his voice filled with worry. "What's wrong?"

"The medical tech," she said. "He left with the emergency pod."

"So?" Sly asked.

"He left the ship," Nyx said. "He's still on Crossmenian Station and we've left the port."

"You're saying he stayed on the station?" Sly asked.

Nyx nodded.

"And you think... Oh, my God. You don't think Ace was in the pod, do you?"

"Yes," Nyx blurted.

"He could be in with the captain," Sly said.

"But I just spoke to Lieutenant Jones. He said Captain Poe doesn't like anyone being in his quarters."

"But we have to check," Sly said.

They hurried to the bridge, but there were only a few officers on duty there, and none of them were Captain Poe. Hurrying on, they went to his cabin and Sly pressed the buzzer.

"What is it, Corporal?" Captain Poe asked through the intercom.

"Sir, I'm looking for Team Leader Evans. I heard he was ordered to report to you once he left the medical bay."

"Are you saying he isn't in medical?"

"That's correct, sir. Has he reported in yet?"

"No, and I don't appreciate hearing that he felt something was more important than following the orders I gave him," Poe snarled angrily. "I want him in here on the double."

"We'll find him, sir," Sly said, but he looked at Nyx with fear in his eyes.

"Down to the engineering level," she said. "The technician said he was putting the pod in storage."

They ran to the lift, which opened and revealed Corporal Sansabar.

"Hey Sands, we need a little help," Sly said.

"I was going to check on Ace," Sansabar said.

Nyx felt a stab of jealousy but pushed it down. She had bigger problems than what was starting to look like a crush the corporal had on Alex.

"He's not in the med bay," Sly said. "Or his cabin. We're trying to find him."

They stepped into the lift and Nyx pressed the icon on the touch screen for the engineering level.

"Did you check his cabin?" Sansabar asked.

"Of course," Nyx said with more venom than she meant to. "We also checked the upper deck. He isn't there either."

"The medical assistant who was working with Alex," Sly said. "Do you know anything about him?"

"No," Sansabar asked. "Why?"

"I saw him leaving with the emergency medical pod," Nyx

said. "And when I checked the security log, it showed him leaving the ship."

"You mean he's on the space station?" Sansabar asked.

"Yeah," Sly said. "And we've already left."

"Then he's AWOL," Sansabar said, the puzzle coming together in her mind. "You think he had Ace in that med pod?"

"He could have," Sly said.

"But why?" Sansabar asked.

That was the one question that Nyx couldn't answer. It made no sense. VP Haley liked Alex and would have gladly taken him along on his next assignment, but he gave Nyx specific orders to ensure that Alex had some down time. And Captain Poe was angry about the mission, but Nyx didn't think he would take it out on Alex. In fact, he seemed surprised that Alex hadn't reported to him yet. Nothing about a kidnapping made sense. It was a mystery; but they hadn't found Alex, and there was a good chance they weren't going to.

CHAPTER THIRTY-ONE

LOMAN WAS ON A COMMERCIAL TRANSPORT. He had splurged on a first-class cabin. The room was small, with a display wall, and three reclining seats made of soft leather. There was a bed behind him, and a stewardess had just prepared him a cold gin martini with a twist. He had his feet up, the liquor warming his entire body. He knew it was only a matter of time before he could close his eyes and sleep all the way back to Arcadia. He wouldn't, of course. Loman didn't consider himself a workaholic, but he genuinely cared about the people who worked under him. And the threat to the company was very real. It was his responsibility to ward off danger that might hurt Ahzco, and more specifically, the hundreds of thousands of people who worked for the company.

He lifted his PIL and opened the messages app. Keeping up with his messages was a full-time job in itself: the budget inquiries, personnel requests, and meetings requests from inside the company and without. He was scrolling through the mail, looking for the most pressing messages, when he saw one from Sergeant Nyx West. He almost kept scrolling. It wasn't unusual after spending time with the people on the front lines that they sent messages that were nice, but not really important. They wanted to thank him or say how inspired they were. It was complimentary, and he didn't take it for granted, but he didn't stop his day to read the messages in most cases. But this time, something made him stop. The heading, which was all he could see of the message, said *EMERGENCY.*

He tapped the message and brought up a screen that looked like an old-fashioned sheet of paper. The message that was written on it was short and to the point.

Mr. Loman Haley, I'm sorry to bother you, but you should know that Alex Evans is missing. We are on our way out of the Crossmenian Sector, and we've searched the entire ship. He isn't here. I believe he was taken by a medical technician named Ernesto Sallizar using an emergency medical pod. I'm going to plead our case to Captain Poe, but if you are still on the Crossmenian Station, we could desperately use your help.

Sgt. Nyx West
Controller

Loman felt a stab of pain in his stomach. It was probably an ulcer, he told himself. The stress of his job was getting worse by the day. Under any other circumstances, he would have just made a note to have the matter looked into. Operators didn't go AWOL very often, and usually when they did, there were signs of mental instability or outside personal issues such as the illness of a family member. But Alex was a different matter. Loman couldn't just write him off or send a memo ordering one of the investigative specialists to look into the matter.

He set the half-finished martini aside and got up from the comfortable chair with a groan. He wasn't a young man and he was feeling the evidence of his recent adventures. He went to the door of this cabin, which slid open as he approached. One of the stewards saw him and stepped quickly up to offer assistance.

"Is something wrong, sir?"

"Actually, I have to get off the ship," Loman said. "How much time do I have."

"They're preparing to board the business class passengers. We've reserved half an hour for that, then another forty-five minutes to board the coach and economy ticket holders. If you're not back by the time they finish, the doors will be closed. We can't wait for you."

"I understand," Loman said. "Show me out, please."

The steward showed him to the private, first class exit. He passed through an open airlock and down a short passageway before going through a door that opened onto Crossmenian Station. There were people everywhere. Most were pulling luggage and moving toward transports that were docked on the station's spoke-like docking arms. Unlike some transit space stations, Crossmenian was small, with separate fueling and resupply stations nearby. Most of the locals were pilots moving goods from the separate stations to the ships that docked at Crossmenian.

Loman went straight to a private computing terminal and closed the booth's doors. His PIL was state-of-the-art, and had he been in Alluenza system near Arcadia, he could have linked the device to his powerful AI in the Ahzco HQ building. Unfortunately, he would have to settle for a less potent, but still useful hack that got him an unofficial list of the ships that were currently docked at the station. He went through the list but didn't recognize any of them, so he ran another program that traced ownership of the vessels. The programs weren't illegal, per se; interstellar ships technically did not have a right to privacy. In fact, it was illegal to fly without a working transponder or accurate reporting information. But most people who cared about their privacy found ways to hide who they were and what they were really doing. One of the most common ways to do so was to register a ship to a company or shell corporation that in most instances, makes it laborious to discover ownership.

For all Loman knew, the med tech Ernesto Sallizar could have gotten on a freighter or technical ship. But Loman couldn't simply run through the station hoping to spot a man with an emergency medical pod. He searched through the list of registries and got lucky. The *Silent Partner* was docked at the station, and the registration was listed as Sigma Services. Loman knew exactly who owned the ship and it was no surprise that they were after Alex. The only question was how much they knew.

Loman hurried from the booth, searching for the berth where the *Silent Partner* was docked. The station itself wasn't large, but the docking arms were long. He found the right platform and hurried down the long corridor to slip A18, but even before he reached the terminal, he could see that the ship was on its way out. The airlock was closed, and a red light showed above it. Loman approached anyway and looked through the small port. He could see a sleek-looking vessel pulling away from the station.

"You just missed 'em," a man nearby said.

Loman turned and saw a member of the station's janitorial staff. He was emptying a waste receptacle.

"By any chance, did you notice a man board this ship with an emergency medical pod?" Loman asked.

"Can't say I even know what that is," the janitor said with a grin. "But there was a fellow pushing a big luggage rack."

"Big enough for a person?" Loman asked.

"Oh yeah, those things can move enough gear for an entire family. I didn't see what was on it. I mean, I see a hundred a day. They just sort of blend together. But it was big. I figured he was a crew member moving luggage or something."

Loman glanced at his PIL. He still had time. He pulled a credit voucher from his pocket and handed it to the janitor.

"That's extremely helpful," Loman said. "Thank you."

"Thank you," the janitor said, looking at the thousand credit marker. It was small, the size of a poker chip, with Ahzco Financial Services printed on its face.

Loman hurried back down the corridor. He had no doubt that Lynn Faulk and her cabal of ultra-rich power brokers were behind Alex's abduction. It couldn't be a coincidence that a ship registered to Sigma Services just happened to be at the Crossmenian Station at the same time that the *Currency* came through and docked for a short time.

Loman realized that he had bigger problems than he realized. Someone in the CDF was helping Lynn Faulk or one of her partners. They could have discovered Alex's special abilities from several people outside of Loman's division within the company. The VP had done his best to keep it secret, but the bomb threat to the Ahzco HQ building had flushed him out. Not that Loman believed the bomb scare to have been concocted for that purpose. In fact, that fiasco had been planned and started before Alex even discovered that he could control more than other operators with his INC.

Loman didn't have to think very hard about who might be in Lynn Faulk's secret circle either. One name rose to the top of the list. Captain Poe had been much too confident, almost arrogant, in dealing with Loman. The insolent captain believed that Loman was not only on the way out, but that he had someone in his corner with even more pull in the company. And Loman had embarrassed Poe, giving the man all the reason he needed to go behind the VP's back.

Still, abducting a sergeant was a big deal. Captain Poe hadn't been acting alone. Ernesto Sallizar was someone else to look into. But all Loman could do at the moment was to get his people on the job. He hurried back to the transport and was taken past the interior section of the ship where passengers were sitting shoulder to shoulder in stiff-looking seats. He felt a pang of guilt about being able to close himself up in a luxurious private cabin, but he didn't have time for feeling guilty. There was no telling what plans Lynn Faulk had for Alex, and Loman owed the boy his life. He would do whatever it took to rescue him from the people planning to seize control of the galaxy.

He dropped into his seat and retrieved his PIL, then composed a message for Ciara Prince. He ordered her to find out all that she could about the *Silent Partner*, most importantly, where it was going. Next, she needed to dive deep into Captain Poe and Medical Technician Ernesto Sallizar. They were pieces of the puzzle and Loman needed to see where they fit in with the bigger players. Finally, he sent orders for Cronus Team to proceed directly from the Helena system to Arcadia. It wouldn't take them much longer to reach the golden planet than it would Loman, and he hoped by the time they arrived to have a plan to rescue Alex Evans.

CHAPTER THIRTY-TWO

ALEX WOKE up on a soft bed. It was strange to be in such a soft bed. The sheets were soft, too, and so thin. His head was pounding, and his mouth was dry. The room was dark, but he could tell he wasn't on the *Currency* anymore. He laid in the soft bed, cocooned in the silk sheets, wondering what had happened to him.

It didn't seem to have ended poorly. In fact, Alex had never experienced such extravagance in his life. Yet, despite the luxurious setting, he knew that something was wrong. He wasn't supposed to be there. In fact, he had no memory of getting there at all. He wracked his brain trying to remember what happened. The last thing he could recall was being in the medical bay of the *Currency* with Ash. He wondered if she was okay. Was it possible that they had both been moved to the place where Alex found himself?

"Hello," he said, his voice a croaking whisper.

There was no reply. He stirred in the bed, pulling back the sheets and trying to remember why he was there. His head hurt, but it wasn't the same burning, piercing pain behind his eyes that he was used to from his INC. And that was strange, too. The room was quiet—no EM waves. He sat up on the edge of the bed, letting his feet hang down to the polished wood floor. The room light came on automatically, and he heard a soft hum from the electrical current. The walls were paneled in dark red stained wood. There were gold finishes around the doors. One led to a closet, another to a small bathroom, and the third, out of the room.

Alex stood up intending to go towards the exit door, but he lost his balance and sat back down. He was dizzy; the room appeared to wobble around and around. He shut his eyes and waited for it to pass. He was beginning to feel a little nauseous when the door opened. The man who walked in wasn't wearing any type of uniform, but he looked familiar.

"Hey there, good to see you up," the man said.

"You're the medical tech from the *Currency*," Alex said, finally able to remember something.

"I was. Now I'm just a wealthy man here to help you. Call me Ernesto."

"I'm Alex," he croaked.

"You need to drink a lot of water," Ernesto said. "You've been out for a while. Nearly twelve hours. You need to rehydrate."

Ernesto handed Alex a large bottle of water. Until he saw the container, Alex hadn't realized how thirsty he was. He popped back the attached cap and sucked greedily at the water.

It flushed through his mouth, cool and sweet, before sliding down his parched throat. He immediately felt better. The headache was still there but diminished and the room stopped spinning.

"Where are we?" Alex finally asked.

"This is the *Silent Partner*. It's a private ship," Ernesto explained as he checked Alex's blood oxygen with a little clip that he applied to the end of Alex's finger. "Quite a step up, eh? I mean, dang, we couldn't afford a ship like this in a million life-times. This kind of luxury is reserved for the very, very rich, my man. So, sit back and enjoy the ride."

"I can't find my PIL," Alex said.

"That's because we didn't bring it," Ernesto said. "But don't worry. We've got everything you need."

"Who is we?" Alex asked. "Why aren't we on the *Currency*?"

"Because Captain Poe gave us an order," Ernesto said. "That's how life is with the CDF, man. It's all, "do this," "do that," "jump to," "on the double." We're better off, I can tell you that for certain."

"What do you mean?" Alex asked.

"What I mean is that you've just been given the golden ticket, Ace. You've been selected to be a key player in the future, man. I admit, I'm just the lucky SOB who happened to be in a position to make things happen, but that doesn't mean I'm not ready and willing to take advantage of the opportunity."

Alex had no idea what Ernesto was talking about. It only made him feel more disoriented.

"Where's Nyx? I need to talk to her."

"Nyx?" Ernesto said, with an almost mocking tone.

"Sergeant West," Alex said.

"I suppose she's still on the *Currency.*"

"Then why am I here?" Alex said, getting angry.

He stood up, put a hand on the polished wall to steady himself, and looked Ernesto in the eye.

"This doesn't make any sense," Alex said. "I don't know how I got here, or why. Someone better start giving me answers."

"Or what?" Ernesto said with a sneer. "You operators are all the same. You think that wearing a battle suit makes you superior? Do you really think that you're actually any stronger than me without that tech?"

Alex wanted to show Ernesto just how strong he was, but he needed answers, and hurting the medical tech wouldn't get them.

"I think you're up to no good," Alex said. "I think this entire setup is phony, and whatever it is you're trying to lure me into won't work."

"Man, you've got this all wrong," Ernesto said, as he headed for the doorway. "But I get it. Disorientation is a side effect of the sedation patch I hit you with. But don't worry, it fades. I just hope you're smart enough to see the opportunity here, man. This kind of luck doesn't come around very often."

The door swished open and Ernesto walked through. Alex started to follow but the door closed and wouldn't reopen. There were no controls that Alex could find. No keypad, no electronic movement sensor, not even a button to press or a hidden panel that could be opened to reveal the controls to the room. He was trapped.

Alex pounded on the door with the palm of his hand. "Hey! Let me out of here!" he shouted.

There was no response, and he could tell from hitting the door that it was made of thick metal underneath a thin veneer of wood. He checked the seams, but there was no way to get a hold on the door and force it open. A quick check of the closet revealed a few bland outfits in solid black. He was still in a thin hospital gown with nothing underneath it. He went to the bathroom, which was small, but well-appointed with a tiled shower, a marble vanity, and more gold fixtures. What was becoming more glaringly obvious was the absence of any electronics. The outer wall of the room had an actual window. He could see that they were in space, but nothing more. It had no touch controls, no way to cover the opening. Not that Alex expected to see people come floating by who might see him changing clothes. There was no display screen, no camera monitoring his activity, no intercom. The room was feeling more and more like a gilded cage to Alex.

He sat on the edge of the bed, trying to think things through. Trying to remember what had happened. Ernesto said that disorientation was a side effect of the sedation patch he had hit Alex with. He took that to mean he had been drugged and taken off of the *Currency* without consent. And he was in a room that was completely bereft of almost all EM waves with no way out. The only thing his INC could register was the barely audible hum of the electric light in the ceiling of the room.

Alex lay back on the bed, looking at the ceiling. It was made of gleaming white material that glowed to provide light. It looked seamless—no panels, no fixtures, no fissures to break through. He was trapped. It was frustrating, but he wasn't completely helpless. He had water and that was helping him. If he was going to escape, he didn't want to do it in a hospital gown. He sipped more water, ran a shower—which felt invigorating—and got dressed in a set of clothes from the closet, which was much larger than the lockers inside of which he was used to keeping his personal goods.

The clothes were simple, yet they fit him perfectly. Almost as soon as he sat down in the new outfit, the door opened. A small, service bot rolled into the room. Part of Alex wanted to bound to his feet and race through the open door, but there was barely room for the robot to pass through, and as soon as it was in the room, the door slid shut again. The service bot was little more than a rolling cart with hot and cold storage. The top was a dome, which slid back to reveal a tray extended out from the open dome, to create a table. Alex didn't need to get up; the service bot created a table for him to eat from. On the tray, he found a plate with thin slices of chicken on a bed of rice, surrounded by colorful vegetables. Next to the plate was a basket of sliced bread. A small dish of soft, golden butter sat between the basket and a glass with sparkling water.

It crossed Alex's mind that the food might be tainted. But why poison him when whoever was behind his abduction, as he had come to think of the situation, could have killed him any number of ways before he even awoke? If the food was compromised, it was probably with some type of drug that would make him more compliant. Yet what did Alex know that someone would need to coax out? He wasn't an officer. He had no clearance for access to secrets. Whatever his captors wanted, it wasn't information.

He took a bite and found the food to be delicious. He felt as if he hadn't eaten in days and devoured everything on the plate, along with all the bread. When he finished and leaned back in the chair, the serving bot retracted the tray and closed the dome. It then turned around and a panel opened, revealing a small basket of fruits, nuts, and candies, along with several bottles of different drinks. He picked out two bottles of soda and took the basket. He put the items on a table beside the chair as the serving bot rolled back toward the door, which opened once again.

Alex watched, trying to learn what he could about the ship on which he found himself. He was stuffed from the big meal and feeling tired again. He would have preferred to go on a walk, but he didn't think that would be an option. Leaping over the robot and trying to make an escape wasn't the best idea either. It was obvious that he was on a ship that was in space, not at a port. There were no other ships around that Alex could see. Even if he could break out of the room that he was being held in, where would he go? He decided to wait and see what would happen.

The robot rolled out of the room and the door closed again. But a few minutes later, the door opened, and a woman walked into the room. She was older than Alex, but it was hard to tell exactly how old. She was beautiful with flawless skin, her face perfectly symmetrical, her body thin, but not too skinny. Her clothes appeared to be perfectly tailored. Likewise, her hair and makeup made her look as if she had just walked out of a salon, or perhaps off of a movie set. She stood just inside the doorway, and Alex rose to his feet to face her. As beautiful as she appeared, Alex didn't find her attractive. In fact, there was a cold cunning in her eyes. It was a bit like looking at a poisonous snake.

"My name is Lynn Faulk," she said. "I'm chairwoman of the Ahzco Board of Directors."

Alex had no idea if she was telling the truth. He didn't know anything about the Ahzco leadership outside of the few people he had met.

"I'm sorry for the way in which you were brought on board," she continued, "but it was absolutely necessary."

"Why?" Alex asked, trying to keep the anger and irritation from his voice.

"Because there are people who are trying to destroy Ahzco," she replied. "People who don't care about the hundreds of thousands of employees who depend on the company—like your parents."

It made him angry that she even knew who his parents were.

"That fiasco on Skandia Seven should never have happened," she went on. "You'll be glad to know that your family has been moved and that they are safe."

"Where are they?"

"En route to a new home," Lynn Faulk said.

"Why did they need a new home?" Alex asked. "Isn't Ahzco going to rebuild the factory on Skandia Seven?"

"That decision is being made by the head of logistics and manufacturing," Lynn Faulk said. "But you've become a wanted man on Skandia Seven. All the detainees are considered criminals, and it's only a matter of time before someone discovered that your parents lived there. I know you wouldn't want them getting hurt because of you."

"Why would they be?"

"I don't think you understand the serious nature of your actions on Skandia Seven."

"I think I do," Alex said. "I was there."

"Precisely. You *were* there. And since your daring escape from the prison transport, the planet has become unstable. There are riots, murders, mass hysteria. People don't know what to believe. None of that is your fault, of course, but I just wanted you to know that we've taken steps to protect the people you care about."

"So why am I here?" Alex said. "What do you want?"

"That's simple, I want your help."

"You didn't have to drug me for that."

"No, I didn't. And again, I apologize for that. But unfortunately, it was necessary. We had to get you off that ship without anyone knowing."

Alex didn't believe a word coming from between Lynn Faulk's beautiful lips. He could tell she was lying; he just didn't know why.

"You have abilities that we don't fully understand," she proceeded. "Abilities that right now, experts are studying in great detail. Not just on Skandia Seven, but in every mega corporation that had people on the *Reaper One.* Soon, the truth about what happened will leak. Most people won't believe it's true, but there will be people of great influence who take notice.

People with resources and power, Alex. People who would stop at nothing to control you."

"People who might drug me and sneak me onto their ship?" Alex asked. "People who would lock me in a room that was completely cut off from all outside information?"

Lynn Faulk smiled. "Precisely. I like that you're smart, Alex. It will make this much easier. Let's dispense with the facade and get to business. I control Ahzco, including the INC in your brain. You can do things with that device that others can't. I want to know what you can do, and I want full control of it. Work with me and you'll be richly rewarded. Resist me and life will be very uncomfortable for you. I'm not an unreasonable woman. As you can see," she waved around the room, "I am a person of means. You can, like many other members of the CDF, take advantage of my patronage, but I want your full, unbridled cooperation."

"I see," Alex said.

"And since we're getting down to brass tacks, let me assure you that I have no qualms about doing things the hard way. I take care of my people, Alex, but if you resist me, I'll have you dissected until I find out exactly what makes you special and how to replicate it. I don't mean to be crude, but I need what you have. It's better, I think, for you to be a unique aberration. It's easier to keep secret, and there is great power in secrets. But it's really up to you. Will you cooperate?"

Alex couldn't believe what he'd just heard, and yet he knew it was true. VP Haley had warned him that there would be people who, if they discovered his power, would stop at nothing to control him. The secret had gotten out, but while people had witnessed his abilities, they didn't understand them. Even Lynn Faulk wasn't sure what he could do. She had locked him a room that was shielded from outside systems, which was smart, but she had revealed a little too much information. She wanted to know what he could do, and it was up to Alex to reveal as little about his abilities as possible. But it wouldn't help him, or the people he cared about, to resist. He would have to play along until an opportunity to escape presented itself.

"Yes," Alex said. "But I want a few things in return."

Lynn Faulk smiled.

"All of life is really just negotiation," she said. "What do you want, Alex Evans?"

"Out of this room, for starters," Alex said. "And I want to know that my family is safe."

"Of course you do. As I said, they're in transit, but as soon as they are safely settled and can communicate with you, I will arrange it. Perhaps even a visit, if possible. As for freedom to move about the ship, well, I can't allow that. Not after what happened in Skandia. You might decide to take control of this vessel and that's not acceptable. We need to build trust, you and I. So, we'll start small."

"A PIL then," Alex said. "I'd like to know what's going on in Skandia, perhaps reach out to my friends."

"I'll have a device brought in, but it won't have connectivity. I can't watch you every minute of the day, Alex, so it's easier to just remove the temptations until we're both satisfied that you're better off working for me. I know it's not ideal, but your abilities are unique and your loyalty isn't certain. So, we'll take it slow. Now, tell me what exactly you can you do."

CHAPTER THIRTY-THREE

"No, ABSOLUTELY NOT," Captain Poe said. "We're almost in the New Helena system."

The group of Operators looked distraught, as they should. He hated their arrogance. On every ship he had served on, the enlisted operators walked around as if the entire vessel was all about them. They did the least work but got the most praise. Holo-films were even made about their exploits. And why? Because they got into mechanized battle suits and shot other heavily armored operators? They knew nothing of real danger, he thought to himself. One wrong move and the entire ship would be lost, including every person on board. Yet he, a senior officer, was supposed to drop everything and turn the entire ship around because one of their number was missing?

"As far as I'm concerned," Poe went on, "Sergeant Evans is AWOL. I'll file my report as soon as we reach New Helena. He'll be someone else's problem then."

"Sir," Corporal Lasiter said, "please reconsider. He could be in grave danger."

"Or he could be sipping drinks at a bar or piled up with who knows what in some sleazy brothel. No," Poe continued, "we will not go back. Sergeant Evans left this ship without permission and without using proper protocol. Now, the bridge is reserved for officers and we will be transitioning through the space tunnel to New Helena soon. I need to focus on getting the ship safely into port."

The group of deflated operators left the bridge. Poe couldn't see her, but he knew that Sergeant Nyx West was just outside in the command corridor. She was busy pulling everyone's strings, but she hadn't gotten the best of Poe. He knew her type, knew exactly what she wanted. It gave him a thrill of pleasure knowing exactly what had happened to her operator.

Corporal Sallizar had carried out Captain Poe's explicit instructions. He had drugged Sergeant Evans and gotten him off the *Currency* with no proof that Evans had even left. Meanwhile, Captain Poe, having issued a direct order for Evans to report to him and having spent the day in his private quarters, ensured that he had nothing to do with the abduction. Plausible deniability was essential when going around the chain of command. But Captain Poe didn't see his actions as traitorous, since he was following a superior's orders. The fact that he had bypassed the pompous vice president of security was of little consequence. Poe had it on good authority that Loman Haley would be out of the company soon. In fact, his benefactor was building something new and he had been assured that he would have a prominent role.

It didn't take a genius to realize that Chairwoman Faulk was involved in the development of a new, centralized government that would oversee all of the autonomous worlds in the Free Trade Association. They would have to vote themselves into the central government, which could take a lot of time, but the best way to bypass that was to present a very real threat. The CDF and other private militaries were the threat. He admired how easily his benefactor had manipulated the media. It supported the supposition that the masses needed leadership; they were too easily swayed. It was, in Captain Poe's opinion, a direct indication of low intelligence. He had carefully monitored the news stories out of Skandia Seven. It didn't take a great mind to see how skewed and biased the news stories were. And yet the masses chose to believe—it was almost as if they wanted to believe—that the CDF and private militaries were truly evil.

The ship passed through the space tunnel, which could put strain on a ship depending on the fluctuating gravitational forces that held them open. Poe waited as the ship passed through the portal, jumping hundreds of light years in the span of a few seconds.

"I want status reports on all systems," Poe ordered. "Lieutenant Jones, you will begin preparations for vessel inspection."

"Aye, Captain," Jones replied.

It was busy work, and could have been delegated to divisional officers, but Poe wanted the turncoat lieutenant off the bridge. Jones had thought himself Poe's equal, taking charge of the ship when VP Haley had done his best to ruin Poe. But one didn't become captain without weathering a few storms, he reminded himself. After the VP was done playing captain, which he couldn't do without trained officers to carry out the actual work of manning the ship, Poe had risen back into authority where he belonged. And Lieutenant Jones was once again a first officer, which was probably a higher rank than he deserved. Poe made sure that Jones felt his displeasure.

The ship would be reassigned after they reached the Helena system. Most of her crew would be sent to other ships, but Captain Poe would stay on until a new commander was selected. At that time, they would perform a ship-wide inspection together, and Poe expected the *Currency* to be in perfect condition. To that end, he would perform an inspection before the crew was dismissed. If there were issues, they would be held responsible before they had the chance to scatter and leave him to clean up their messes.

"All systems report no change, Captain," the chief engineer announced.

"Very good. How long until we reach the next tunnel?"

"Nine hours, twenty-eight minutes, sir," the navigation officer said.

"Outstanding, Delnore, you have the con. If anyone needs me, I'll be in my quarters."

Poe left the bridge and walked to his private quarters. He had plenty of time for a meal, a shower, and a solid eight hours of sleep. Command had its privileges after all, and Captain Poe was resolved to enjoy every last one of them.

CHAPTER THIRTY-FOUR

"You knew he would say no," Nyx said.

"I had to try," Sly said.

"It's not like Alex is still at Crossmenian Station just waiting to be found," Nyx said. "There's a plot here. If we're going to help him, we have to find a way to uncover who's behind the abduction."

"Has it occurred to anyone that finding Ace could get us all fired?" Hanes pointed out. "I mean, I owe the guy, but it doesn't make sense for us to stick our necks out too far."

"Nice," Sansabar said.

"I'm just saying what you're all thinking," Hanes insisted.

"Not all of us," Sly said.

"There's the door, pinhead," Ash said.

She was sitting up in a chair with a medical apparatus that glowed with therapy light. Her upper body was swathed in a loose-fitting gown so that the puckered scars from her lacerations and surgeries could get the full benefit of the light. Her body was held rigid in the special chair, but at least she could move around and feed herself. The nerve block had been removed once the swelling had subsided, but she had to restrict her movements. Light therapy was only effective on certain systems. The nerves in her spine would continue to be at risk until her body adapted to the titanium rods used to fuse her spinal cord.

At first, being released from the med bay had brightened her spirits, but she struggled with feeling responsible for Alex's abduction. She had been one bed over, but still completely unable to help her friend as Ernesto Sallizar drugged him and smuggled him off of the ship. She didn't have the patience to deal with Corporal Hanes's selfish worries about his career. Sly slid his hand over and held hers. They had decided it was okay to show a little affection in public. If people hadn't realized they were lovers, then they were probably blind, she thought. And she was all too aware of just how quickly life could change. She didn't want to waste time trying to keep up appearances. Cronus team was acting independently from any one squad or battalion. If they were assigned to one with a persnickety CO, she would deal with that, but until then, it was good to feel Sly's hand in hers. He had a way of grounding her and taking the edge off of the painful emotional extremes at which she functioned.

"How do we do that?" Sly asked. "We have no resources. We don't even get to say what our next assignment will be."

"VP Haley told me he was ordering time off for Alex once we reached New Helena. I'm sure that goes for the entire team."

"And we'll be reassigned to another ship," Sansabar said. "We probably won't be able to help."

"Don't say that," Ash said. "The best chance we have is networking. We have to make sure that everyone we know is looking for Ace."

"He can't have just disappeared into thin air," Nyx said.

They were gathered in the operators' ready room. It was far away from Captain Poe, who Nyx claimed was somehow behind the abduction. It gave them a sense of privacy and was large enough for all of them. Nyx was the only non-operator, so it made sense, although Ash felt oddly out of place. Until her therapy was done, she couldn't suit up. And being in the ready room made her want to fly so badly that she could taste it.

"We have to get the word out," Ash said. "Write messages to everyone we know in the CDF."

"I heard there's a reward out for Alex," Hanes said. "Not officially, of course, but on the dark net. He's been labeled by the authorities on Skandia Seven as an instigator."

"That doesn't help," Sansabar said.

"I'm just saying, it may not be a plot or whatever. Maybe he was taken back to the Skandia system and turned over to the authorities," Hanes explained.

"Either way, we have to find him," Ash said.

"I'll contact his family," Nyx said.

She pulled out her PIL and swiped the screen to activate it. Her eyes immediately widened in surprise."

"What is it?" Ash asked.

"Vice President Haley wrote me back," she said.

"Really?" Sly said. "I thought that was a super long shot."

"Alex saved his bacon, remember?" Ash said.

"He says he found out who took Alex!" Nyx said. "He's coming to New Helena and we're supposed to wait for him."

"When?" Sly asked.

"I don't know," Nyx said.

"We can wait," Ash said. "But we can't depend on anyone to do this for us. If there really is a plot, we don't know who we can trust."

"She's right," Sly said. "He might be telling us to wait because he's in on it."

"Monitor Ace's status," Sansabar said. "If he gets listed as AWOL, we'll know."

"That's what Captain Poe said about him," Sly said. "If he has his way, we'd all get thrown out of the CDF."

"Good thing he's not in charge," Ash said.

"So, we wait?" Nyx asked.

"It won't hurt to keep our ears to the ground," Sly said.

"We can be discreet," Ash added.

"Well, some of us can," he teased her.

She liked his teasing. It made her feel like she belonged. It made her feel like he knew her, that they were more than just colleagues; they were friends. Of course, she and Sly were more than friends, but she knew people whose romantic involvement didn't guarantee intimacy, or even genuine concern. Ash had been used most of her life. Her parents were busy people who rarely had time for her. It was one of the reasons she pushed so hard at everything she did. Recognition came from being the best, and Ash longed to be seen and heard. She didn't want to be invisible.

"The most important thing is to stay connected," Ash said. "If the VP, or even just some other officers are involved, they'll try to split us up."

"Then we can't trust the Ahzco network," Sly said. "They could be monitoring it."

"It's best if we meet in person," Nyx said. "Twenty-four hours after we make port, we should meet at the Bosun Brewery. It's in the Helena system space port."

"Sounds good to me," Hanes said.

"We'll regroup and decide what to do next," Ash said.

Everyone nodded. It was a plan, and while it might not get them any closer to actually finding Alex, they all desperately wanted to feel like they were doing something to help.

CHAPTER THIRTY-FIVE

"So you can control vehicles," Lynn Faulk said.

"I can control some systems," Alex said. "If I'm close enough. As you're aware, some control systems are very integrated. It really depends on the system."

"But you discovered the explosives in the basement of the Ahzco HQ building," she insisted. "Those weren't vehicles. They didn't even have computer systems."

"They were electric powered detonators," Alex said, trying to stay ahead of the Chairwoman. "They have a very unique signature, and I'm very attuned to my INC, as you could probably guess."

Lynn Faulk nodded. There was a polite smile on her face, but in her eyes, Alex could see that she didn't believe him.

"I have a device in my pocket," she said. "I'm going to power it on. I'd like you tell me what it is."

"I will," Alex said. "If it's something I can connect to."

She reached inside her jacket, and Alex heard the device hum to life. He felt an intense desire to sync to the EM waves that were suddenly radiating from her inner jacket pocket, but the device was strange. It had a small, but powerful power supply, and radiated an almost painfully high-pitched whine. Alex couldn't help but wince.

"I don't know," he said. "Please, turn it off."

She removed the device, which was hardly larger than the battery that powered it. She held it out on the palm of her hand.

"This is a frequency jammer," she said. "There's a much more powerful one connected to the ship's computer system, set as a failsafe. Should the system be infiltrated, it would go off."

"Larger than that one," Alex said, letting his genuine fear bleed into his voice.

"Much larger," she said. "I'm afraid I'm having a little trouble believing your story. You see, I have the official reports from the Carthage system. Not the redacted files that most Ahzco employees saw, but the full reports. I know that you were instrumental in stopping the Zen Tech ships."

"I was," Alex said, trying to convince Lynn Faulk that his abilities were only a fraction of their true strength. "But my abilities are enhanced in the Titan battle suit. I don't know why. And if you read those reports, you know that I accidentally lost control of the Zen Tech freighter and crashed their systems."

She nodded, but he could see the doubt in her eyes.

"I know you took full control of the prison transport."

"I did," he agreed.

"And you did more than fly the ship."

"That ship was fully automated," Alex said. "All I had to do was tell it where to go. And I was on board the ship. You can't get much closer to the operating system than that."

"You don't sound proud of what you accomplished," she said.

"I'm proud of the people I saved," he said. "I'm proud of the way things turned out. The commandos from Skandia Seven were intent on killing us if they couldn't take us captive."

"I feel like you aren't being completely honest with me, Alex. Unfortunately, that leaves me with little choice."

"I'm not sure how else to convince you," Alex said. "There's nothing I can do inside this faraday cage you've got me trapped in."

"Alright," she said, suddenly getting to her feet, "let's take a walk."

Alex nearly jumped out of his chair. Lynn Faulk didn't look back at him, and Alex quickly caught up with her. Just outside the door, he was hit with a variety of strange sounds. Some were familiar, others were just gibberish, but he realized that Lynn Faulk was using jamming technology to overwhelm his INC. Ten steps in, his heart was pounding as if he'd been sprinting, and it didn't take long for the red-hot stabbing pain behind his eyes to return.

Outside the doorway was a spiral staircase. His room was in the equivalent of a tower on the massive yacht. The ship was so large that it felt like he was on a space station. There were windows in various places around the tower. One looked out over the ship, which stretched for what seemed like two entire kilometers. There was even a shuttle mounted on the bow.

"Is this all just for you?" Alex asked.

"This is my primary space craft," Lynn Faulk said. "I travel extensively, as you probably know."

Alex didn't know. He had never heard of Lynn Faulk, although he was sure she had to have been listed on some of his father's paperwork. Growing up, Ahzco was like the government. It was this huge, powerful organization that had direct control of their lives. As an employee, his father got periodic paperwork from various departments, but Alex had never felt any desire to read them.

"It's amazing," Alex said.

"It's necessary to keep up a certain level of respectability," she explained as she led the way down the stairs. "Ahzco is just one of many interests I manage."

They went down to an atrium with a transparent roof. There was a large dining table, along with several additional luxurious seating areas, all surrounded by a long circular track.

"This is the grand concourse. It has everything you need. Space to move, as well as dining and seating areas. We should finish our conversation."

"Sure," Alex said.

She led him to a group of thick, wooden chairs, with stuffed cushions and heavy-looking polished stone ashtrays. In the middle of the sitting area was an automated cigar humidor.

"Can you work this?" Lynn Faulk said, pointing to the humidor.

"What is it?" Alex asked. He could feel the simple device's EM waves. Syncing to it would be easy. In fact, he could have easily connected to the ship's computer system. He could feel a powerful main control computer, and several separate systems. It made sense; the ship itself was huge, and Alex could only guess at what measures a woman like Lynn Faulk had to take to keep her business private. The temptation to sync to the main system and learn all he could about her massive ship was huge, but he knew that opening himself to the INC would also bombard him with the cacophony of EM waves from the jamming frequencies. He felt like it was safer to just play dumb as long as possible.

"This?" Alex said, pointing at the humidor.

"Yes," she said. "Try to connect to it. It's a simple device, but computer controlled. You should be able to sync your Implanted Neural Controller to it."

Suddenly the noise of the jamming frequencies stopped. Alex didn't know why, but it seemed that Lynn Faulk was controlling it. He let his INC connect to the humidor. There were over a thousand cigars in the device, which kept track of each type and size. The computer controls also kept tight watch over the temperature and humidity inside the device.

"Okay," Alex said. "I did it."

There was something else in the humidor, a secondary system. It was small, barely anything at all. Just a simple reporting program piggybacking on the primary computer system. Alex knew that someone was paying attention, someone who could tell Lynn Faulk exactly what he was doing to the computer-controlled device.

"I want an El Hombre Santo," she said.

Alex skimmed through the different types of cigars. There were options from a dozen different planets, but he found the kind she wanted and placed the order. The machine whirred for a few seconds, then the top opened and a cigar was sitting on a little stand. Lynn Faulk picked it up, looked at the band, and smiled.

"Impressive," she said. "Do you smoke?"

"No, ma'am," Alex replied.

"Pity," she said, pulling a small tool from the side of the humidor and snipping the tip of the cigar. "They can be expensive, but it is an elegant way to enjoy oneself."

A steward appeared. He was tall, broad shouldered and well-muscled in a tight-fitting uniform that seemed even tighter than the compression fatigues Alex was used to wearing. He produced a lighter from a hidden pocket and handed it to Lynn Faulk.

"Can I get you anything, my lady?" the steward asked.

"Brandy please," Lynn Faulk said. "Alex, would you care for a drink?"

"No thank you," he said.

The steward bobbed his head and hurried away.

Lynn Faulk fired the lighter, which shot up a blue flame that looked more like a small torch. She worked the cigar around, drawing in smoke through the tobacco to light it equally. When she was done, she took in a long draw and then blew out a cloud of smoke.

Alex stayed connected to the humidor and let the watchdog program monitor his actions. He did nothing, just kept the connection. With the jamming frequency turned off, it was easy to hear and identify the different systems on the ship. It was a big place, with many electronic devices, all of which emitted

EM waves, but Alex could easily pick out the more powerful computing systems. There was one overarching computer monitoring program that linked the others together, but each was protected with security programs and firewalls. They were not an issue for Alex, but he also detected the same monitoring program humming in the background of all the ship's individual systems. They didn't trust him, and he would have to watch himself at every turn.

"You have the freedom to move around down here, but please don't go down to the lower decks," Lynn Faulk said. "Anything you need will be provided by the ship's crew. Don't hesitate to ask."

"Okay, that is great," Alex said. "May I ask a question?"

"Yes?"

"What, exactly, do you want me to do?"

"What do you feel like you could do?"

"I'm an operator," Alex said. "I'd like to get back to my team."

"That isn't going to happen," she said. "You are too valuable. For now, let me think on the best way to use your talents. When I come to a decision, you'll be the first to know."

Alex didn't think that sounded very promising, but he had to bide his time. He was essentially a captive on a huge ship. And while he didn't think the safety measures could stop him from taking control of the vessel, he still couldn't see how it would benefit him. There was nowhere to go.

CHAPTER THIRTY-SIX

LOMAN WAS on an Ahzco ship en route to the Helena system, studying a report given to him by his investigative team via an encrypted message. The news wasn't really all that surprising. Loman had learned long ago that most people were predictable if you knew what they wanted and what means were at their disposal.

It was no mystery what Lynn Faulk wanted. She was an incredibly wealthy woman who wanted the one thing her riches could not purchase for her outright—power. And it was no surprise to realize that she was behind the mysterious Sigma Services company or that she had found out about Alex's special abilities. What he didn't know was how she planned to use him to increase her power... but he had a good guess. Ciara Prince had discovered the flight plan for Lynn Faulk's super yacht, the *Silent Partner*. At first, it seemed inconspicuous—just a wealthy mogul making the rounds to manage her various enterprises. But Ciara Prince had gone the extra mile, checking on the other members of the cabal behind the idea of a central-ized government to oversee the entire galaxy. Rubin Coifmere and Quintessa Vandross had no travel plans, but media magnate Francis Parlaon was also traveling. And with their itineraries side by side, Lynn Faulk's plan became clear.

Travel plans could always change, but if the two ultra-rich moguls stayed on course, their ships would pass through the Gobal Sector at the same time. Loman had the Gobal Sector pulled up on his PIL. It was a unique section of space, with a thriving tourist business taking sightseers into the Olympus Nebula from a small space station that most people called the Temple. What made that sector of space truly unique was the distance between space tunnels. It was a well-kept secret that passing through the Gobal Sector would allow travelers to by-pass many of the more highly trafficked spaceways. The tunnels in the Gobal section were relatively close together; just a few hours at reasonable speeds separated the passageways to other systems. A ship could pop into the system and be gone again in a fraction of the time it took to traverse most systems.

Loman sat back in his seat. He was on a small transport ship with a group of researchers returning from a conference in the Oxfirth system. He had ensconced himself in the rear of the passenger cabin and was ignored by the other passengers. It gave Loman time to consider what Lynn Faulk might be planning.

One possibility was that she might pass Alex off to Parlaon, but Loman didn't think so. She obviously knew about Alex's special abilities, but no one else did, which gave her an advantage over her partners. They needed each other to gain control over the FTA's free planets, but Loman knew that Lynn Faulk didn't like for anyone to outshine her. Parlaon was, like most of the ultra-rich, very private. But his ownership of several news agencies, production studios, and an entertainment distribution company made him a popular figure in the media. Some people hated him while others loved him, but Loman guessed that jealousy was driving Lynn Faulk to take drastic measures against him.

Parlaon had done his part and stirred the media frenzy. It couldn't be proven conclusively, but it was widely believed that he took an active role in setting the agendas for the news agencies he controlled through his company, Matrix Media. Besides his wealth, it was his ability to manipulate the so-called mainstream media that made him valuable. Once that was done, his usefulness would diminish, and Lynn Faulk wasn't the type to share her power.

Unfortunately, there was no way for Loman to get to the Gobal sector in time to stop her plan. He couldn't say that he knew for certain what she was up to, but it didn't take a lot of imagination to guess that she might use Alex to sabotage Parlaon's ship. If the media magnate disappeared or was killed in a space accident, it would increase Lynn Faulk's influence. She might even sacrifice Alex to the media, pointing out that his actions were the result of an unregulated private military bent on holding onto their power, whatever the cost.

But knowing Lynn's probable next move didn't make his any clearer. The only way he could actually save Alex was to wait until the young operator made his move to break free of

Lynn Faulk's control. She was a powerful woman, even chair of the board at Ahzco, but that didn't mean that Loman didn't have secrets, too. If he could wrest Alex from her clutches, Loman was confident that he could get the young operator to safety.

He chuckled to himself at the very idea of Alex hiding. Just as Loman could predict Lynn Faulk's behavior, he could also predict Alex Evans's reaction to the idea of hiding. It might be for his own good, but the boy wasn't the type to settle in obscurity just to avoid risk. He wouldn't sit by and let others fight his battles for him. It was one of the things that Loman most admired about Alex.

The problem, as Loman saw it, was that he needed a fast ship with a full complement of operators who were at his complete disposal. He didn't view himself as a general with an army to lead into battle, but as more of a captain trying to prevent the war in the first place. Colonel Chastain was gathering every available resource she could in the Askerria Sector, and that didn't leave him with a lot of options.

He knew there were several older ships in the Helena Prime system that hadn't been used in a while. There were two Mora-class vessels in the system. They were considered obsolete, having been in service longer than Loman had been in the CDF. But the ships were functional; all he needed was a crew. Best of all, the ships were fast. Loman sent an order to begin the process of preparing the *Drachma*. His message wouldn't go through until the passenger ship actually reached the Helena System, but it was placed in the queue and would be transferred instantly as soon as the messaging app connected with the CDF's servers in system.

His next message was to all the officers, controllers, technicians, and operators still in the Helena system. Most would be on leave of some sort, or like the crew of the *Currency,* awaiting new orders. He wouldn't conscript anyone to his crew if he could help it. Instead, he requested volunteers for a special detail which he would lead personally. As VP of security, he was the highest ranking officer in the CDF, but that didn't mean he was respected or loved by the troops that carried out his orders. In some cases, he was hated, a fact which his last experience in the Helena System with Chief McKinna and the disgraced Colonel Bixby proved beyond all doubt. Loman hated to admit it, but he had made mistakes in the past. Some had cost people their lives, directly as a result of his orders. And in every organization, there were some people who didn't like the way things were run. It wasn't his goal to please everyone, but to keep the company employees and assets safe from harm. And at the moment, the biggest threat, by far, was the idea of a central government that would work to break up the mega-corporations with a growing army of their own.

Loman added the message to his outbox and focused his mind on where he should go first. Once he had a ship and a crew, his first priority had to be getting Alex back, even if that meant a direct confrontation with Lynn Faulk and the *Silent Partner.*

CHAPTER THIRTY-SEVEN

ALEX HAD RETURNED to his room. Perhaps it was the fact that he was still recovering from the abduction—and certainly, climbing the long, winding staircase back up to the room in the tower didn't help—but Alex was exhausted. He was surprised to find that someone had been in the room. The bed was made, the food he had taken from the small serving bot was neatly arranged on the table. The bathroom had been cleaned, and fresh towels hung up. It was both luxurious and suspicious. Alex had no doubt that the room had also been searched from top to bottom. There might even be some type of surveillance equipment, but he couldn't sense any EM waves with his INC. Either way, he couldn't do anything about it. He was just as much a prisoner on the luxurious *Silent Partner* as he had been on the *Reaper One*. He fell into bed and went to sleep immediately.

Sometime later the door opened, and Ernesto Sallizar stepped in.

"Wake up, Sergeant. Your presence is requested downstairs."

"What?" Alex asked.

"Our benefactor wants you downstairs in ten minutes," Ernesto said. "Hop to it. We can't afford to get on her bad side."

Alex sat up in the bed, rubbing his eyes. He had no way of knowing what time it was or how long he had slept. All he knew for certain was that he still felt tired. Ernesto dropped down into the chair where Alex had eaten dinner. It was the only seat in the small room.

"Please," Alex said. "Make yourself at home."

"Like I said, we have ten minutes and those stairs take some time," Ernesto said. "Get moving."

Alex wanted to punch his abductor right in the face, but he had to bide his time carefully. An opportunity to put Ernesto Sallizar in his place would come, and he would be ready when it did. He threw back the silky covers and got out of bed. He went into his little bathroom and freshened up, then walked across his room and put on fresh outfit.

"Not bad digs, eh?" Ernesto said. "A major improvement over the *Currency*."

"I suppose," Alex said.

"You suppose? Really?" Ernesto said. "You should be thanking me, Sergeant. You couldn't afford a single journey in a ship like this if you saved every spare credit for the rest of your life."

"This isn't a free ride you know," Alex said as he slipped on the lightweight garments. "Lynn Faulk wants something in return."

"So does everyone," Ernesto said. "That doesn't make her bad."

"It does when you don't have a choice."

"My God, you are such a child, you know that?" he sneered. "Are you really going to blow the opportunity of a lifetime because she didn't ask. You operators are so full of yourselves. I'd gladly help her kick you out the airlock, but without you, she doesn't need me. So why don't you get your act together, Evans? Otherwise, I'll be forced to make sure you're in line a different way."

"We're at threats already?" Alex asked.

"If that's what it takes," Ernesto said. "Let's move!"

"You know I outrank you, right?" Alex asked.

"Yeah, that's ridiculous," Ernesto said, leading the way down the winding staircase. "You're just a kid, and someone decides you should be giving me orders? I don't think so. You know the doctors would come into a ship and couldn't find a band aid, much less a laser scalpel or a light therapy machine. They can't start an IV, they have no concept of actually carrying out their own instructions, and yet they're in charge. I know more medicine than any doctor I ever met, but does anyone consult me? Oh, hell no. I'm just the med tech."

"Why not go to medical school?" Alex asked.

"Sure, pay millions of credits to learn what I already know," he sneered. "I'll pass."

Alex knew exactly who Ernesto Sallizar was in that moment. His bitterness had pushed him into making a life-altering mistake. He could never go back to the CDF. Not after abducting Alex and joining Lynn Faulk's secret war. If there was one thing that was true about the situation in which Alex found himself, it was that Lynn Faulk had grandiose ideas about her own importance. She thought she was above the law, above her peers, above everyone. Perhaps it was because of the money, or maybe it was just something deep inside of her that needed to be the most important person in every situation. The odd thing was, Alex assumed that she *was* the most important person in most interactions. People probably bowed and scraped before her and deferred to her ideas over their own just to get into her good graces. Alex didn't feel the desire to get to know her any better. He just wanted off her ship and out of her control.

They reached the bottom of the tower and moved across the wide concourse to a small dining table where there was a man in uniform already seated. The uniform wasn't CDF, or any private military that Alex recognized. He had dark eyes, and his hair rose straight up from his head before curling back down again.

"Alex Evans—meet General Cordair, Sigma Services," Ernesto said.

General Cordair looked up and his eyes narrowed as he stared hard at Alex.

"Nice to meet you, sir," Alex said, not quite sure what the protocol was for addressing a senior officer from another service.

"Sergeant Evans, I believe," Cordair said. "He outranks you, Corporal."

"I'm not a corporal anymore," Ernesto said. "I've told you that. I'm out."

"Very well, we'll take it from here, Sallizar. Go crawl back under a rock for all I care."

Ernesto walked away, cursing under his breath. Alex watched him leave for a moment, then turned back and caught sight of Lynn Faulk striding toward them. Alex looked down. There was something about her that made him feel ill.

"You've met," Faulk announced as she reached the table. "Very good. Sergeant Evans—have a seat. I've decided to bring you into my new organization, Sigma Services."

"I'm in the CDF," Alex said.

"You were, and now we need to transfer you over. Sigma is the elite, the best of the best. And because you're going to be instrumental in what we're doing, we'll make you an officer. How does Lieutenant Evans sound?"

"Thank you," Alex said, nodding to hide the fury he felt inside.

Who did Lynn Faulk think she was to just decide what he would do and who he would work for? But he couldn't confront her until he had an exit strategy. The best idea was to just play along.

"Alright, so we're a few hours out from the Gobal Sector," Lynn Faulk said. "If we've timed things right, we'll pass Francis's ship, the *Starstruck III*. I want you to disable his ship, Lieutenant."

"What?" Alex asked.

"We have a Titan suit that you will take out and approach his vessel with," Lynn went on, completely ignoring the shock in Alex's voice and the look of surprise on his face. "You get close, take control of her computer systems, send the vessel off course, and most importantly, disable the communications system."

"I don't know if I can do that," Alex said.

"Oh, I think you can," Lynn Faulk said. "Let's not be coy, Lieutenant. You didn't disable that Zen Tech freighter in the Carthage system by accident. You have a powerful gift and we're going to utilize it. I want this to look like an accident."

"You want me to kill innocent civilians?" Alex asked.

"Oh, believe me, there is nothing innocent about Francis. The man's a pig and everyone knows it," Lynn Faulk explained. "You'll be doing the universe a favor by taking him out. Now, once you knock his ship off course and disable the systems, you will return to the *Silent Partner* without being seen. We cannot stop or make concessions for you just in case someone, some-where is watching. You'll have to board without help."

"I don't know if I can do that," Alex said.

"Can't, or won't?" Lynn Faulk asked, her eyes narrowing. Little wrinkles appeared at the corner of her eyes that had somehow escaped the facial contouring procedures. It was a sure sign of her anger, and Alex scrambled to explain himself.

"As you know, ma'am, a mechanized battle suit is intended to be controlled with an operator and a controller," Alex said. "How will I do it without help?"

General Cordair sat forward. "I'll be your controller for this mission, Lieutenant."

"We've thought this through, Alex. I've got schematics and engineering specifications for the *Starstruck*. She's a well-built yacht, and the computer system has a potent security suite, but I'm sure you can find a way around it. The general will help in any way he can. Now, I'll leave the details to the two of you."

She got to her feet and Alex saw her cast a look at General Cordair, who gave her an almost imperceptible nod. He didn't know if they were sending him on a suicide mission, or if it was all just another test of his loyalty. For the life of him, Alex couldn't understand why she thought he would be loyal to her at all.

The general waited until she was gone before continuing with mission specifics.

"We have one issue, as I see it," he said, pausing as a server approached the table with a pitcher of orange juice, two glasses, and a tray of baked goods. She set everything down, and the general winked at the server. Alex saw a smile light up the server's face as if she had just stepped out into the sunshine. He hadn't even noticed how attractive she was until she was already leaving.

"An issue?" Alex said.

General Cordair poured two tall glasses of orange juice before he answered. "We can't have you leave the ship in the Gobal sector," he finally explained. "You're going to have suit up, exit the *Silent Partner*, and then follow us through the space tunnel."

"That's impossible, sir," Alex said. "The Titan MBS isn't engineered for that kind of stress."

"Well, it hasn't been tested," Cordair said. "That doesn't

mean it won't survive. Besides, the odds of a gravitic event putting stress on your suit is less than twenty percent."

Alex couldn't argue with the statistics. In fact, he had never really paid much attention to the science behind the tunnels that connected star systems. Still, even he knew that ships occasionally suffered damage from passing through the tunnels.

"We'll cross over and go radio silent once we're in the Gobal Sector. You can use the *Silent Partner's* exhaust to hide your approach. We should be able to slow the *Starstruck*. Ms. Faulk will reach out to Mr. Parlaon, allowing you to make contact with their ship. It's my understanding that your ability is most potent when you can make contact with the vessel."

Alex nodded. He had known that the secret of his ability would eventually get out, but to be confronted with the reality that people were talking about him was unsettling.

"Wait for our ship to clear," General Cordair continued. "We need to make sure no one can blame us for the *Starstruck's* demise."

"I understand," Alex said, feeling dirty about just being aware of such a heinous plan.

"We'll continue through the space tunnel and you can follow once you're certain the *Starstruck* is beyond saving."

"Can I ask you a question, sir?" Alex said.

"Sure," General Cordair said, pulling off a bit of a savory treat from one of the baked goods on the tray and popping it into his mouth.

"Why are we doing this? I mean, this isn't like any kind of military operation I've heard of. We don't attack civilians, sir."

"Oh, don't believe the propaganda, Lieutenant," Cordair

said. "No one is innocent in this galaxy. And just because Francis Parlaon owns news agencies instead of corporations doesn't make him any different from the titans of industry who enslave worlds and keep their employees dependent on the company store."

Alex nodded. He understood the system. His father had been trapped by it on NP8261, and if Alex hadn't been able to join the CDF, he would be stuck there still. There were realities that people considered unsavory in every age. And that didn't mean that Alex liked it, or agreed with Ahzco's policies, but the CDF wasn't asking him to ambush a civilian ship and kill every soul on board.

"Eat up," General Cordair said. "When you're finished, we'll get you into your new Titan suit. It's got a few improvements that you'll want to familiarize yourself with. I think you're going to like it."

Alex didn't think he would like it, but he ate anyway. It was clear that he was probably having the last meal he would ever eat. If anything went wrong on this mission, the only certainty was that Lynn Faulk would leave him on his own and never look back.

CHAPTER THIRTY-EIGHT

Nyx looked around the table, a sense of despair setting in. They had been talking for over an hour and there was nothing they could do. They all wanted to help, but they were powerless.

Normally the Helena System was a busy place, with a variety of military space crafts and passenger vessels bringing researchers and admins to the heart of the CDF. TROY was the code name for the massive space station that orbited Helena Prime. Nyx had spent plenty of time on the station, training and waiting to be paired with an operator. She had spent the first free time she had ever had with Alex on TROY, but since being relieved of duty on the *Currency*, it seemed that the entire system was being abandoned. There was almost no one left on TROY except for admins and retired CDF personnel who had permits to run its various stores, clubs, restaurants, and entertainment venues.

Nyx wasn't sure what she had hoped for—perhaps a ship that would be sent to find Alex—but even if the vice president himself had ordered a search, there were no other ships available in the system except for the *Currency*.

"We have to do something," Sansabar said. "Sitting around talking about it isn't getting us anywhere."

"We could charter a ship," Sly said. "If we all pooled our credits, we could charter a ship to take us back to Crossmenian Station."

"And then what?" Ash said. "Whoever took Ace isn't hiding him on the space station."

"We need more intelligence," Nyx said. "We don't even know what our next assignment is going to be."

"I thought you said we'd be on leave," Hanes said. "My PIL still shows me waiting for assignment."

"Mine too," Sly said.

"That's what I was told, but I don't know for sure," Nyx said.

She could feel the tears of frustration trying to well up in her eyes. The last thing she wanted was to break down crying in front of her friends. Yet, it was the fact that she had friends in the first place that made her feel so strongly. They were closer to her than any group had ever been. Growing up on a scientific space station, there weren't many children her age. Those that she met were short-term stays, meaning that their parents were only there for a set amount of time to study some anomaly before moving on to another project somewhere else. One of the reasons she had joined the CDF was the hope that she could make friends and have some type of social life, but controllers were natural introverts. Most spent all day, every day, at their consoles. They watched the galaxy from their computer monitors where they felt safe. But when Nyx had been paired with Alex, everything changed. She had a friend who she felt she could relate to and who truly cared about her. Not only that, but traveling with Cronus Team and being in the field with them allowed her to befriend Sly and Ash, even Sansabar and Hanes. They were more than just a team; they were a group of friends. And yet they were being crushed under the guilt of having lost Alex. She feared that if they didn't discover a way to go and find him, the friendships they had formed might not be strong enough to survive.

Her PIL pinged in her pocket, alerting her to a message. There was nothing unusual about that, and she might have ignored it, except that hers wasn't the only PIL that chimed. Everyone in the group heard the chimes go off at the same time. Nyx looked around the nearly empty bistro. There were a few other off-duty CDF members, and they too pulled out their PIL's to check on a message.

"Weird," Nyx said, before looking down at her Personal Information Link.

"No way," Sly said.

"Is he serious?" Ash asked.

Nyx scanned the message. It was from Vice President Loman Haley, requesting volunteers to join a special task group. She wanted to jump to her feet and run out of the restaurant to sign up at that very moment. She didn't need a sign or personal message from the VP to know he was going to find Alex.

"This is it," she said softly.

"It's what?" Hanes asked.

"It's what we've been looking for," Nyx said.

"Did you see that he's activated the *Drachma*," Sly said. "How old do you think that ship is?"

"Pretty old," Sansabar agreed.

"It's a Mora-class ship," Ash said. "They're fast."

"Light armor," Hanes said. "Laser cannons only."

"He'll be going to find Alex," Nyx insisted.

"How can you be so sure?" Ash asked.

"Yeah, he's the Vice President of the entire division," Sly said. "Surely he's got more important responsibilities."

"Maybe," Nyx said. "But think about who we're talking about. Think about what he can do. Losing him really isn't an option."

"She has a point," Sly said.

"Well, look," Hanes said. "I'm all for helping Ace, if that's possible, but volunteering for additional duty isn't really what I signed up for."

"Coward," Sansabar snapped.

"What are you, lazy or something?" Ash asked.

"I'm not a coward and I'm not lazy," Hanes said. "But if we volunteer for this special assignment, we won't have a say in what we do. They might go looking for Ace, or they might do something else. We won't know. We're not officers. No one is taking us into their confidence. I mean, what if the VP ran into another problem already. He might have forgotten all about one sergeant that's gone missing."

"Alex is not just a sergeant," Nyx said.

"He and the VP are pretty close," Sly said.

"Yeah, Ace saved VP Haley's life right here on this station," Ash said. "There's no way the bossman forgets that Ace is missing."

"Maybe, but maybe not. Why don't a few of you volunteer," Hanes said. "If it's like you think it is, let the rest of us know."

"I'm in," Sansabar said.

"Me too," Sly replied.

"You think he'll take me?" Ash asked.

She was still wearing a back brace and was supposed to avoid physical duty for at least another week.

"Only one way to find out," Nyx said.

She replied to the message and volunteered. Part of her didn't think it would matter that she didn't have an operator, but she had to be realistic. The VP had been friendly with her on the *Currency*, but she was a bit like a fish out of water. There wasn't a lot she could do without an operator, and he might not want her on the ship.

"If we're going right back out," Sly said. "I need to buy some snacks."

"I need to write a few messages," Ash said.

"We don't even have berths yet," Hanes said. "Is anyone else catching a shuttle down to Sparta?"

Sansabar rolled her eyes.

"Let's get our errands done, then meet back here," Nyx said.

The rest of the group agreed. They paid for their drinks and hurried out of the little bistro. It took less than an hour to get a reply saying that she'd been accepted to the VP's taskforce. She was to report to the shuttle bay on Delta level where she would be taken out to the *Drachma*. When she stopped at the bistro, Sansabar and Sly were waiting for her.

"Where's Ash?" Nyx asked.

"Getting special permission to join the group," Sly said. "Her acceptance was conditional, based on whether or not she could get clearance from a physician in the infirmary."

"You think she'll get it?" Nyx asked.

"If she doesn't, I wouldn't want to be that doctor," Sly said.

They left the bistro and hurried down to the shuttle bay on Delta level where they were ferried across with a dozen other crew members. Two were technicians, but the rest were officers. Nyx recognized several from the *Currency*. When the shuttle docked in the *Drachma's* hangar, they filed out and were met by a beaming Lieutenant Rory Jones.

"Welcome aboard," he said. "We've got a lot of work to do. Follow me."

For the next six hours, Nyx worked harder than she had since basic training. The Drachma was still in working order, but had to be loaded with supplies. Everything from linens to food and water had to be brought on board the older ship. There were signs of age everywhere Nyx looked. The metal had a patina to it. Every corner was overrun with dust and cobwebs. In various places, the lights were out or flickering. And everyone worked, including the officers. Nyx even saw VP Loman Haley carrying a crate of supplies at one point.

When the ship was finally fully stocked, and enough crew had been brought on board to man the ship, VP Haley made an announcement on the ship's intercom.

Crew of the Ahzco ship Drachma. *Welcome and thank you for volunteering. Our first order of duty is getting this ship ready to leave the system, and we are close to meeting that requirement. The Mora-class ships were built to be fast, and that's what we'll be doing. Moving fast, dealing with issues, and moving on as quickly as possible. This is now my flagship, and you are my crew. I will work with you in whatever way I can to make this ship as efficient and effective as possible, but we are only as strong as our weakest link. I hope you'll join me in committing to doing our very best to make this ship, and our mission, the standard by which every other vessel in the Ahzco fleet is measured.*

If you have messages to send, do that now. We will be underway within two hours. Please report to your divisions and carry out all of the assigned tasks with enthusiasm and professionalism. This is Commander Loman Haley. Welcome aboard and good luck to all of us.

"I guess we should check in," Sansabar said.

"Yeah, where do we do that?" Sly asked.

"Let's check the ready room," Nyx said. "Any word from Ash?"

"No," Sly said. The disappointment in his voice was almost painful.

"There's still time," Sansabar said, even though they all knew that Ash's time was almost up.

They walked from the supply room down a long corridor to the operators' ready room. Nyx knew that it wasn't exactly where she was supposed to be, but she didn't want to leave her friends. She was the only controller in their group. They walked into the room where about twenty people were already gathered. Most were from Oscar Company. The only two members not present that Nyx could see were corporal Hanes and Master Sergeant Montgomery.

The operators were all looking around, talking to one another. Nyx felt completely out of place and was about to leave when Loman Haley walked in. He saw her and went right to where she stood.

"Commander on deck!" Nyx shouted, once the shock of seeing the VP wore off.

The room fell silent and every operator came to attention. Nyx did as well, standing stiffly and staring toward the wall, trying not to look at Haley.

"Well, if I didn't believe you were the right choice for this, you just proved that are," Haley said softly. "Controller West, would you do me the honor of being the acting chief, at least until we can get Evans back in our ranks?"

"Sir?" Nyx said, hardly daring to look his way.

"I need someone I trust, and who knows their way around the operations division," Loman said. "We don't have any officers on board to do the job. I know it's a lot to ask, but I need you, Sergeant. What do you say?"

"Of course," Nyx said. "Thank you, sir."

"Thank you," Loman said, before raising his voice to speak to the entire group. "Thank you all for volunteering. I really have no idea what to expect, but these are dangerous times, as you all know. Leading from an office on Arcadia is no longer an option for me. As long as I'm in charge, I'll be out front with each and every one of you. Once we get underway, we'll be starting an intense training regimen. I expect every one of you to work hard day and night. We'll take on more crew when we can, but for now, you'll all be pulling double, sometimes triple duty. I apologize for that, but it can't be helped. We're on the verge of a war, the likes of which the galaxy has never seen before. And we have to be ready.

"Sergeant Nyx West will be acting chief for the foreseeable future. I will be working side by side with her to make sure the operators on this ship are the best of the best. For now, I want you to help the technicians get every MBS on this ship prepped and ready. Once we leave this system, we'll be in dangerous territory. Every ship we see could be an enemy and we can't take anything for granted. That is all," VP Haley announced.

"We'll make you proud sir," Sly said.

All of the other operators all cheered. There was something about the vice president that made people want to perform at their best. Nyx could only hope to imitate him and make sure the operators were ready if they were called on.

"Chief West—follow me please," Haley said.

She followed him out of the ready room, and they walked side by side down the corridor.

"I have an idea where to find Sergeant Evans," Haley said quietly. "But I need some confirmation. Can you message him?"

"Yes sir," Nyx said. "But I've been checking my messages. He hasn't responded."

"He will, when he can. I want him to know we're out there and we're listening."

"Yes, sir. Of course."

"Very good. You're an officer now, West. You can't befriend the operators. You have to keep some distance."

"I understand."

"I knew you would. Also, I'm having a planning meeting with senior officers. In this instance, that means you. Meet me on the bridge in ten minutes."

"Yes, sir."

"And West, I'm glad to have you aboard."

"It's my pleasure," Nyx said. "Thank you for having me."

"This is you," he said, pointing to a barracks room.

She went inside and he walked on down the corridor. The room was similar to the barracks on the *Republic*, a large room with alcove bunks for the operators on the right side, and two private rooms on the left. There was a digital display beside the first room. It said *CHIEF WEST*. Nyx had never considered becoming an officer. All she really wanted was to partner with a good operator. She had gotten that with Alex, but circumstances had changed. After fearing that there wouldn't be a place for her on board the *Drachma*, she was glad to discover that she could grow into a new role.

After finding her rucksack among the luggage piled into one corner of the barracks and stowing it on the bunk in her room, she hurried to find the bridge and attend her first officer's meeting.

CHAPTER THIRTY-NINE

ALEX NOTICED the differences in the Titan MBS immediately. Unlike the normal battle suits, the one deep in the bowels of the *Silent Partner* was painted stark black. Without any exterior lights, she would be almost invisible in outer space. The other big change was the gun arms, which had been replaced with articulated, almost human-looking arms with rotating pincers for hands.

"No guns?" Alex asked as he walked around the battle suit.

"No need," General Cordair said. "Your mind is the weapon... right?"

Alex nodded, but it felt strange to go into a dangerous situation with no way to defend himself if the need arose. A rolling set of stairs was pushed up to the Titan and Alex climbed up and quickly settled himself into the battle suit.

"We added one more element to this battle suit," the general continued. "It was Faulk's idea, not mine. But she's footing the bill for all this, so what the hell, right?"

Alex didn't answer.

"In place of the traditional killswitch that's supposed to cut you off from controlling the Titan, we put in an explosive charge."

"So if I don't do exactly what she wants..." Alex said.

"She's a woman who knows her mind and wants things done her way," the general said. "Once she trusts you a little more, I'm sure we can remove it. I just wanted you to know."

"Threats are no way to build trust," Alex said.

"Maybe not the best way," Cordair replied. "But they can be effective."

The general and the engineering staff left Alex alone in the small hangar where the Titan MBS was located. He felt as if he was sitting in a casket. It was insane to think he would do anything for Lynn Faulk knowing that she could kill him with the press of a button, and that there was nothing he could do about it. It was possible that using his abilities, he could sever the connection between the battle suit and General Cordair's control console, but odds were high that the canny Lynn Faulk had thought of that, too. The chances of setting off the charges in the battle suit were just too high. He really had no choices. If he refused to go out and do the job she wanted done, they would kill him. If he failed to carry out the plan as she wanted it done, they would set off the charges in the battle suit. It didn't have to be a big blast either, just enough to compromise the suit would be enough. If the Titan was opened to hard vacuum, even just a hairline fracture, it would kill him.

Alex pressed the button to activate the battle suit's systems. It came to life around him, the inflated padding swelling up around his body. His hands slid easily down into the arms of the battle suit and took hold of the control sticks that would operate the pincer hands. The clam-like body of the suit closed around him, and for a moment, he was in complete darkness. The hum of the suit's EM waves was like a familiar song. He let his Implanted Neural Controller sync to the suit's operating system and the Titan became part of him.

The suit's external cameras fed live video straight into his brain, which translated the data into sight. Alex lifted his arms and looked at the Titan's hands. He used the joystick to rotate the pincers. The trigger closed the clamps together, while a thumb toggle moved them apart.

What do you think of her?

The voice in his head was different. It still sounded like his own thoughts, but there was a cocky edge to the voice that was different. It felt out of place.

"I don't think of the suit as a vehicle," Alex said. "Once you're synced, the Titan becomes an extension of your own body."

Well, what do you think of your new super powered body? I guess now your physical self can keep up with your super powered brain.

The general wasn't wrong. Alex liked having arms and hands. He would have liked to have had a few weapons, too, and he could see that there were mounts on the arms for weapons, but they hadn't been added. It was unlikely that Lynn Faulk, or anyone else on her gigantic ship, trusted him. If he had weapons, he could immediately fly out and turn them on the *Silent Partner*.

He let his mind go over every system in the enhanced battle suit. Everything was online. He had plenty of power and oxygen. The only things he didn't have were weapons, and he soon discovered the explosives. There were several small charges, all connected on a single circuit. Even if he could isolate one, the others would detonate. It was a clever system. Alex couldn't see an immediate way around it, and the consequences were too high for experimentation.

Alright Lieutenant, we're approaching the space tunnel. I'm going to open the hangar and let you out. Remember, we won't continue to broadcast once we're in the Gobal Sector, but we'll be monitoring everything you do.

"Roger that," Alex said. At least he wouldn't have the general's voice in his head distracting him from the job at hand."

You've got five hours of oxygen, so don't waste time. Remember, you follow us. Don't make contact with the Silent Partner *until you've passed through the second space tunnel.*

Alex just hoped the pressure of flying through the tunnel in a battle suit didn't overwhelm the Titan's armor or set off the explosive charges.

"I've got it," Alex said.

Outstanding, General Cordair replied as the hanger doors opened. *You're free to begin your mission. Good luck, Lieutenant Evans.*

Alex didn't reply, but he did walk toward the hangar doors. It was difficult not revel in the feeling of strength and power that came from being in a Titan. Outside the super yacht, space stretched out in an endless panorama of twinkling stars. Alex jumped away from the ship and passed through the *Silent Partner's* artificial gravity field. He used the suit's thrusters to steady himself in zero-gravity and rotate around to face the huge ship. It was the first time he was able to get a sense of the enormous spacecraft's true size. He had seen its length and breadth from the tower, but from outside the ship, he could see how tall she was. The Titan battle suit had targeting software that showed the actual size of an object. The *Silent Partner* was covered with running lights that made it easy to see in the darkness of space. She was thirty meters from the keel to the concourse, and that didn't count the tower or the elevated bridge.

He watched the ship drift past him. Turning and watching it wasn't difficult, but it made him feel somewhat isolated. Fear was working at his mind. What if the charges went off accidentally? What if his Titan malfunctioned? What if he was crushed by the pressures of flying through the space tunnel? It took an act of sheer will power to set his fears aside and focus instead on what could go right. He had a few ideas. The first was connecting to the *Starstruck's* computer system and sending Nyx a message. He wondered if she was thinking of him. He missed her intensely, but not just her. He wondered what Sly and Ash were doing. Was Ash well enough to rejoin Cronus Team? He didn't know. When he'd seen her in the medical bay, her entire body unable to move because of the nerve block the doctors had administered, she seemed small and weak. But if he knew anything about her, it was that Ash would never settle for a small life. She would find a way to overcome any deficit and that realization was encouraging. He was facing a lot of unknowns, but he would find a way to turn things around. Lynn Faulk had the upper hand for the moment, but Alex could find a way to turn the tables. His abilities gave him an edge that she couldn't match. Not even all of her riches could make her his equal when it came to controlling technology.

The ship was several kilometers away when the space around it began to shimmer. It wasn't a glow exactly, but there was movement, as if a creature with glossy black scales was swirling around the enormous ship. Suddenly, almost as if she had never been there at all, the *Silent Partner* disappeared. Alex wondered if it was possible for him to simply turn and run, but they were in a large system and hours from the nearest settlement. Odds were good that he would run out of air before he could reach another ship or space station. And if he didn't pass through the portal, could General Cordair somehow detonate the charges? It was too great a risk to run. Instead, despite the danger of the space tunnel and the mission he had been tasked with in the Gobal Sector, Alex knew he only had one choice. He would follow the *Silent Partner* and find a way to thwart Lynn Faulk's plans for him, and for the galaxy.

He activated the Titan's thrusters and flew toward the space tunnel. There were buoys marking the edges of the enormous passageway. They were so far away that to Alex, they looked like stars, but they were blinking on and off in a coordinated pattern. He felt his skin prickle with fear as he flew toward the dark portal. He had no way of knowing what flying through a space tunnel was like, or if he would even survive, but the only way to find out was to keep going. He flew into the portal and disappeared from sight.

EPILOGUE

LOMAN HAD GONE through the volunteers and vetted them as best he could. He was certain of his officers. Not just because he had recently flown with them in the *Currency* and brought them safely through what could have been a very dangerous mission, but because he had spent the most time having his investigators check them out. None had ties to Lynn Faulk, or the group of ultra-rich financiers with plans to take over the galaxy.

He walked onto the bridge of the *Drachma*, which was vastly different from the updated ships off the line in the CDF fleet. The Mora-class ships were built in a style that Loman had to admit was impressive. There were the usual stations for the various officers to monitor the ship and their individual systems, but the walls in the bridge, which was a round room in the center of the ship, were covered with incredibly high-resolution screens. It was almost like the bridge was open to the outside of the ship. Loman could turn in any direction and see a real time video feed that showed the space outside. The screens were all connected, so the image flowed seamlessly. The result was breathtaking.

His station on the bridge was a seat on a small elevated platform that could swivel, equipped with a set of controls built into the arms. Loman went straight to the captain's chair but didn't sit. Instead, he stood behind the chair and looked around the bridge. There were eight people present—six system officers, plus Lieutenant Rory Jones, who would be Loman's XO, and acting Chief West, who would serve as the commander of the operations division that included the controllers, technicians, and operators. It was a small team, but he could already feel the synergy. Perhaps it was proximity to the head of the CDF, or maybe it was being part of a special task force that would be operating differently than most other CDF posts, but either way, his officers seemed excited to be there.

"Alright, we're finishing up the final preparations before we return the *Drachma* to active service," Loman said. "I want to remind everyone that his is an old ship. She's fast, but lightly armored, and things are bound to go wrong. We will keep our heads and stay positive and solution-oriented. Is that clear?"

"Yes, Commander," they all said in unison.

There were very few things that were as exciting as the sound of enthusiastic troops that were so disciplined, they even answered as one. Loman could feel his sense of pride in them growing already, and they hadn't even left port.

"I know that a lot of you are wondering why I've called for you to join me on this special task force," Loman said. "And while there's a time for confidentiality, that time has come and gone. I'm going to tell you exactly what we're facing. And, when I'm done, if any of you no longer wish to continue with this task force, then we will see you off the ship, no questions asked."

Loman knew that wasn't exactly true. He would have to isolate anyone who left and make sure they were assigned to someplace where they couldn't cause him trouble. But he would cross that bridge when he had to.

"Not long ago, my agents, working to investigate the attacks against Ahzco planets and personnel, discovered a group of wealthy moguls who had joined together and funded a number of disruptive, even violent attacks."

There were glances of shock and surprise, but no one spoke. They were hanging on his every word and he didn't blame them. He had felt the same way when Ciara Prince had explained her findings to him.

"We know two things for certain," Loman continued. "This cabal has formed a company called Sigma Services, which claims to be a security firm, but is actually a front for illegally funded groups that are disrupting the CDF and other private military organizations. Secondly, we know that these ultra-rich individuals are behind the media attacks on private military organizations and are calling for a centralized government."

"Wait," acting Chief West said. "Are you saying there's a group of people manipulating the media in order to gain control over the proposed centralized government?"

"I know it sounds a bit outlandish, but I'm afraid it's true. We're facing an attack on the liberty of the entire galaxy, and while our mandate is to protect Ahzco employees and assets, we can't stand by and let this tiny group of wealthy moguls create a governing entity that would break up our company.

"Sigma Services is actively purchasing private military assets from companies that their agents have pushed to the brink of bankruptcy. At this very moment, private militaries are moving into the Askerria Sector with plans to fight for the rich mineral rights to the asteroid field there."

"Doesn't Lewan Enterprises hold the permits to mine that sector?" Lieutenant Rory Jones asked.

"Indeed, they do. But they've been persuaded to pull out of the Askerria Sector. I believe the intention is to let the various private militaries fight each other over the riches in the asteroid field and weaken their security forces to such an extreme that the new centralized government can then sweep in and take control of their parent companies."

Loman let that thought sink in before continuing.

"So, they let us fight each other, and then buy what's left of the biggest losers' security fleets," Nyx said. "And they use those assets, under their own firm's name, against the victors."

"Yes," Loman said. "Sigma Services is already buying up as much military tech as it can get. Once the cabal is in charge, they can give the security contract to whoever they choose."

"And they used the promise to return the rights of the Askerria sector to Lewan Enterprises," Lieutanant Rory Jones said. "That's a diabolical plan."

Loman was impressed at how quickly his new crew was putting things together. He didn't have to give them every detail. They could see the danger and the corruption for themselves.

"Colonel Chastain is gathering as much of our CDF forces as we can spare in the Askerria system, but not to fight," Loman said. "It's merely the best way to hide our strength from the backers of the new government, who will be operating under the assumption that we're there to fight the other private militaries. Instead, we will be going there with the intention of sharing this information and hopefully, recruiting other companies to join us in resisting government oversight of Ahzco. If they want to take our planets and break up the company, they'll have to go through the CDF to do it."

"So, we're starting a war?" the communications officer asked.

"We're not starting a war," Loman said. "We're hoping to prevent one. But if we fail to prevent it, then we need to be able to move fast and make sure we're in the best position to fight. I know that the media and public opinion of the CDF are against us. Everything we do is being twisted to make us look like aggressive, war-mongering barbarians. But as things stand, this is our best chance to prevent the loss of everything we've worked for."

He paused again, letting each member of his crew think things through for themselves. When he spoke again, it was with an earnestness he hoped they could hear in his voice.

"I've spent my entire adult life working to make Ahzco employees safe," he said. "I've fought to ensure that the CDF has the resources and the autonomy to carry out our mandate without interference and with the best equipment that can be manufactured. I do not believe that turning the company over to government control will make things better for anyone involved. And please hear me. This has nothing to do with money. It has everything to do with our freedom and the right of the company that employs us to do business as they see fit. If any of you disagree with me, I honestly respect your opinion and would never ask you to continue with me. But time is of the essence, and I must ask that you leave the ship now, so we can carry on. I want every member of this command staff to be fully committed to fighting the tyranny of this supposed central government idea."

He waited, hardly daring to breathe. There was a chance they might all leave him. In fact, even if just one left, it would cripple what he was trying to do. He needed them all to carry out his plans. One by one, they made eye contact. There were slight nods of approval and small smiles. Loman's gaze settled on Nyx last of all. Her face bore a look of determination that Loman found inspiring.

"I think I speak for us all," Lieutenant Jones said, "when I say we're with you, sir."

"All the way," Nyx said.

"Excellent. You all have my eternal gratitude. And I'm committed to making sure we do everything we can to succeed. To that end, let's cast off the moorings and get the *Drachma* under way."

"The last shuttle is docking now," Jones said, "with Corporal Timmons on board."

"Outstanding," Loman said. "As soon as we have everything secure, take us out."

All around him the officers turned to their stations. There was a buzz of activity as they began calling out orders and answering questions. Loman moved around to the front of the captain's chair and sat down. The seat wasn't comfortable. It was stiff and seemed strangely designed, but that was a good thing in his mind. He might be the head of the CDF, but the last thing he could afford to do was get comfortable. There were too many people depending on him. And their enemy was too devious, too resourceful, and already a few steps ahead of them.

"Sir?" Nyx West said, approaching his station at the center of the bridge. "May I ask a question?"

"Is it about Sergeant Evans?" Loman asked.

She nodded. It didn't surprise him. There was something about Alex Evans that was like gravity. He drew people into his orbit. Loman thought it was impossible not to like the brave, young operator.

"Finding him is our first priority," Loman said. "All of our plans depend on him."

There was a look of relief on Nyx's face, but in Loman's mind, a fear had already taken root. What if they couldn't find Alex? Or worse yet, what if Lynn Faulk had already corrupted him? Loman knew the odds were stacked against them, but without Alex Evans and his unique abilities, they had no chance at all. If they couldn't get him back, the war would be over before it even began.

AUTHOR'S NOTE

Thank you for reading Skandia Seven. The fifth and final book of the Ace Evans series is coming in August 2020.

Join my mailing list at http://www.tobyneighbors.com/contacts.html to get updates on new books as soon as they become available.